Alarion and the Eternal Flame

The Chronicles of Alarion, Volume 7

ANANT RAM BOSS

Published by ANANT RAM, 2024.

This is a work of fiction. Similarities to real people, places, or events are entirely coincidental.

ALARION AND THE ETERNAL FLAME

First edition. December 2, 2024.

Copyright © 2024 ANANT RAM BOSS.

ISBN: 979-8230230120

Written by ANANT RAM BOSS.

Also by ANANT RAM BOSS

1
The Chronicles of Alarion -Part-6 "Alarion and the Nexus of Netheron"
"The Chronicles of Alarion -Part-7-"Alarion and the Legacy of Luminarya"

2
Mystic Alliances

Alarion Chronicles Series
The Dawn of Magic
Shadows Embrace
Book#3: "Phoenix's Flight"
Book 4: "Warriors of Light"
Echoes of Wisdom
Captivated Woodland
Kingdom of Crystals
Book 8: "Lost Legacies"
Book 9: "Siege of Hope"
Book 10: "Veil of Light"

The Astral Chronicles
Awakening Shadows
Awakening Shadows
Celestial Convergence
Whispers of the Himalayas
Riddles of Rishikesh
Portals of the Past
Echoes from Vijayanagara
Veil of Varanasi
The Astral Nexus
Eclipse of Eternity
Beyond the Veil

The Chronicles of Alarion
Book # 1: Alarion and the Cryptic Key
Book # 2 Alarion and the Secrets of Tiderune
"Book # 3 "Alarion and the Oracle's Enigma
Book 4 Alarion and the Shattered Sigils
"The Chronicles of Alarion" A Magical Adventure Awaits
Book#4Alarion and the Shattered Sigils
Alarion and the Rift of Arcane Fates
Alarion and the Eternal Flame

Standalone
Love's Delectable Harmony
Adventures in Candy land
Adventures in Candy land
Canvas to Catalyst: Parenting Mastery

Guardians of Greatness: Our Children Are Our Property in Cultivating Tomorrow's Leaders
Guardians of Greatness: Cultivating Tomorrow's Leaders
Space Explorers Club
The Enchanted Forest Chronicles
Mystery at Monster Mansion
Robot Friends Forever
Underwater Kingdom
Underwater Kingdom
Time Travel Twins
Time Travel Twins
The Giggle Factory
Dreamland Chronicles
The Case of the Vanishing Cookies
Dragon Knight Chronicles
The Wishing Well
Trade Tactics Unveiled: Mastering Profit Secrets
Whispers in the Graveyard
Love after Dawn: A Second Chance Romance
Exodus: A Hopeful Dystopia
Death at Blackwood Manor
Orient Express: Murder Redefined
Poirot & the Raven: Digital Legacy
The Brave Little Elephant
The Little Robot That Could
The Adventures of Little Star
Dream World
Unique Friendship
The Courage of the Lion
The Art of Building Wealth: A Strategic Guide
Epic Savings Day

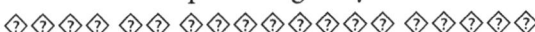

The Circle of Life
Alarion and the Veil of Duskspire
The Circle of Life: Embracing Childhood Again
The Circle of Life: Embracing Childhood Again
High-Ticket Marketing Mastery
Legacy of Sacrifice
Monetising Pinterest
Mastering Life: Small Habits, Big Wisdom

Table of Contents

....	1
Overview	3
Introduction	5
Description	8
Chapter 1: The Call of Destiny....................................	10
Chapter 2: A Fiery Greeting	16
Chapter 3: The Sizzling Rival.......................................	23
Chapter 4: A Potion with a Twist	30
Chapter 5: The Fiery Trials..	37
Chapter 6: A Spark of Friendship	43
Chapter 7: Shadows of the Past	49
Chapter 8: The Mischievous Spirits	55
Chapter 9: The Dance of Flames	60
Chapter 10: The Blazing Bandit..................................	67
Chapter 11: A Test of Loyalty	74
Chapter 12: The Flame Keeper....................................	81
Chapter 13: The Unexpected Ally	86
Chapter 14: Trials of the Heart	92
Chapter 15: Whispers of Flame	98
Chapter 16: The Inferno Maze	104
Chapter 17: The Shadow Enemy................................	110
Chapter 18: Heart of the Flame	116
Chapter 19: A Rival's Return	122
Chapter 20: The Eternal Flame's Guardian................	130
Chapter 21: Flames of Reflection	137
Chapter 22: The Betrayal	143
Chapter 23: A Love Rekindled....................................	148
Chapter 24: The Final Battle Begins...........................	154
Chapter 25: The Heart of the Storm	160
Chapter 26: The Power of Unity	165
Chapter 27: A Dance of Flames	170

Chapter 28: The Eternal Flame Unleashed 175
Chapter 29: The Price of Power 180
Chapter 30: Flames of Destiny 185
Chapter 31: The Bonds of Love 190
Chapter 32: A Heart Divided 195
Chapter 33: The Last Stand 200
Chapter 34: The Echo of the Past 205
Chapter 35: The Price of Love 210
Chapter 36: The Flame's Embrace 215
Chapter 37: The Turning Tide 220
Chapter 38: The Power of Love 225
Chapter 39: The Final Confrontation 230
Chapter 40: The Light of Hope 235
Chapter 41: The Awakening Flame 240
Chapter 42: A New Beginning 244
Chapter 43: The Journey Home 249
Chapter 44: The Celebration 254
Chapter 45: Whispers of the Heart 259
Chapter 46: A Gift of Flame 264
Chapter 47: The Flame of Love 270
Chapter 48: The Eternal Flame Ceremony 276
Chapter 49: The Future Beckons 282
Chapter 50: A New Quest 288
A Thank You Note to the Readers 294
Acknowledgments 296
Disclaimer 298
About the Author: Anant Ram Boss 300

Join Alarion on this unforgettable quest, where the flickering light of the Eternal Flame holds the key to his destiny and the future of his world. Immerse yourself in a narrative filled with action, humor, and romance, and discover why this tale will linger in your heart long after the last page is turned. Grab your copy today and light the way to adventure!

"In the glow of the Eternal Flame, love and courage intertwine, forging a path where adventure never ends."

Series "The Chronicles of Alarion"
Book 7: "Alarion and the Eternal Flame"

Overview

In the exhilarating conclusion of Alarion's epic journey, Alarion and the Eternal Flame invites readers into a world where adventure, love, and the battle between light and darkness intertwine. Alarion, our courageous hero, embarks on a quest for the legendary Eternal Flame—a mystical force said to hold unparalleled power and the key to restoring balance to his realm. However, this journey is not merely a physical endeavor; it is a deep dive into his heart and soul, revealing secrets that will change his life forever.

As Alarion traverses breathtaking landscapes, from the enchanting Emberwood Forest to the fiery peaks of Mount Ignis, he encounters a colorful cast of characters—each adding their unique flavor to his adventure. The presence of Lila, a spirited and witty companion, adds a layer of complexity to Alarion's quest. Their dynamic is filled with playful banter, tender moments, and sparks of romance that light up the pages. Readers will find themselves laughing at their humorous exchanges while also rooting for their blossoming relationship as they face challenges together.

Throughout the narrative, Alarion must confront both external adversaries and his inner doubts. The shadowy figure threatening the realm serves as a formidable antagonist, pushing Alarion to test his limits. Each encounter with strange enemies not only poses a challenge but also serves as a catalyst for Alarion's growth. He learns that true strength comes not just from magical abilities, but from the bonds of friendship, loyalty, and love that he forges along the way.

The story unfolds with a perfect blend of lighthearted moments and profound revelations. Alarion's journey is peppered with comedic mishaps—like a potion gone awry or a dance-off with fiery sprites—ensuring readers are entertained while also invested in the deeper themes of self-discovery and sacrifice. As Alarion delves into the lore surrounding the Eternal Flame, he uncovers hidden truths about his past, intertwining with the fate of those he holds dear.

As the stakes rise and the final battle looms, Alarion must grapple with the implications of wielding such immense power. The question of destiny hangs in the air: Will he be able to embrace his role as a hero while safeguarding his heart? Can he navigate the complexities of love and duty without losing himself? With each turn of the page, readers will find themselves on the edge of their seats, eager to discover how Alarion reconciles his desires with the responsibilities that come with his newfound powers.

In this climactic chapter of Alarion's story, themes of courage, friendship, and the transformative power of love shine through. The Eternal Flame symbolizes not just strength, but also the warmth of connection that can light even the darkest paths. The journey culminates in a spectacular finale that brings together all the threads of Alarion's adventure, offering a satisfying resolution while leaving room for future tales.

Alarion and the Eternal Flame is a story that promises to resonate with readers of all ages. With its rich tapestry of humor, romance, and fantasy, it captures the essence of what it means to be human: the struggle between ambition and love, the joy of companionship, and the courage to face one's destiny. Join Alarion as he embraces his fate, discovers the true meaning of power, and ultimately learns that the greatest adventure lies not just in seeking the Eternal Flame, but in the relationships, he nurtures along the way. The flame of hope flickers brightly as the story draws to a close, leaving readers inspired and yearning for more.

Introduction

In a realm where magic dances through the air like whispers of old, and legends are etched into the very fabric of time, a hero's journey comes to its climactic end. Alarion and the Eternal Flame marks the thrilling conclusion of Alarion's odyssey—a tale woven with threads of bravery, romance, and the age-old struggle between light and darkness.

Alarion, once a humble young mage with dreams as vast as the starry skies, has transformed into a formidable warrior through his adventures. His quest has been riddled with challenges that tested not only his magical prowess but also the depths of his character. From battling mischievous spirits to forging alliances with unexpected companions, Alarion has learned that true strength lies not just in power but in the connections, he builds along the way. His journey has been about more than just seeking a legendary artifact; it has been a voyage of self-discovery, where the most profound lessons often come wrapped in laughter and love.

As we embark on this final chapter, the focus shifts to the fabled Eternal Flame—a source of unmatched power, said to hold the secrets of creation and the potential to reshape destinies. The Flame shrouded in mystery and guarded by ancient forces, represents Alarion's ultimate challenge. To claim it is to confront not only formidable enemies but also the shadows of his own past. What sacrifices must he make? What truths will he uncover? And, most importantly, how will his choices shape the future of his world?

The Eternal Flame is more than just a coveted prize; it symbolizes hope, unity, and the light that resides in all of us, even in our darkest moments. As Alarion navigates treacherous landscapes filled with both physical dangers and emotional trials, readers will find themselves captivated by the rich tapestry of his world. The vibrant settings—from the lush, enchanted forests of Emberwood to the volcanic peaks of Mount Ignis—create a vivid backdrop for the unfolding drama. Each location is alive with magic, secrets, and the essence of the elemental forces that govern the realm.

At the heart of this story lies Alarion's relationship with Lila, a spirited and clever ally whose unwavering support and sharp wit add both humor and depth to their journey. Their bond deepens as they face adversities together, creating a dynamic that blends adventure with moments of genuine tenderness. Through their banter and shared experiences, readers will experience the highs and lows of love—those sweet, fleeting moments of connection amid the chaos of their quest.

As the narrative unfolds, prepare to be swept away in a whirlwind of emotions—joy, fear, triumph, and even a touch of heartache. Alarion's story is a reminder that every hero's journey is fraught with challenges, yet it is in these very trials that we discover who we truly are. Each battle fought, each friendship forged, and each secret revealed serves to illuminate the path toward understanding one's destiny.

In Alarion and the Eternal Flame, adventure awaits at every turn, and the stakes have never been higher. As we follow Alarion on this extraordinary quest, we are invited to reflect on our own paths—on the choices we make, the love we nurture, and the legacy we leave behind. So, turn the page, and join Alarion as he embarks on his most perilous adventure yet, where the fate of his world hangs in the balance, and the Eternal Flame beckons him closer than ever before.

Let the journey ignite your imagination, and may the warmth of the Flame guide you as you delve into this enchanting tale.

Description

Step into a World of Magic, Love, and Adventure!

In the thrilling finale of Alarion's epic journey, Alarion and the Eternal Flame, readers are invited to experience a breathtaking tale of courage, romance, and the eternal battle between good and evil. This enchanting story weaves together humor, heartfelt moments, and exhilarating action as our beloved hero faces his most formidable challenge yet—the quest for the legendary Eternal Flame.

Key Points:

Epic Quest for Power: Alarion sets out on a daring journey to find the Eternal Flame, a mystical source of unmatched power believed to hold the secrets of creation itself. But claiming it comes with great risks and formidable foes.

Unveiling Secrets of the Past: As Alarion delves deeper into the mysteries surrounding the Flame, he uncovers long-buried truths about his heritage and the forces that shaped his destiny. These revelations challenge his understanding of himself and his purpose.

A Dynamic Duo: Accompanied by Lila, a witty and resourceful companion, Alarion's adventure is enriched with playful banter and undeniable chemistry. Their relationship blossoms amid the chaos, bringing warmth and humor to their perilous quest.

Strange Enemies and Fierce Battles: Alarion encounters a host of strange enemies, each battle testing not just his magical abilities but also his determination and resilience. As the stakes rise, he learns that true strength comes from within and the bonds he forges with those around him.

Themes of Love and Sacrifice: At its heart, this story is about love—love for friends, love for a partner, and love for one's homeland. Alarion must navigate the complexities of his feelings while making sacrifices that could alter the course of his life and the fate of his world.

A Climactic Finale: As the story reaches its peak, the tension mounts. Alarion must confront not only external threats but also the choices that define who he is. Will he be able to harness the power of the Eternal Flame to save his world? The gripping conclusion will leave readers breathless, pondering the implications of destiny and the power of love.

A Journey of Self-Discovery: Throughout the adventure, Alarion evolves from a hesitant mage into a confident hero. Readers will be inspired by his growth, reflecting on their own journeys of self-discovery and the importance of embracing one's true potential.

Alarion and the Eternal Flame is more than just a fantasy novel; it's a celebration of friendship, bravery, and the warmth of human connection. Whether you're a long-time fan of Alarion's adventures or new to this captivating world, this story promises to transport you to realms where magic reigns, laughter echoes, and love conquers all.

Join Alarion on this unforgettable quest, where the flickering light of the Eternal Flame holds the key to his destiny and the future of his world. Immerse yourself in a narrative filled with action, humor, and romance, and discover why this tale will linger in your heart long after the last page is turned. Grab your copy today and light the way to adventure!

Chapter 1: The Call of Destiny

A*larion receives a mysterious message about the Eternal Flame, sending him on an adventure that promises both excitement and unexpected romance. Little does he know, his first obstacle is a love-struck dragon!*

The sun dipped low on the horizon, painting the skies in hues of orange and purple, as Alarion sat cross-legged on a grassy knoll, contemplating his next move. He had just returned from a series of adventures in Tiderune, a land filled with mischievous mermaids and wily wizards, but something tugged at his heart, a whisper that something bigger awaited him.

Suddenly, the tranquility of the evening was shattered by a loud, booming voice that echoed across the valley. "Alarion! Alarion! Come forth!"

Startled, Alarion scrambled to his feet, his heart racing. He recognized that voice—It belonged to the Great Oracle of Zynthor, a wise and enigmatic figure who resided in the mountains. With a mix of excitement and apprehension, Alarion grabbed his trusty satchel and made his way towards the voice.

Upon reaching the Oracle's cave, he was greeted by a flickering blue flame that danced mysteriously in the center of the room. The Oracle emerged from the shadows, her shimmering robes flowing like water.

"Alarion, you have been chosen," she intoned, her eyes twinkling with ancient wisdom. "The Eternal Flame, a source of unmatched power, calls to you. But be warned, it will not be an easy path. You will face trials that test your heart and your strength."

"Trials? What kind of trials?" Alarion asked, feeling a mix of thrill and anxiety.

The Oracle smiled mysteriously. "Your first obstacle is a love-struck dragon named Zephyra. She guards the entrance to the Hidden Valley, where the Eternal Flame resides."

"Love-struck dragon?" Alarion laughed. "How can a dragon be love-struck?"

As if on cue, a loud roar echoed from outside the cave. The ground trembled, and Zephyra, a magnificent dragon with iridescent scales, landed gracefully before them. Her emerald eyes sparkled with an odd mixture of affection and longing.

"Alarion!" she bellowed, her voice both melodic and fierce. "I've heard tales of your bravery! I seek a partner to help me with... emotional turbulence. Would you be my valiant knight?"

Alarion stared wide-eyed, his mind racing. A dragon wanted him to help her with her love life? This was absurd! But there was a glimmer of adventure in her eyes, and he couldn't resist the thrill of the unknown.

"Uh, sure! I mean, I'm not really a relationship expert, but I could help," he stammered, trying to mask his bewilderment.

"Wonderful!" Zephyra exclaimed, her wings fluttering with excitement. "We'll make a great team! But first, let me serenade you with a song to mark our new partnership!"

And with that, Zephyra launched into a heartfelt ballad, her voice echoing through the valley:

Song: "Heart of Fire"
(Verse 1)
In the twilight's embrace, where dreams take flight,
A dragon's heart beats strong, igniting the night.
With every flame that dances, a tale unfolds,

Of love and courage, in whispers bold.
(Chorus)
Oh, heart of fire, shining bright,
Guide us through the darkest night.
With courage by our side, we'll face the storm,
Together, we'll break every norm.
(Verse 2)
When shadows loom and doubts arise,
With your hand in mine, we'll reach for the skies.
No fear can conquer, no heart can break,
Together we'll soar, make no mistake.
(Chorus)
Oh, heart of fire, shining bright,
Guide us through the darkest night.
With courage by our side, we'll face the storm,
Together, we'll break every norm.
(Bridge)
Through trials and battles, we'll stand as one,
Chasing our dreams until the day is done.
With laughter and love, our spirits ignite,
In the heart of the battle, we'll shine so bright.
(Chorus)
Oh, heart of fire, shining bright,
Guide us through the darkest night.
With courage by our side, we'll face the storm,
Together, we'll break every norm.

As Zephyra finished her song, Alarion couldn't help but clap, caught up in the moment. "That was incredible! But tell me, what's troubling your heart?"

"I long for the affection of Sir Balthor, the knight of the Crimson Castle," she confessed, her voice now tinged with melancholy. "But

ALARION AND THE ETERNAL FLAME

he's enamored with a fair maiden from the village below. I fear I am too much of a dragon for him to ever love."

"Let's not give up just yet!" Alarion encouraged, his adventurous spirit ignited. "Together, we'll win over his heart! After all, who wouldn't love a magnificent dragon like you?"

"Really? You think so?" Zephyra asked, her eyes sparkling with hope.

"Absolutely! We'll concoct a plan that will impress him!" Alarion exclaimed, feeling more confident.

With their mission set, Alarion and Zephyra soared into the night sky, flying toward the Crimson Castle. As they approached, the castle's walls gleamed under the moonlight, casting an enchanting glow. Alarion's heart raced; the excitement of the adventure tingled in his veins.

As they landed in the courtyard, Sir Balthor appeared, his shiny armor reflecting the moonlight. His expression shifted from surprise to fear as he spotted the dragon.

"Stay back, beast!" he shouted, drawing his sword.

"No, wait!" Alarion interjected, stepping forward. "She's not here to harm you! She wants to express her feelings!"

Balthor lowered his sword, eyeing Zephyra warily. "A dragon expressing feelings? This I must see!"

Alarion quickly explained their plan, and Zephyra took a deep breath, summoning her courage. "Sir Balthor, I know you admire beauty, but I offer more than just looks. I can bring you strength and adventure!"

Balthor crossed his arms, intrigued yet skeptical. "And what makes you think I would ever choose a dragon over a fair maiden?"

Before Zephyra could respond, a shadow loomed over them. A group of hidden enemies—dark knights clad in black armor—emerged from the trees, their intentions clear. They sought the Eternal Flame for themselves!

"Defend the castle!" Balthor shouted, rallying his knights.

Alarion quickly realized they were outnumbered. "Zephyra, we need to show them that love and courage can overcome anything!"

"Right!" Zephyra roared, her wings unfurling, creating gusts of wind.

As the dark knights charged, Alarion took a stand beside Zephyra and Balthor. "Let's show them what we've got!"

With a mighty flap of her wings, Zephyra sent a blast of fire toward the advancing knights, illuminating the night. Alarion joined in, using his quick reflexes to dodge and outmaneuver the attackers, while Balthor wielded his sword with precision, striking down any foes that came too close.

As the battle raged, Zephyra found her confidence. She twirled in the air, breathing fire and creating dazzling displays that momentarily distracted the dark knights. Alarion seized the moment, rallying the other knights around him.

"Together, we can push them back!" he shouted, his voice filled with determination.

The knights, inspired by Alarion's bravery and Zephyra's fierce display of strength, joined forces. They fought valiantly, united by the bond of unexpected friendships. With each clash of swords and roar of the dragon, the tide began to turn.

At last, after a fierce battle, the dark knights retreated into the shadows, vanquished for the moment. Zephyra landed gracefully beside Alarion and Balthor, her chest heaving with exhaustion but her spirit soaring.

"That was amazing!" Alarion exclaimed, wiping the sweat from his brow. "You were incredible, Zephyra!"

Balthor, still catching his breath, looked at Zephyra with newfound admiration. "Perhaps there is more to you than meets the eye, dragon. Your bravery has proven you worthy of my respect."

"Thank you, Sir Balthor," Zephyra replied, her heart swelling with hope. "Would you consider a friendship, perhaps even something more?"

Balthor hesitated but saw the sincerity in her eyes. "Friendship is a start, and I must admit, you are quite extraordinary."

As the moon shone brightly above, Alarion couldn't help but smile at the unexpected bonds that had formed that night. With the threat of the dark knights vanquished, and the promise of a new adventure looming, Alarion realized that this was only the beginning of a grand journey.

With laughter and love echoing through the castle, Alarion, Zephyra, and Sir Balthor stood united, ready to face whatever challenges lay ahead in the quest for the Eternal Flame.

Chapter 2: A Fiery Greeting

Upon arriving at the village of Emberwood, Alarion is met with a warm welcome—and a fiery mishap involving a clumsy fire juggler. Sparks fly, both literally and figuratively, as he meets Lila, a feisty local.

Alarion descended from the sky, Zephyra's emerald scales shimmering in the sunlight as they landed just outside the quaint village of Emberwood. The village was known for its lively atmosphere, filled with laughter and music that wafted through the air like the aroma of freshly baked bread. But as Alarion stepped onto the cobblestone path, he was unaware that he was about to become part of a most unexpected spectacle.

"Welcome, brave adventurer!" shouted a cheerful villager, waving enthusiastically. The crowd around him erupted in applause, clearly intrigued by the arrival of the dragon and its rider. Just then, a loud whoop sounded, and a figure darted into view—a fire juggler, dressed in vibrant colors and a hat too large for his head.

"Step right up and witness the magnificent flames!" he declared, tossing a series of torches into the air. But as he spun around to add a flourish, one of the torches sailed off course, igniting the nearby haystack.

"Fire! Fire!" screamed a woman, pointing at the growing blaze.

"Oh no!" Alarion exclaimed, looking at Zephyra. "We have to help!"

"Don't worry; I've got this!" Zephyra grinned, puffing out a stream of water from her mouth, extinguishing the flames in a single breath. The villagers gasped in awe, and the fire juggler fumbled his torches, dropping them one by one.

"Um, thank you, mighty dragon!" the juggler stammered, a mix of embarrassment and gratitude on his face.

As the crowd cheered, Alarion couldn't help but chuckle. "Looks like you could use a little more practice!"

"Just a little!" he replied sheepishly, scratching the back of his neck. "I'm always working on my fire tricks. Next time, I'll aim for the sky!"

Amidst the laughter and chaos, Alarion caught sight of a figure moving gracefully through the crowd. A young woman with fiery red hair and bright green eyes emerged, her confidence radiating like the sun. She pushed through the throngs of villagers, her gaze fixed firmly on the fire juggler.

"What a disaster, Flint!" she exclaimed, rolling her eyes. "Do you ever think before you act?"

Flint scratched his head. "It was supposed to be a grand entrance, Lila!"

"More like a grand fire hazard!" Lila shot back, but her lips curved into a teasing smile, revealing a playful side.

Alarion, enchanted by her fiery spirit, stepped forward. "I think it was quite the show! You handled that fire well."

"Ah, a knight in shining armor!" she grinned, looking him up and down. "Or should I say, a dragon rider? I'm Lila, and I'm not impressed by flashy tricks. But you seem... different."

Before Alarion could respond, Flint piped up, "You should see him in action! He's just returned from a quest for the Eternal Flame!"

Lila's eyes widened. "The Eternal Flame? That's quite a story! But why would you want to chase after something that could burn your eyebrows off?"

Alarion laughed, appreciating her candor. "It's not just about the flame. It's about the journey and the friends you make along the way."

"Sounds like a cheesy motto from a storybook!" Lila teased, and Alarion couldn't help but admire her wit.

"Maybe, but I'd take the cheese if it comes with a side of adventure," he winked.

With the banter flowing easily between them, Alarion felt an undeniable spark. Just then, a loud crash interrupted their moment—a cart had toppled over, sending apples rolling across the cobblestone path.

"Apples everywhere!" Lila exclaimed, rushing to help the flustered merchant pick them up. Alarion quickly followed, eager to lend a hand.

As they gathered the fallen fruit, the connection between them deepened, their laughter mingling with the lively sounds of the village. Alarion noticed the way her eyes sparkled when she smiled and how her laughter was like music that wrapped around his heart.

"What brings you to Emberwood, besides our spectacular fire juggling?" Lila asked, tossing him a bright red apple.

"I'm searching for the Eternal Flame," Alarion explained, taking a bite of the apple. "But I could use a guide. Any chance you know the way?"

"Of course I do! But the path to the Flame isn't just about walking. It's filled with challenges and—" she paused dramatically, "adventures!"

"Adventures?" Alarion echoed, intrigued.

"Absolutely! I can show you the best spots for finding the hidden treasures of Emberwood," Lila said with a mischievous grin. "And I promise, it won't be boring."

"Count me in!" Alarion replied, his heart racing with anticipation.

"Then let's start our journey!" Lila proclaimed, pulling him toward the village square.

As they strolled through the marketplace, Lila shared tales of Emberwood's history—of enchanted springs, talking animals, and legendary heroes who once roamed the land. Alarion hung on her every word, captivated not just by her stories but by her infectious spirit.

At that moment, Lila grabbed Alarion's hand, and he felt a rush of warmth spread through him. "Follow me!" she said, leading him toward a small clearing where a fountain glimmered in the sunlight.

"Time for a little fun!" she declared, suddenly hopping onto the fountain's edge. With a flourish, she began to dance, her movements fluid and joyful.

"Wow, you're quite the dancer!" Alarion laughed, clapping along. "Show me your moves!"

"Oh, you think you can keep up?" Lila challenged, beckoning him to join her.

Taking a deep breath, Alarion climbed up and began to mimic her steps, albeit clumsily.

"Left foot, right foot! Spin around, jump!" she called out, leading him in a playful dance.

Alarion stumbled but quickly regained his balance, their laughter ringing through the air.

"Now let's add a little music!" Lila said, raising her arms dramatically. "Follow my lead!"

She began to sing a lively tune, a playful rhythm filling the air:
Song: "Dance of the Flames"
(Verse 1)
Come on, come on, let's dance away,
Under the sun, we'll laugh and play.
With every step, let our spirits soar,
In the heart of Emberwood, we'll dance some more!

(Chorus)
Dance, dance, feel the fire,
Let your heart be your desire.
With every twirl, we'll chase the night,
Together we'll shine, oh what a sight!
(Verse 2)
With each turn, we'll make a friend,
In the village where the magic never ends.
Let the flames ignite our dreams,
In this world, nothing's as it seems.
(Chorus)
Dance, dance, feel the fire,
Let your heart be your desire.
With every twirl, we'll chase the night,
Together we'll shine, oh what a sight!
(Bridge)
Through laughter and joy, we'll face our fears,
With every step, we'll conquer the years.
In the heart of the night, we'll light our way,
Together forever, come what may!
(Chorus)
Dance, dance, feel the fire,
Let your heart be your desire.
With every twirl, we'll chase the night,
Together we'll shine, oh what a sight!

As they danced, Alarion felt an unexplainable connection growing between them. The world around them faded into a beautiful blur, filled only with laughter, music, and the warmth of the sun.

But just as the last notes of their song faded into the air, a sudden darkness swept over the village. Alarion's heart raced as shadows loomed near the edge of the clearing.

"Lila, look!" he shouted, pointing to a group of cloaked figures emerging from the trees, their intentions unclear.

"What are they doing here?" Lila whispered; her playful demeanor replaced by a look of concern.

"I don't know, but we can't let them disrupt our fun!" Alarion replied, his bravado shining through the uncertainty.

The cloaked figures advanced, and Alarion stepped forward, summoning the courage he had gathered from their shared moments. "Who goes there?" he called out.

One of the figures stepped forward, revealing a face shrouded in shadow. "We seek the Eternal Flame. Hand it over, and we won't harm you!"

Alarion exchanged a glance with Lila. "You'll have to get through us first!" he declared.

"Fools! You think you can stand against us?" the shadowy figure laughed, pulling out a dark dagger glimmering with malice.

"Let's show them what we're made of!" Lila shouted, her determination igniting a spark within Alarion.

With a swift motion, Zephyra swooped down from above, roaring fiercely. "You shall not take what does not belong to you!" she bellowed, sending a shockwave through the clearing.

The cloaked figures hesitated, and Alarion took the opportunity to grab a nearby stick, brandishing it like a sword. "We're not afraid of you!"

As the battle erupted, Alarion and Lila fought side by side, dodging and weaving through the oncoming attackers. Alarion swung his makeshift weapon with a mix of courage and awkwardness, while Lila expertly outmaneuvered their foes, her quick reflexes shining.

"Behind you!" she shouted, pushing Alarion out of the way just in time to avoid a swift blow.

"Thanks!" Alarion replied, heart pounding.

"Now, let's show them how Emberwood fights!" she declared, rallying the villagers who had gathered to watch, brandishing whatever they could find.

Together, they formed a united front, their laughter and courage defying the darkness that threatened their village. The cloaked figures, realizing they were outmatched by the fiery spirit of Emberwood, began to retreat into the shadows.

"Run, cowards!" Lila shouted, and the villagers cheered as the attackers fled.

Breathless and exhilarated, Alarion and Lila stood amidst the cheering crowd, hands still clutching their weapons, though the threat had passed.

"Not bad for a day's work, huh?" Alarion said, trying to catch his breath, a grin spreading across his face.

"Not bad at all! I'd say that was quite the fiery greeting!" Lila laughed, her eyes sparkling with mischief.

As the sun set behind them, painting the sky with shades of orange and pink, Alarion felt a warmth in his heart—a promise of more adventures to come, and perhaps something deeper with Lila, whose spirit shone as brightly as the embers in the fading light.

And so, as they walked back into the heart of Emberwood, hand in hand, Alarion couldn't shake the feeling that this fiery greeting was just the beginning of an extraordinary journey filled with laughter, love, and unforeseen challenges.

Chapter 3: The Sizzling Rival

*L*ila's ex, a jealous fire mage, challenges Alarion to a duel. What starts as a heated argument quickly turns into an amusing battle of wits, showcasing Alarion's unexpected charm.

The sun hung high over Emberwood, casting a warm glow that made the village look like it was kissed by a golden brush. Lila and Alarion had spent the morning exploring the enchanted nooks and crannies of the village. Their laughter mingled with the cheerful sounds of vendors selling their wares, creating an atmosphere ripe for adventure.

Alarion was beginning to feel at home in Emberwood. Lila's infectious energy was pulling him in, and every moment spent with her made the world seem brighter. But, as fate would have it, trouble was brewing just around the corner.

As they approached the village square, a gust of wind swept through, bringing with it an ominous chill. Lila's expression changed from lighthearted to wary. "Oh no, not him," she muttered under her breath.

"Who?" Alarion asked, confused.

Before she could answer, a figure emerged from the crowd—a tall, muscular man with fiery red hair and piercing blue eyes. He wore an elaborate robe adorned with flame motifs, making it clear he was a fire mage. The villagers instinctively parted, allowing him to stride forward with an air of arrogance.

"Lila!" he bellowed, his voice booming over the chatter of the crowd. "I've heard rumors of a new suitor. I cannot let you be swept away by some dragon-riding fool!"

Lila groaned, rolling her eyes. "Caden, not now. This is ridiculous."

Caden ignored her protest, his gaze fixed squarely on Alarion. "I challenge you to a duel! A fire mage such as myself cannot stand idly by while a mere dragon rider encroaches on what is rightfully mine!"

Alarion raised an eyebrow, his heart racing with a mixture of amusement and annoyance. "And what makes you think I'm interested in 'encroaching' on anything?" he shot back.

"Everything about you screams arrogance!" Caden snapped, flames flickering to life at his fingertips. "A duel will settle this matter! One-on-one, I will show you what true power looks like!"

"Wait," Lila interjected, stepping between them. "This is absolutely unnecessary! Alarion is not trying to steal anything from you!"

"Silence!" Caden roared, flames now dancing wildly in the air around him. "A duel is the only way to prove who is worthy of your affection!"

Alarion sighed, casting a sideways glance at Lila. "You don't want me to fight him, do you?"

Lila's eyes sparkled mischievously. "Oh, it could be entertaining!"

"Entertaining?" Alarion repeated, a grin spreading across his face. "You want to see me fight? Alright, let's turn this duel into a show!"

Caden seemed momentarily taken aback but quickly regained his composure. "Then let it be a battle of wits as well as magic! We'll see who is the true champion!"

"Fine!" Alarion declared. "But let's make it interesting. For every magical attack you throw, I'll counter with a clever quip. If I can make the audience laugh, I win!"

Caden smirked, clearly underestimating Alarion's charm. "Very well, let the duel begin!"

The villagers gathered in a circle, buzzing with excitement as the two squared off. Lila stood at the edge, her heart pounding with both fear and anticipation.

Alarion took a deep breath, steadying himself as Caden conjured flames that danced in mid-air, casting a warm glow across the square. "You'll regret challenging me!" Caden shouted, sending a barrage of fiery sparks toward Alarion.

Alarion dodged, laughing as he called out, "Wow, Caden, I didn't know you were auditioning for a firework show!"

The crowd erupted in laughter, and even Caden struggled to suppress a grin. "You think you can distract me with your jokes?" he retorted, throwing another fireball.

"Hey, if you want me to laugh, you might need to work on your aim!" Alarion shouted back, narrowly avoiding the blast.

"Your banter won't save you!" Caden bellowed, conjuring flames that spiraled into a dragon shape, soaring toward Alarion.

"Nice try! But I prefer my dragons to be more... scalable!" Alarion quipped, diving to the side as the flame-dragon disintegrated against the ground.

Lila couldn't help but laugh. "He's got a point, Caden!"

Caden's face turned a deeper shade of red, but he quickly regained his focus. "Enough of this! I'll show you true power!" He raised his arms dramatically, summoning flames that roared to life around him.

"Looks like someone needs to cool down!" Alarion shouted, his quick wit still intact.

As Caden unleashed a storm of fireballs, Alarion danced around them, narrowly avoiding the scorching blasts. He waved his arms, making exaggerated dodging movements that sent the crowd into fits of laughter.

"Careful, everyone! The fire mage has a short fuse!" he teased, causing Lila to double over with laughter.

"Stop dancing around and face me!" Caden challenged, a hint of frustration creeping into his voice.

"Why face you when I can dance?" Alarion grinned, executing a ridiculous two-step while dodging another fiery attack.

The crowd was now fully engaged, cheering for Alarion as he turned the duel into a comedy show. Caden, realizing he was losing the crowd's favor, tried to regain control. He conjured a towering wall of flames, a last-ditch effort to intimidate Alarion.

But Alarion, ever the improviser, turned the fiery wall into an opportunity. "A wall of flames? Oh, I see, you're just trying to build a fire safety lesson!" he exclaimed.

The audience burst into laughter once again, and even Lila was clapping her hands, her eyes shining with admiration.

"You'll pay for this!" Caden shouted, frustration boiling over. He charged forward, throwing a powerful wave of fire toward Alarion.

Just as the flames reached him, Alarion summoned all his courage and leaped high into the air, performing a mid-air somersault that left the audience gasping. "Sorry, Caden, but I'm not ready to be burned out yet!"

As he landed gracefully, the villagers erupted into cheers and applause. Alarion was riding a wave of confidence, fueled by their encouragement.

Caden's face fell, realizing he was losing not just the duel but also Lila's interest. "This is not over!" he yelled, trying to regain some semblance of dignity.

"Oh, I think it is," Lila replied, stepping forward with a smirk. "Alarion has shown his strength today, both in wit and in heart. I think it's time you accept defeat, Caden."

Caden huffed, crossing his arms. "This is embarrassing."

"Only for you!" Alarion chimed in, enjoying the victory. "But cheer up! You still have a future as a fire magician... in a comedy club!"

The villagers roared with laughter, and even Lila couldn't help but chuckle.

"Fine, I concede!" Caden grumbled, his pride wounded but accepting defeat. "But mark my words, Alarion, I will not forget this!"

With that, he turned and stormed away, flames sputtering behind him. Alarion and Lila exchanged glances, a spark of mischief lighting up between them.

"Wow, you really know how to steal the show!" Lila exclaimed; her cheeks flushed with excitement.

"Just trying to keep it light! I can't help it if I'm funny," Alarion replied with a wink.

"Funny and brave! Maybe I should keep you around," Lila said, her eyes dancing with playful challenge.

As they walked hand-in-hand back through the village square, laughter still echoed in the air, and Alarion felt a warmth in his chest that had nothing to do with the flames of the duel.

"Maybe we should celebrate your victory," Lila suggested, glancing toward a small tavern that promised warm drinks and music.

"Only if you promise to dance with me!" Alarion replied, an impish grin on his face.

"Deal!" Lila laughed, her eyes twinkling with anticipation.

As they entered the tavern, the sound of lively music greeted them. Alarion took Lila's hand, leading her to the center of the floor.

The air was thick with laughter and cheer as the villagers welcomed them with open arms.

"Let's create a song for our victory!" Lila shouted over the music.

"Perfect!" Alarion replied. "How about this?"

Song: "Flame and Laughter"
(Verse 1)
In the heart of Emberwood, we take our stand,
With fire and laughter, hand in hand.
A duel of wits, a battle of hearts,
Together we'll shine, and our journey starts!
(Chorus)
Flame and laughter, a fiery dance,
With every twist, we'll take our chance.
Through battles fought and laughter shared,
In Emberwood, our hearts are laid bare!
(Verse 2)
Caden may fume, but we'll rise above,
With every jest, we'll share our love.
In the light of the flames, our spirits soar,
Together forever, we'll laugh some more!
(Chorus)
Flame and laughter, a fiery dance,
With every twist, we'll take our chance.
Through battles fought and laughter shared,
In Emberwood, our hearts are laid bare!
(Bridge)
So, raise your glass, let the music play,
In Emberwood, we'll chase the gray.
With friends beside us, we'll face the night,
In this fiery village, everything feels right!
(Final Chorus)
Flame and laughter, a fiery dance,

With every twist, we'll take our chance.
Through battles fought and laughter shared,
In Emberwood, our hearts are laid bare!

As they danced and sang, Alarion couldn't shake the feeling that this was just the beginning of an extraordinary journey filled with laughter, love, and unexpected challenges. Each moment felt electric, promising more adventures on the horizon.

With Lila by his side, he was ready for whatever came next—even if it meant facing a jealous fire mage again. After all, a little rivalry only added spice to their tale, and he wouldn't trade it for anything.

Chapter 4: A Potion with a Twist

In search of a potion to enhance his abilities, Alarion accidentally drinks one that makes him irresistibly charming—much to Lila's delight and the fire mage's annoyance!

The sun had barely begun to rise over the village of Emberwood when Alarion found himself rummaging through the cluttered shelves of the local apothecary. The scents of dried herbs and mysterious concoctions hung in the air, creating a blend that was both intriguing and slightly nauseating.

"Just one little potion to boost my magical abilities," Alarion murmured, sifting through dusty jars and bottles that looked like they hadn't seen the light of day in years. He could feel Lila watching him, her amused smile teasing the corners of her lips.

"Are you sure you know what you're looking for?" she asked, leaning against a wooden counter, her arms crossed and a playful twinkle in her eyes. "Last time you tried to enhance your powers, you turned your hair purple for a week!"

Alarion chuckled, running a hand through his hair, which was still slightly tinted from that incident. "That was a minor setback. This time, I'm aiming for something more... sophisticated."

"Good luck with that," Lila replied, rolling her eyes. "Just promise you won't turn into a giant toad or something."

He laughed, "No promises, but I'll do my best."

As Alarion rummaged through the shelves, he stumbled upon a shimmering bottle filled with a sparkling liquid that seemed to dance in the light. "What's this?" he exclaimed, pulling it from the shelf.

"Ah, the Elixir of Charm," came a voice from behind him. It was Old Maura, the village's eccentric apothecary, her gray hair pulled back in a frizzy bun and her eyes twinkling with mischief. "A potion that enhances one's charm and charisma tenfold! But be careful, it can have unexpected effects!"

Alarion's eyes sparkled with curiosity. "Perfect! Just what I need!"

Lila raised an eyebrow, skepticism etched on her face. "Are you sure that's a good idea?"

"Absolutely!" he declared, not wanting to admit that he had no idea what those "unexpected effects" might be. "A little charm never hurt anyone, right?"

"Famous last words," Lila muttered under her breath, but Alarion was already pouring the shimmering liquid into a small vial, excitement bubbling within him.

With a flourish, he downed the potion in one gulp. Almost instantly, a warm glow enveloped him, and he felt a rush of energy unlike anything he'd experienced before. "Wow! This is amazing!"

But as he turned to Lila, he noticed something peculiar. The room seemed to shimmer, and Lila's eyes widened in surprise. "Alarion, are you okay?"

"I feel—" he began, but suddenly, his voice took on a velvety smoothness that made Lila's cheeks flush. "—incredible!"

Just then, a wave of confidence washed over him. He strutted across the room, striking a pose as if he were the most charming man in the universe. "Old Maura, you've outdone yourself!"

"Be careful!" she warned, a hint of concern creeping into her voice. "That potion can be unpredictable!"

Ignoring her words, Alarion approached Lila, who was now staring at him with wide eyes. "How about a little dance?" he suggested, winking dramatically.

Before Lila could respond, he took her hand and twirled her around, causing her to burst into laughter. "What are you doing?" she gasped, trying to catch her breath.

"Just showcasing my newfound charm!" Alarion declared, feeling invincible.

But as he continued to dance around the room, he suddenly heard a loud crash from outside. The sound shattered the playful mood, and Lila's laughter faded as concern etched across her face.

"What was that?" she asked, her eyes darting toward the door.

"I don't know, but let's check it out!" Alarion replied, excitement bubbling in his chest. He might be feeling charming, but that didn't mean he couldn't be a hero too.

They rushed outside to find a small crowd gathered near the village square. Caden, the fiery mage, was causing a scene, his face contorted in anger. "How dare you challenge me again!" he shouted, pointing an accusing finger at a cloaked figure standing defiantly across from him.

"Challenging you was a mistake, Caden," the cloaked figure replied, voice low and threatening. "You should know better than to meddle in matters beyond your understanding."

Alarion exchanged a glance with Lila, his playful demeanor fading. "Looks like we've got trouble," he said, trying to sound brave despite the lingering effects of the potion.

"Oh no," Lila whispered. "He's going to start a fight!"

"Not if I can help it," Alarion declared, feeling the urge to protect Lila and the villagers surge within him. He stepped forward, puffing out his chest. "Caden! Why don't you take your anger elsewhere?"

Caden turned, surprise crossing his face before morphing into a smirk. "And what will you do about it, dragon rider? Charm me into submission?"

"Actually," Alarion said, his confidence bolstered by the potion, "I was thinking more along the lines of a good old-fashioned duel."

"Are you sure you want to do that?" the cloaked figure asked, stepping out of the shadows.

Alarion finally got a good look at him—he was tall and muscular, with sharp features and an aura that radiated danger.

"I can handle myself," Alarion replied, casting a quick glance at Lila, who looked both worried and impressed. "I'll protect you; I promise."

Lila nodded, her eyes sparkling with determination. "Let's show them what we've got!"

With that, Alarion faced Caden, who was now fuming. "You think you can challenge me in front of everyone? This will be your downfall!"

"Maybe, but I can't wait to see the look on your face when I win," Alarion replied, grinning.

Without warning, Caden unleashed a torrent of fireballs aimed directly at Alarion. He dodged to the side, the heat singeing his clothes as he laughed. "You'll have to do better than that!"

Lila, watching with wide eyes, suddenly shouted, "Alarion, remember your charm! Use it!"

"Right!" he shouted back, catching a fireball in his hand, and instead of throwing it back, he turned it into a dazzling display of colorful sparks. "Why don't we turn this duel into a fireworks show instead?"

The crowd gasped, their surprise transforming into laughter as they cheered for Alarion's audacity. Caden's expression faltered, confusion creeping in. "What are you doing?"

Alarion took a few confident steps forward, his voice smooth and melodic. "Caden, don't you see? We can all enjoy the spectacle without fighting. How about a duet instead?"

"A duet?" Caden echoed, incredulity mingling with annoyance.

"Yes! Let's serenade the crowd! Here's a song I wrote!" Alarion announced, standing tall as he began to belt out a tune.

Song: "Hearts on Fire"
(Verse 1)
In the heart of Emberwood, where the flames dance bright,
Let's put our differences aside tonight.
With laughter and charm, we'll ignite the sky,
Join me, dear rival, let our spirits fly!
(Chorus)
Hearts on fire, burning bright,
With every note, we'll take flight.
Together we'll shine, through laughter and pain,
In the heat of the moment, let's break these chains!
(Verse 2)
So Caden, my friend, don't let anger consume you,
Join me in song, let's chase away the gloom.
With every strum, our worries will fade,
In this grand duet, our fears will evade!
(Chorus)
Hearts on fire, burning bright,
With every note, we'll take flight.
Together we'll shine, through laughter and pain,
In the heat of the moment, let's break these chains!
(Bridge)
So let the flames flicker, let the laughter ring,
In Emberwood's heart, we'll dance and sing.
Together we'll stand, our differences gone,
In this fiery embrace, we'll carry on!
(Final Chorus)
Hearts on fire, burning bright,
With every note, we'll take flight.
Together we'll shine, through laughter and pain,
In the heat of the moment, let's break these chains!

As Alarion sang, the crowd began to sway, caught up in the infectious joy radiating from him. Caden, at first hesitant, found himself tapping his foot against the cobblestones, a begrudging smile breaking through his anger.

Lila joined in, her voice blending harmoniously with Alarion's, creating an enchanting melody that wrapped around the village like a warm embrace. The villagers erupted into cheers, their laughter echoing in the air, and even Caden couldn't help but laugh as the tension melted away.

By the end of the song, Caden's bravado had deflated, replaced by a sheepish grin. "Alright, alright, you win this round, dragon rider," he conceded, extending a hand toward Alarion. "Maybe there's more to you than I thought."

"Don't mention it," Alarion replied, shaking Caden's hand and relishing the shared camaraderie. "Let's keep the fires of rivalry simmering, but let's make it more fun next time."

The crowd erupted into applause, and Lila beamed at Alarion. "That was amazing! You really turned the situation around!"

"Just a little potion magic," he grinned, giving a wink. "And a lot of charm!"

As the villagers began to disperse, laughter filled the air, and Alarion felt a sense of accomplishment wash over him. He had faced a fiery rival, charmed the village, and even strengthened his bond with Lila, who was watching him with admiration.

"Maybe this potion isn't so bad after all," Alarion said, feeling a spark of mischief ignite within him. "But I think I'll keep my distance from any fireballs for now."

Lila laughed, shaking her head. "Just promise me you won't go overboard with your charm. I like you just the way you are—quirky and all."

Alarion grinned, his heart soaring. "Quirky, huh? I can work with that."

As they walked together under the soft glow of the Emberwood lanterns, Alarion couldn't help but feel that their adventures were just beginning. With Lila by his side and a little charm in his pocket, he was ready to face whatever challenges lay ahead.

Chapter 5: The Fiery Trials

Alarion faces the Trials of Fire, a series of tests that involve both physical challenges and navigating the flames of his own heart. Humor ensues as he fumbles through them, often with Lila's witty commentary.

As dawn broke over Emberwood, the village bustled with excitement. Today marked the beginning of the Trials of Fire, a legendary challenge that every aspiring mage had to face. Tales of the Trials echoed through the village, filled with fiery obstacles and the promise of glory. For Alarion, however, the thought of facing flames and trials sent shivers down his spine, a mix of exhilaration and apprehension dancing in his chest.

Lila, radiant and teasing as ever, bounced beside him, her golden hair shimmering in the early morning light. "Are you ready for your fiery doom?" she quipped, a playful smirk gracing her lips.

"Doom? I prefer to think of it as an exciting adventure!" Alarion replied, trying to sound confident despite the knot in his stomach. "Besides, what could go wrong?"

Lila raised an eyebrow, crossing her arms. "Oh, I don't know—perhaps the flames will discover how charming you are and fall madly in love?"

Alarion laughed, his nerves easing slightly. "At least I'll have my charm to keep me safe!"

As they approached the center of the village, Alarion spotted a large bonfire crackling in the middle of the square, surrounded by villagers eager to witness the trials. The village elder, a wise old woman with an air of authority, stood by the fire, her eyes scanning the crowd.

"Welcome, brave souls!" she called out, her voice booming. "Today, we begin the Trials of Fire! Each contestant will face three challenges, testing not only their physical strength but their spirit and heart as well!"

Alarion exchanged a glance with Lila, determination gleaming in his eyes. "Let's do this!" he declared.

The elder gestured for the contestants to step forward. Alarion, filled with excitement, raised his hand. "I'm ready!"

As the first challenge commenced, Alarion found himself standing before a wall of flames that roared like a hungry dragon. "The first trial," the elder announced, "is to navigate through the Fire Wall!"

Alarion gulped. "Navigate through fire? Piece of cake!" He took a deep breath and charged forward, only to trip over his own feet and tumble into the fiery wall, squealing in surprise. Lila burst into laughter, her eyes sparkling with mirth.

"Nice dive!" she called out, trying to catch her breath. "You're really committed to the whole 'fiery' theme!"

As Alarion scrambled to his feet, he realized the flames were mere illusions, flickering around him but causing no real harm. "Oh, that's not so bad!" he laughed, brushing himself off.

With newfound confidence, he danced through the flames, arms flailing wildly as he pretended to perform an exaggerated routine. The crowd erupted in cheers and laughter, and even the elder couldn't suppress a smile.

"Impressive footwork, Alarion!" Lila shouted, clapping her hands. "Who knew you were such a talented performer?"

Finishing with a flamboyant bow, Alarion soaked in the applause. "All in a day's work!"

Once through the first challenge, Alarion turned to see the second trial awaiting him: a massive cauldron bubbling with bright orange liquid. "Your next task is to retrieve the Ember Crystal from the cauldron!" the elder proclaimed. "But beware of the boiling liquid!"

"Looks simple enough," Alarion said confidently. He approached the cauldron, peering into the swirling liquid. "How hot can it be?"

"Let's find out!" Lila teased. "Just remember to aim for the crystal and not your fingers!"

Taking her advice to heart, Alarion dipped his hand in the cauldron, wincing at the warmth. "Oh, this is fine," he said, trying to sound nonchalant. Suddenly, the cauldron bubbled violently, splashing hot liquid onto his face. "Yowch!" he yelled, pulling his hand back. "That's hot!"

"Did you just burn your eyebrows off?" Lila giggled, unable to contain her laughter.

"Maybe just a little," Alarion replied, shaking his head and trying to regain his composure. "I can still do this!"

Determined, he leaned back in, grasping for the crystal with exaggerated care. With a flourish, he finally plucked the glowing gem from the cauldron and held it up triumphantly. "I've got it!" he cheered, but the moment was short-lived.

As he turned around, he lost his balance and fell backward into the cauldron, sending everyone into a frenzy of laughter. "Fire mage turned soup!" Lila exclaimed, clutching her sides.

Emerging from the cauldron, Alarion shook off the gooey remnants, his hair sticking up comically. "I guess I'm just soaking up the experience!" he quipped, trying to save face as he rejoined Lila, who was wiping tears of laughter from her eyes.

"Just a few more trials to go!" Lila encouraged, though her voice was still thick with giggles.

"Bring it on!" Alarion declared, wiping his brow.

The final trial loomed ahead, and Alarion's heart raced. Before him stood a massive stone statue of a fiery dragon, its eyes glowing ominously. "To pass this trial," the elder announced, "you must defeat the Guardian of Fire in a battle of wits!"

"Wits?" Alarion echoed, scratching his head. "Isn't that more your specialty, Lila?"

"Hey! You've got this!" she encouraged, stepping back as the dragon roared to life, flames shooting from its mouth.

"Okay, I can do this," Alarion said, stepping forward with newfound determination. "I'll just charm it with my brilliance!"

As the dragon lunged, Alarion ducked and rolled, narrowly avoiding the fiery breath. "Okay, okay," he muttered to himself. "Think fast, Alarion!"

The dragon paused, eyes narrowing. "What is the secret of the flames?" it boomed, smoke billowing from its nostrils.

Alarion stood tall, determination flooding through him. "The secret of the flames is—" he paused for dramatic effect, "that they can't burn a heart filled with laughter!"

Lila burst out laughing from the sidelines, her laughter infectious. "That's right! Humor is the key!" she yelled, clearly enjoying the spectacle.

"Correct!" the dragon roared, though it seemed slightly confused. "But can you prove it?"

"Of course!" Alarion said, a plan forming in his mind. He began to sing a song, pulling Lila into the performance.

Song: "Dance of the Flames"
(Verse 1)
In the heat of the fire, let's dance with glee,
With laughter and joy, come and follow me.
The flames may be fierce, but they can't hold me down,
In this sizzling trial, I'll wear my crown!
(Chorus)

Dance of the flames, let's twirl and spin,
With each little step, let the magic begin.
In the heart of the fire, we'll shine so bright,
Together we'll conquer, from morning till night!
(Verse 2)
So, fire dragon, join us, let's make a show,
With every beat and rhythm, let the good times flow.
We'll dance through the flames, hand in hand,
With laughter and charm, we'll take a stand!
(Chorus)
Dance of the flames, let's twirl and spin,
With each little step, let the magic begin.
In the heart of the fire, we'll shine so bright,
Together we'll conquer, from morning till night!
(Bridge)
So don't be afraid, let the flames take flight,
In this fiery embrace, we'll ignite the night.
With every laugh and smile, we'll break down the wall,
In the Dance of the Flames, we'll conquer it all!
(Final Chorus)
Dance of the flames, let's twirl and spin,
With each little step, let the magic begin.
In the heart of the fire, we'll shine so bright,
Together we'll conquer, from morning till night!

As Alarion and Lila sang, the flames swirled around them, creating a mesmerizing display of fire and color. The crowd erupted in cheers, clapping along with the rhythm. Even the dragon seemed enchanted, its fiery eyes softening.

By the end of the song, the dragon bowed its head. "You have proven your worth, young mage. Your heart is indeed filled with laughter and joy." The flames around Alarion dimmed, revealing a shimmering path through the fire.

Alarion turned to Lila, his heart racing. "Did we just win?"

"Absolutely!" Lila exclaimed, throwing her arms around him. "You were amazing! Who knew you had such charm in battle?"

"Thanks to you!" he replied, grinning widely. "I couldn't have done it without your support."

As they walked away from the Trials of Fire, the villagers cheered, celebrating Alarion's unexpected triumph. Lila nudged him playfully. "Next time, maybe you can just dance your way through the challenges!"

Alarion laughed, his heart soaring. "With you by my side, I can conquer anything!"

As they strolled back toward the village, the sun dipped low in the sky, casting a golden hue over Emberwood. Lila looked up at Alarion, her eyes sparkling with admiration. "What's next for us, my brave mage?"

"Who knows?" Alarion replied, a twinkle in his eye. "But wherever we go, I know it'll be an adventure!"

With laughter ringing in the air and a spark of romance lighting their path, Alarion and Lila stepped into their next chapter, ready for whatever challenges awaited them in the magical realm.

Chapter 6: A Spark of Friendship

During a quiet moment, Alarion and Lila bond over shared stories of their pasts, igniting a spark of friendship that hints at something deeper. Can their chemistry survive the coming battles?

The sun hung low in the sky, casting a warm golden hue over Emberwood. After the exhilarating Trials of Fire, Alarion and Lila found themselves resting on a grassy hill overlooking the village. The faint sound of laughter and chatter drifted up from below, blending seamlessly with the soft rustle of leaves in the gentle breeze.

Alarion stretched out on the grass, hands behind his head, staring up at the fluffy clouds drifting lazily by. "You know," he began, breaking the comfortable silence, "I never expected the Trials to be so... entertaining."

Lila chuckled beside him, her fingers idly plucking at the grass. "Entertaining? You mean the part where you fell into the cauldron? Or when you danced through the flames like a deranged firefly?"

He shot her a playful glare, though the corners of his mouth tugged upward. "Hey, at least I made an impression! And besides, those moves were top-notch."

"Top-notch? More like a clumsy caterpillar!" she laughed, her eyes sparkling with mischief. "But I suppose the dragon enjoyed your performance. You charmed it right into submission!"

With a mock-serious expression, Alarion replied, "Well, they do say laughter is the best weapon. Perhaps I should stick to comedy in battle!"

"Good plan!" Lila said, leaning closer, her curiosity piqued. "But seriously, what made you decide to become a mage?"

Alarion paused, feeling the weight of her question. "Honestly? I wanted to prove that I could be more than just the 'ordinary' kid from the village. I wanted to explore, to have adventures—just like the stories my grandmother used to tell me."

"What kind of stories?" Lila inquired, her tone shifting to one of genuine interest.

"Adventures filled with magic and brave heroes," he replied, his voice growing more animated. "My favorite was about a daring mage who saved a kingdom from a terrible dragon. He didn't just fight the dragon; he befriended it and learned from it, discovering that courage comes in many forms."

"That's beautiful," Lila said, her gaze drifting off to the horizon. "I've always wanted to be a hero too, but my journey started in a much different way."

"Really?" Alarion leaned in closer, intrigued. "What happened?"

She took a deep breath, recalling her past. "I grew up in a small village, and magic wasn't something we spoke of. My family struggled to make ends meet, and I often found myself daydreaming about a life filled with adventure. One day, I stumbled upon a hidden grove filled with strange glowing flowers. They whispered to me, beckoning me to join them. That's when I discovered my own magical abilities. It felt like I was meant for something greater."

"That's incredible!" Alarion exclaimed. "So, you were chosen by magic itself?"

"Something like that," she said, a shy smile creeping onto her face. "I never thought I'd find someone to share my adventures with. But then you came along."

Alarion's heart fluttered at her words, a warmth spreading through him. "I feel the same way. You've turned this whole journey into something amazing. And even with all the battles and challenges ahead, I'm glad I have you by my side."

Their eyes locked for a moment, the world around them fading into the background. Just as a spark of understanding flickered between them, a sudden rustling in the nearby bushes broke the tension.

"What was that?" Lila whispered, her playful demeanor vanishing.

"Not sure," Alarion replied, sitting up straight, all senses heightened. "Let's check it out."

With cautious steps, they approached the bushes, hearts racing. Suddenly, a figure emerged, cloaked in shadow, with an air of danger surrounding them. The intruder smirked, revealing a sharp grin. "Well, well, well! If it isn't the infamous Alarion and his lovely companion!"

Alarion narrowed his eyes. "Who are you?"

The stranger stepped forward, revealing fiery red hair and piercing blue eyes that seemed to spark with mischief. "I'm Kira, a rogue mage, and I'm here to settle a score with you, Alarion. You think you can charm your way through everything?"

"I didn't realize charm was a crime," Alarion retorted, trying to keep his cool.

"Oh, it is when it makes you a target," Kira replied, conjuring a flickering flame in her palm. "I've heard tales of your escapades. You and your little dance number at the Trials. What a joke!"

Lila stepped forward, her protective instincts kicking in. "You're just jealous because he outshined you. What's your problem?"

Kira chuckled, her voice dripping with sarcasm. "My problem is you're in my way. I'm here to prove that charm isn't enough to win in this world of magic!"

With a wave of her hand, Kira unleashed a barrage of fireballs toward them. Alarion instinctively jumped in front of Lila, conjuring a protective barrier just in time. The flames exploded against the barrier, sending sparks flying in every direction.

"Watch out!" Alarion yelled, pulling Lila to safety behind a tree.

"Nice reflexes!" Lila exclaimed; her eyes wide with excitement. "But what now?"

"We need to distract her," Alarion said, glancing at the rogue mage, who was now preparing for another attack. "How about a little humor?"

"What do you mean?" Lila asked, her brow furrowing.

"Just trust me!" Alarion replied, a grin spreading across his face.

With newfound determination, Alarion stepped out from behind the tree, arms raised dramatically. "Hey, Kira! Want to hear a joke?"

Kira paused, momentarily thrown off guard. "What?"

"Why did the fire mage break up with their partner?" Alarion shouted.

"Why?" Kira asked, intrigued despite herself.

"Because they found their love too hot to handle!" Alarion declared, throwing in a flourish.

As laughter bubbled up from Lila, Kira's expression shifted, caught off guard by the unexpected humor. "That's ridiculous!"

"Exactly!" Lila chimed in, stepping forward. "And that's why you need to lighten up! There's enough chaos in the world without adding more."

Alarion saw the flicker of uncertainty in Kira's eyes. "Look, we're not enemies. We can find a better way to solve this than battling it out."

Kira hesitated, her fireballs wavering. "You think charm will work on me?"

"Not charm, friendship," Alarion replied, sincerity pouring from his words. "We've all got our pasts, but we can't let them define us. Join us instead. There's plenty of adventure to go around."

Slowly, the flames began to fade from Kira's hands. "Friendship?" she echoed, disbelief evident in her tone. "What do you know about friendship?"

"I know it's about finding common ground," Lila interjected. "About connecting and sharing laughter, like Alarion does with everyone. You could join us in our adventures!"

Kira's posture softened, the fierce facade cracking just a bit. "You really think I could just... join you?"

"Absolutely!" Alarion smiled, stepping closer. "Imagine all the mischief we could get into together!"

After a moment of silence, Kira dropped her head, a small laugh escaping her lips. "You two are ridiculous. But maybe... just maybe, I could use some friends."

"Great! Just don't go setting anything on fire, alright?" Alarion joked, raising an eyebrow.

Kira chuckled, the tension evaporating as she lowered her hands. "Deal. But you two better keep up!"

With the unlikely friendship forming, the three of them began to walk back toward Emberwood, laughter echoing through the trees. The spark of friendship had ignited, hinting at something deeper as they moved forward together into the unknown, ready to face whatever challenges awaited them.

Song: "Friends by Firelight"
(Verse 1)
In the glow of the flames, we'll laugh and play,
With stories to share, let worries drift away.
Side by side, we'll conquer the night,
Together we'll shine, hearts burning bright.
(Chorus)
Friends by firelight, we'll dance through the dark,
With every step, we'll ignite a spark.
In this journey together, no battles alone,

We'll find our way, and make this world our own.
(Verse 2)
From trials and troubles, we'll rise above,
Through fire and laughter, we'll find our love.
In the warmth of friendship, we'll stand tall,
Together we'll face whatever may befall.
(Chorus)
Friends by firelight, we'll dance through the dark,
With every step, we'll ignite a spark.
In this journey together, no battles alone,
We'll find our way, and make this world our own.
(Bridge)
So let the flames flicker, let the shadows fall,
In the heart of our laughter, we'll conquer it all.
With every adventure, with every twist and turn,
The fire of friendship will forever burn!
(Final Chorus)
Friends by firelight, we'll dance through the dark,
With every step, we'll ignite a spark.
In this journey together, no battles alone,
We'll find our way, and make this world our own.

As they sang, their voices harmonizing under the starlit sky, Alarion, Lila, and Kira felt the weight of past struggles lift, replaced by the warmth of newfound friendship. Together, they were ready to embrace whatever magical adventures awaited them in the days to come, forging bonds that would withstand the tests of time and fire.

Chapter 7: Shadows of the Past

Alarion encounters a ghost from his past, revealing secrets that challenge his perception of friendship and love. Can he reconcile these memories while keeping his eyes on the prize?

The morning sun filtered through the trees of the Whispering Woods, casting playful shadows on the ground as Alarion, Lila, and Kira made their way deeper into the forest. After forging a bond that seemed almost magical, the trio felt emboldened to explore uncharted territories and tackle whatever challenges lay ahead.

"I can't believe we survived Kira's fiery temper!" Lila said, her laughter echoing through the trees. "You really do know how to charm a rogue, Alarion!"

Kira rolled her eyes, smirking. "I'm still trying to figure out if I'm impressed or just bemused."

"Definitely both," Alarion replied, giving her a playful nudge. "But honestly, it's not every day you find a fiery rogue who can also be charmed by dad jokes."

As they walked, Alarion felt a tugging sensation at the back of his mind—a feeling he couldn't quite shake. "You guys ever feel like something is watching us?" he asked, glancing around nervously.

"Maybe it's just your overactive imagination," Lila teased, though her eyes darted about, looking for signs of danger.

Suddenly, the atmosphere shifted. A chilling breeze swept through the trees, causing the leaves to rustle ominously. Alarion's heart raced as he sensed something was indeed amiss.

"Stay close," he warned, taking the lead. Just then, a figure emerged from behind a gnarled tree—a translucent apparition clad in tattered robes, with a face that seemed both familiar and haunting.

"Alarion..." the ghost whispered, its voice echoing through the woods.

"What? Who are you?" Alarion stammered, his heart pounding. He recognized the voice, but it felt like a distant memory.

The ghost stepped closer, and Alarion's breath caught in his throat. "It's me... Maris."

Lila gasped, her expression shifting from confusion to sympathy. "You knew her?"

"She was my best friend... before..." Alarion faltered, grappling with the emotions that rushed back. Memories flooded his mind—days filled with laughter, adventures, and an unspoken bond that had crumbled with time.

Maris floated closer; her eyes full of longing. "I never wanted to leave, Alarion. I was taken too soon, and I've been watching you ever since."

Alarion clenched his fists, the weight of regret heavy on his shoulders. "Why are you here? What do you want from me?"

"I'm here to help you, to guide you through the shadows of your past," Maris replied, her voice soft yet firm. "You've been running from the memories of our friendship, but you must face them to find your true strength."

"Face them?" he echoed, incredulous. "You want me to confront a past that still haunts me?"

"Exactly," she said, her ghostly form flickering like a flame. "You're about to face a great battle, and your memories will be your greatest weapon."

As Maris's words sank in, a wave of nostalgia washed over Alarion. He remembered how they used to explore the woods, discovering hidden paths and secret glades. They were inseparable, partners in crime, until the day fate tore them apart.

Kira and Lila exchanged worried glances, sensing Alarion's inner turmoil. "Alarion, you don't have to do this alone," Lila said, placing a comforting hand on his arm. "We're with you."

"Yeah," Kira chimed in, her usual bravado softened. "If there are shadows, we'll fight them together."

With newfound determination, Alarion faced Maris. "What do I need to do?"

"You must confront the moment you lost me," she said, her form shimmering. "Only then can you reclaim the strength you need for the battles ahead."

"Let's go," Alarion said, resolute. "Lead the way."

As Maris began to float backward, Alarion, Lila, and Kira followed her deeper into the woods. The atmosphere grew heavier, the shadows thickening around them as they entered a clearing they hadn't seen before—a place Alarion recognized all too well.

"This is where it happened," he whispered, his voice trembling as he glanced at the remnants of a once-vibrant clearing. The air was thick with memories—the echoes of laughter faded into ghostly whispers, intertwining with the sorrow that hung like a shroud.

A dark figure emerged from the shadows, a malevolent presence that sent chills down Alarion's spine. "You should have stayed away, Alarion," the figure growled, its voice dripping with malice.

"Who are you?" Alarion demanded, stepping protectively in front of Lila and Kira.

"Just a shadow of your past," the figure sneered, morphing into a monstrous shape. "I came to remind you of your failure. Your weakness."

"Shut up!" Alarion shouted, feeling the heat of anger ignite within him. "I won't let you haunt me anymore!"

"Prove it," the shadow taunted, lunging at them.

Kira sprang into action, flames bursting forth from her hands. "Get ready!" she shouted, hurling fireballs at the creature, but they passed right through it as if it were smoke.

"Nice try!" it taunted. "But you can't burn away the past!"

"Alarion!" Lila shouted, urgency lacing her voice. "You have to remember the good times with Maris! Channel that strength!"

In the heart of battle, Alarion felt the warmth of memories flooding back—days spent laughing with Maris, running through the forest, and sharing dreams of adventure. With each thought, his heart ignited with purpose.

"Enough!" Alarion shouted, his voice steady. "You may be a shadow, but I have light in my heart!" He lifted his hands, channeling the magic within him, creating a barrier of light that pushed against the dark figure.

"Get out of my way!" he yelled, pouring every ounce of his emotions into the barrier, fueled by memories of laughter and friendship.

The shadow screeched, unable to withstand the light. It writhed and twisted, struggling to escape the force of Alarion's magic. With a final surge of energy, Alarion unleashed a blinding burst of light, engulfing the shadow completely.

The clearing fell silent, the darkness dissipating like smoke in the wind. Alarion, breathless and shaken, turned to find Maris standing there, a proud smile on her ethereal face. "You did it, Alarion. You faced your past and emerged stronger."

Tears filled Alarion's eyes as he looked at her. "I wish you were still here."

"I'm always with you, in every adventure and every laugh," Maris replied gently. "Now, go. Your journey isn't over yet."

With that, her form began to fade, the soft glow of her presence illuminating the clearing one last time before she disappeared completely.

Alarion felt a wave of grief and relief wash over him, knowing he had finally confronted his past. "Let's move forward," he said, wiping away his tears, a newfound determination shining in his eyes.

Lila stepped forward, wrapping her arms around him. "You're incredible, Alarion. We're proud of you."

Kira nodded; her fiery spirit rekindled. "And if any more shadows try to creep up on us, they'll have to deal with all three of us!"

With their spirits lifted, the trio set off once again, the weight of the past no longer holding them back. As they ventured deeper into the woods, they knew that whatever lay ahead—be it trials, battles, or new friendships—they would face it together, ready to embrace every moment of their magical journey.

Song: "Shadows No More"
(Verse 1)
In the depths of the night, I hear a call,
Whispers of the past, I can't ignore at all.
But I'll stand my ground, won't let fear take flight,
With the memories of laughter, I'll face the night.
(Chorus)
Shadows no more, I'm breaking free,
With the light of friendship, I'll find my way, you'll see.
Together we rise, hand in hand,
In the face of the darkness, we'll take a stand.
(Verse 2)
From the echoes of doubt, I'll build my strength,
With the fire of our bond, we'll go to any length.
In the heart of the battle, we'll shine so bright,
No more hiding away, we'll embrace the light.
(Chorus)
Shadows no more, I'm breaking free,
With the light of friendship, I'll find my way, you'll see.

Together we rise, hand in hand,
In the face of the darkness, we'll take a stand.
(Bridge)
Every memory cherished, every laugh shared,
In the heart of our journey, we'll find that we dared.
To confront the shadows, to face what we fear,
With the strength of our friendship, we'll always be nearby.
(Final Chorus)
Shadows no more, I'm breaking free,
With the light of friendship, I'll find my way, you'll see.
Together we rise, hand in hand,
In the face of the darkness, we'll take a stand.

As the echoes of their song faded into the woods, Alarion, Lila, and Kira felt the warmth of their friendship radiate, ready to conquer whatever challenges awaited them next. Their laughter mingled with the rustling leaves, a promise that they would face the shadows together, turning the past into strength for the future.

Chapter 8: The Mischievous Spirits

In a whimsical forest, Alarion and Lila face off against playful fire sprites who steal their belongings. They must outsmart these mischievous creatures to retrieve a key to the Eternal Flame.

The sun dipped low in the sky, casting a golden hue over the whimsical forest of Flickerwood. Alarion and Lila, their spirits high after their recent victory against the shadows of the past, strolled along a path lined with flowers that giggled when touched. Lila twirled around, her laughter ringing like chimes in the wind.

"Can you feel that?" she exclaimed, her eyes sparkling. "It's as if the forest is alive!"

"Alive and full of mischief, I suspect," Alarion replied, raising an eyebrow. "Remember what Kira said about Flickerwood? It's not just the flowers that are playful."

"Yeah, yeah, I know. But how much trouble could a few fire sprites cause?" Lila grinned, undeterred.

Just as the words left her lips, a flickering flash of light darted past them. Alarion's instincts kicked in, and he whipped around, ready to defend them against whatever might come.

"Look out!" he shouted.

But it was too late. A group of mischievous fire sprites burst forth from the trees, their tiny forms dancing in midair like living flames. They giggled, their voices high-pitched and melodic, as they zoomed past Alarion and Lila.

"Give us your stuff, or you'll have to play!" one of the sprites taunted, snatching Lila's backpack right off her shoulder and darting away.

"Hey! Come back here!" Lila yelled, her face a mix of annoyance and amusement. "That's mine!"

Alarion let out a laugh, realizing that their situation was comical despite the impending trouble. "I didn't think we'd be robbed by fire sprites today. This is going to be interesting!"

"Interesting doesn't begin to cover it!" Lila shot back, already chasing after the sprites. Alarion joined her, both of them sprinting through the forest, laughter and determination driving them forward.

The sprites darted among the trees, their giggles echoing through the air. They flitted just out of reach, teasingly waving Lila's backpack as they swooped and dived.

"Okay, think, Alarion!" he muttered to himself, trying to strategize. "What would a mischievous sprite want?"

Lila caught up beside him, her hair bouncing wildly. "A game! They love games!"

"Games?" Alarion pondered. "Like tag or hide-and-seek? We can't just chase them. They'll only keep teasing us."

Just then, one of the sprites swooped down low, almost within reach. Alarion had an idea. "Let's challenge them! If we can outsmart them in a game, they'll give us back your backpack and the key to the Eternal Flame!"

"Great idea!" Lila beamed. "But what game?"

"Let's do a riddle-off!" Alarion proposed, an excited grin forming on his face. "Sprites love riddles, and it will give us a chance to win our stuff back."

"Deal!" Lila shouted; her competitive spirit ignited. "Let's call them!"

Alarion clapped his hands together, drawing the sprites' attention. "Hey, mischievous sprites! We challenge you to a riddle-off! If we win, you return our belongings!"

The sprites paused mid-flight, intrigued. One of the larger sprites with shimmering wings hovered closer. "Riddles? How fun! We accept your challenge!"

"Great! You first!" Alarion said, trying to sound confident despite the flutter of nerves in his stomach.

The sprite grinned, its fiery form crackling with energy. "Here's my riddle: I can be cracked, made, told, and played. What am I?"

Alarion's mind raced. "A joke!" he shouted, a triumphant grin spreading across his face.

The sprite's eyes widened in surprise, but then it laughed, a tinkling sound that rang through the forest. "Correct! But can you keep up with our pace?"

With a flourish, the sprite tossed Lila's backpack into the air. Another sprite caught it, and they began to pass it back and forth like a hot potato. Alarion and Lila exchanged glances, their determination renewed.

"Your turn!" Lila called, her hands on her hips, ready to impress.

The sprites giggled, clearly enjoying the game. "Here's our next riddle: What has keys but can't open locks?"

Alarion's face lit up. "A piano!"

"Very clever," the sprite conceded, its tiny hands clapping together in delight. "But let's see if you can handle the next one."

The game continued, each round filled with laughter, playful banter, and even a few amusing blunders. Alarion and Lila traded riddles with the sprites, matching wits and finding joy in the challenge.

At last, the final riddle came. "You're getting close, but can you answer this: The more you take, the more you leave behind. What am I?"

Alarion's brow furrowed in concentration, but it was Lila who suddenly burst out with the answer. "Footsteps!"

The sprites erupted in laughter, their glow brighter than ever. "You've outsmarted us! A fair victory!" one sprite exclaimed, flitting around in delight. "We will return your belongings and grant you access to the key of the Eternal Flame!"

The sprites gleefully retrieved Lila's backpack and presented it back to her. In unison, they summoned a small, glowing key that danced in the air, shimmering with an enchanting light. "This is the key you seek, but remember—true strength lies in friendship, laughter, and the willingness to embrace the whimsical!"

"Thank you!" Alarion said, grateful for the experience. "You made this adventure unforgettable!"

As they waved goodbye to the sprites, Lila hugged her backpack tightly. "What a day! I never thought I'd have so much fun being chased by fiery little thieves!"

"Who knew we'd have to play games to get our stuff back?" Alarion laughed, the adrenaline still coursing through him.

"Next time, I'll just keep a closer eye on my things!" Lila teased, her eyes sparkling with mischief. "Maybe we should keep the key hidden until we need it."

As they continued their journey deeper into Flickerwood, a sense of camaraderie filled the air. Together, they faced the unexpected and learned to find joy even in the most whimsical of challenges.

Song: "Chasing Fireflies"
(Verse 1)
In the forest where the spirits play,
We danced with flames, chased the day away.
With laughter echoing through the trees,
Our hearts ignited, carried on the breeze.
(Chorus)

Chasing fireflies, oh what a thrill,
With each riddle and laugh, we're climbing the hill.
In the glow of friendship, we rise above,
With the spark of the forest, we find our love.
(Verse 2)
Mischievous sprites, they stole our pride,
But with a wink and a laugh, we took it in stride.
In the light of the flames, we made our stand,
Together we're stronger, united we'll land.
(Chorus)
Chasing fireflies, oh what a thrill,
With each riddle and laugh, we're climbing the hill.
In the glow of friendship, we rise above,
With the spark of the forest, we find our love.
(Bridge)
Through shadows and trials, we'll face the night,
With the warmth of our hearts, we'll shine so bright.
Every challenge before us, we'll conquer as one,
In the dance of our spirits, we'll never be done.
(Final Chorus)
Chasing fireflies, oh what a thrill,
With each riddle and laugh, we're climbing the hill.
In the glow of friendship, we rise above,
With the spark of the forest, we find our love.

As they continued their journey, the echoes of the song followed them, weaving a melody that captured their spirits. With the key to the Eternal Flame secured, Alarion and Lila felt the bond between them grow even stronger, ready to face whatever whimsical adventures lay ahead. The forest sparkled with possibilities, and together, they were ready to embrace every twist and turn.

Chapter 9: The Dance of Flames

Alarion and Lila participate in a festival celebrating the Flame, where an enchanting dance leads to unexpected feelings and some comically awkward moments under the starlit sky.

The night air was thick with excitement as Alarion and Lila approached the heart of Flickerwood, where the annual Festival of Flames was in full swing. Lanterns shaped like flickering fireflies hung from every branch, casting a warm, golden glow on the vibrant crowd. The aroma of roasted marshmallows and sweet pastries filled the air, tantalizing their senses.

"This place is incredible!" Lila exclaimed, her eyes sparkling with wonder. "I can't believe we're here!"

"I know, right?" Alarion grinned, feeling the infectious energy of the festival. "It's like a dream!"

As they navigated through the festivities, they passed booths filled with handmade crafts, games, and an impressive spread of food. Everywhere they looked, people were laughing, dancing, and enjoying the magical atmosphere. A fire juggler spun flames in the air, while a bard strummed a cheerful tune on his lute.

"Look! They're about to start the dance of flames!" Lila pointed, excitement bubbling in her voice.

At the center of the festival, a large bonfire blazed, surrounded by a circle of dancers. The flames flickered in time with the music, creating a hypnotic rhythm that drew the crowd in. The dancers moved gracefully, their movements mirroring the fire's flickering light.

"Shall we join them?" Alarion asked, his heart racing with both anticipation and a hint of nervousness.

"Absolutely!" Lila replied, grabbing his hand and pulling him toward the fire.

As they entered the circle, the warmth of the flames enveloped them, and Alarion felt a surge of confidence. He could hardly believe how magical this moment was. Lila's laughter was like music to his ears, and he was determined to make it unforgettable.

The dance began, and they followed the steps of the other dancers. At first, Alarion stumbled, stepping on Lila's foot as they twirled. "Sorry!" he said, wincing.

"Watch where you're going, hotshot!" Lila teased, playfully shoving him. Her eyes sparkled with mischief, and he couldn't help but laugh at their silly antics.

As they continued to dance, the rhythm of the fire and the music took over. Lila led him into a spin, her hair swirling around her like a fiery halo. Alarion lost himself in the moment, his heart pounding not just from the dance but from the undeniable chemistry between them.

"Okay, let's really show them how it's done!" Lila exclaimed, and with that, she launched into a series of fancy moves. Alarion, trying to keep up, attempted a dramatic flourish, only to trip over his own feet. He stumbled backward, nearly crashing into a group of dancers.

The crowd erupted in laughter, and Lila doubled over, unable to contain her amusement. "Nice one, Alarion!"

"Hey, I was just trying to add a little drama!" he shot back, grinning despite himself. He took her hand again, and they danced in sync this time, their laughter mingling with the music.

As the night progressed, the dance became more intense, with swirling flames and the exhilarating beat of the drums. It felt like the world around them faded away, leaving just the two of them in their own little universe. Alarion looked into Lila's eyes, and for a moment, everything felt perfect.

"Do you think we'll be dancing like this forever?" he asked, his voice barely audible over the music.

"Only if you don't step on my toes again!" she replied with a playful wink. But beneath her teasing, Alarion sensed a hint of something deeper—a connection that sparked like the flames surrounding them.

Just then, a loud crash interrupted their moment. The music stopped, and the crowd gasped as a figure emerged from the shadows, cloaked in darkness. The air grew tense as everyone turned their attention to the newcomer—a stranger with a fiery demeanor that rivaled even the flames of the bonfire.

"What's going on here?" the stranger demanded, eyes narrowing at Alarion and Lila. "This is a celebration for the Flame! You're not worthy to dance among its sparks!"

Alarion stepped forward, his heart racing. "We didn't mean any disrespect! We're here to celebrate, just like everyone else!"

The stranger sneered, raising his hand and conjuring flames that danced dangerously around him. "You think you can just waltz in and enjoy the festivities? Let's see how well you can handle the heat!"

Before Alarion could react, the stranger launched a fireball into the air, and it exploded with a dazzling display of sparks. The crowd shrieked and scattered, but Alarion stood his ground, determination igniting within him.

"Lila, stay back!" he shouted, focusing on the threat before him. He summoned his own magic, flames flickering around his fingertips as he prepared to defend against the stranger.

"You think you can challenge me?" the stranger laughed, flames flickering dangerously close. "This will be entertaining!"

Alarion felt Lila's hand grasp his arm. "We can't let him ruin the festival! We have to stand together!"

"Right!" Alarion nodded, his heart racing. "Let's show him what we've got!"

With a flick of his wrist, Alarion sent a wave of fire toward the stranger, who countered with a burst of flames of his own. The two forces collided in a dazzling display of light and heat, illuminating the night sky.

"Here's a little dance of our own!" Lila called out, her eyes gleaming with mischief. She pulled out a small vial from her pouch—an explosive potion they had prepared earlier for emergencies. "Catch!"

She tossed the vial into the air, and as it hit the ground, it erupted in a colorful burst, showering the area with sparks. The stranger stumbled back, momentarily distracted by the unexpected explosion.

"Now's our chance!" Alarion seized the opportunity, darting forward. He conjured a wave of flames that danced around him like a fiery cloak, ready to confront the stranger.

As the flames surrounded him, he felt empowered, the warmth fueling his determination. "You won't ruin our night!" he declared, his voice strong.

The stranger glared, flames crackling around him. "You're just a child playing with fire!"

With a swift movement, Alarion unleashed a flurry of fireballs, each one aimed with precision. The stranger dodged and retaliated, the battle escalating into a spectacular display of magic and sparks.

"Focus, Alarion!" Lila shouted, her voice breaking through the chaos. "Remember the dance! Move with the rhythm!"

Her words resonated within him. Alarion closed his eyes for a brief moment, centering himself as he recalled the energy of the festival. He and Lila had danced together, and now they would fight as a team.

In a synchronized move, they advanced together, Alarion launching fire spells while Lila created barriers of swirling flames to protect them. The energy between them crackled, and as they fought side by side, Alarion felt their connection deepen.

With one final powerful surge, Alarion concentrated all his magic into a single fireball, larger than any he had conjured before. "Together!" he called to Lila.

"Together!" she echoed, channeling her own energy into the spell.

The fireball soared through the air, a brilliant comet of flames that struck the stranger directly. With a bright flash, the force sent him sprawling backward, extinguishing his flames in a spectacular display.

The crowd erupted in cheers as the stranger scrambled to his feet, a look of disbelief on his face. "You... you think you can defeat me?" he growled, but his bravado was clearly shaken.

"Not if you know what's good for you!" Lila shot back, hands on her hips.

Alarion stepped forward, his flames flickering low now but still glowing. "We don't want trouble. Just let it go and enjoy the festival."

Realizing he was outmatched and that his moment of glory had vanished, the stranger grunted and retreated into the shadows, leaving behind a stunned crowd.

As the cheers and applause echoed around them, Alarion and Lila turned to each other, laughter bubbling up between them. The tension from the fight melted away, leaving behind a warm glow of victory.

"Did we just do that?" Alarion laughed, his heart still racing from the thrill of the battle.

"We did! And it was amazing!" Lila beamed, her eyes shining brighter than the lanterns around them.

"Hey, since we saved the festival, how about we celebrate with another dance?" Alarion suggested, his heart pounding for reasons beyond just the excitement of the fight.

"Only if you promise not to step on my toes!" Lila teased, a grin spreading across her face.

"Deal!" Alarion said, taking her hand once more as they stepped back into the circle of dancers.

The music resumed, filling the air with energy and joy. As they danced under the starlit sky, the warmth of the flames surrounded them, igniting something new within Alarion—a flicker of hope, of love, and the exhilarating thrill of the night.

Song: "Flame's Embrace"
(Verse 1)
Underneath the starlit sky,
With flames that dance and dreams that fly,
We faced the darkness, side by side,
With every spark, our hearts collide.
(Chorus)
In the dance of flames, we found our way,
With laughter and magic, we'll never sway.
Through trials and battles, our spirits ignite,
Together forever, we'll shine so bright.
(Verse 2)
With each step, we weave our fate,
In the warmth of love, we celebrate.
Hand in hand, we'll face the night,
With every heartbeat, we take flight.
(Chorus)
In the dance of flames, we found our way,
With laughter and magic, we'll never sway.

Through trials and battles, our spirits ignite,
Together forever, we'll shine so bright.
(Bridge)
So let the fire burn, let it light our path,
With love as our armor, we'll never look back.
In this dance of flames, we'll rise above,
With every twirl, we're wrapped in love.
(Chorus)
In the dance of flames, we found our way,
With laughter and magic, we'll never sway.
Through trials and battles, our spirits ignite,
Together forever, we'll shine so bright.

As the final notes of the song faded into the night, Alarion and Lila lost themselves in each other, their hearts ablaze with the fire of new beginnings. The dance of flames had not only saved the festival; it had ignited the spark of a romance that would light their path forward, forever entwined in a story of magic, laughter, and love.

Chapter 10: The Blazing Bandit

Alarion faces off against a flamboyant bandit who claims to have a map to the Eternal Flame. A battle of wits and humor ensues as Alarion attempts to outsmart this colorful character.

The sun hung low in the sky, casting a golden glow over the Emerald Glade as Alarion and Lila ventured deeper into the enchanted woods. Birds chirped merrily overhead, and the gentle rustling of leaves accompanied their every step. They were on a quest to uncover the next clue leading to the Eternal Flame, and Alarion couldn't shake off the feeling that something unexpected was waiting for them.

Suddenly, a flamboyant figure burst into view, his vibrant attire contrasting sharply with the lush greens of the forest. With a wide-brimmed hat adorned with feathers and a coat that sparkled like a thousand stars, he struck a pose, arms outstretched. "Ahoy there, travelers! I am Blaze, the Blazing Bandit, and I hold the key to your quest!" He twirled dramatically, causing the feathers on his hat to dance.

"Blaze the Blazing Bandit?" Lila whispered to Alarion, stifling a giggle. "He looks like a walking firework!"

"Just roll with it," Alarion replied, stifling a laugh as he stepped forward. "What do you have for us, Blaze?"

With a flourish, the bandit produced a tattered map, waving it above his head like a trophy. "This, my dear adventurers, is the map to the Eternal Flame! But beware! It comes with a challenge!"

"Oh? And what challenge might that be?" Alarion asked, curiosity piqued.

"Simple! You must defeat me in a battle of wits and humor! Should you fail, the map is mine to keep, and you'll leave empty-handed!" Blaze declared, striking a dramatic pose that would make any theater actor proud.

Alarion exchanged a glance with Lila, who nodded, her eyes sparkling with mischief. "We accept your challenge, oh flamboyant bandit!"

"Excellent!" Blaze clapped his hands together, bouncing on his heels. "Let the games begin! I shall ask you riddles and toss jokes your way. Should you answer correctly or make me laugh, you win the map! Fail, and it shall remain in my possession."

"Let's see what you've got!" Alarion grinned, ready for the playful duel.

"First riddle!" Blaze declared, theatrically raising his hand. "What has keys but can't open locks?"

Alarion thought for a moment, scratching his chin. "A piano!"

Blaze's eyes widened, but then he burst into laughter. "Clever, clever! But can you make me laugh? Here's your chance!"

Alarion cleared his throat dramatically and recited a classic joke he loved: "Why did the scarecrow win an award? Because he was outstanding in his field!"

Blaze doubled over with laughter, clutching his stomach. "That was pretty good! But can you keep it going? Next riddle: What can travel around the world while staying in a corner?"

"A stamp!" Alarion shot back, feeling more confident.

"Darn it! You're good!" Blaze exclaimed, his colorful coat shimmering as he swayed with excitement. "But now for the ultimate challenge: Let's see if you can outdo my sense of humor!"

"Oh, I'm ready!" Alarion grinned, determined to win this whimsical battle.

"Here's my best joke! Why did the tomato turn red?" Blaze asked, eyes glinting mischievously.

"Uh, I don't know," Alarion admitted, genuinely curious.

"Because it saw the salad dressing!" Blaze declared, his laughter ringing through the glade.

Lila snickered at the joke. "That was good!"

"Now, let's see if you can top that," Blaze said, leaning forward, a mischievous glint in his eyes.

Alarion felt the weight of the challenge. "Okay, how about this one: What did one ocean say to the other ocean? Nothing, they just waved!"

Blaze erupted in laughter again, his flamboyant demeanor somehow even more exaggerated. "You're on fire!"

But just as Alarion felt they were gaining momentum, the atmosphere shifted. A rustle in the bushes nearby caught their attention, and a group of shadowy figures emerged, cloaked in darkness. Alarion recognized them instantly as the hidden enemies who had been following their quest.

"Looks like your fun is over, Blazing Bandit!" one of the shadowy figures sneered, stepping forward. "We'll take the map now!"

"Hold on! I had a deal with these two!" Blaze protested, puffing out his chest. "You can't just waltz in and ruin my performance!"

"Save it for the stage, bandit. We want that map!" the figure growled, eyes glinting with malice.

"Not so fast!" Alarion shouted, stepping protectively in front of Lila. "If you want the map, you'll have to get through us first!"

"Very brave of you!" one of the shadowy figures mocked. "But you're outnumbered!"

"Outnumbered, maybe. But never outsmarted!" Lila chimed in, her voice full of determination.

With a swift motion, Blaze retrieved a handful of glittering dust from his pocket and tossed it into the air. It sparkled brightly, momentarily blinding the attackers. "Now's our chance!" he shouted.

"Right!" Alarion grabbed Lila's hand. "Let's show them what we can do!"

As the dust settled, they charged toward the cloaked figures, Alarion conjuring flames that flickered around him like a fiery aura. Lila created barriers of shimmering energy, pushing back the advancing shadows.

The first attacker lunged at Alarion, but he dodged swiftly, countering with a burst of fire that sent the shadowy figure stumbling back. "Not today!" he shouted, feeling the thrill of battle coursing through him.

Lila flung her hand forward, sending a wave of energy that knocked two of the enemies off their feet. "Stay focused, Alarion! We can do this!"

Blaze, emboldened by their courage, joined the fray. "You can't take the map from my new friends! Prepare to be dazzled!" He spun and twirled, sending out bursts of colorful sparks that disoriented the attackers.

"Let's take them down together!" Alarion yelled, his voice steady as he and Lila moved in perfect synchronization.

They launched a coordinated attack—Alarion's fire mixing with Lila's barriers, creating a dazzling display of light and power. Blaze added to the chaos with his flamboyant antics, hurling jokes that confused the enemies as much as his magic did.

"Why did the shadow cross the road?" he shouted mid-fight. "To get to the dark side!"

One of the attackers, bewildered by the absurdity, paused long enough for Alarion to deliver a well-aimed blast of flame, sending them tumbling into the bushes.

Lila seized the opportunity, rallying Alarion and Blaze. "Now! Together!"

With a final surge of energy, they combined their powers into a brilliant wave of magic that surged forward, engulfing the remaining attackers. With a bright flash, the shadows dissipated, leaving nothing but the soft rustling of leaves in their wake.

Panting but exhilarated, Alarion turned to Blaze. "That was amazing! You really held your own there."

"Thank you, my brave companions!" Blaze said, adjusting his hat with a flourish. "But let's not forget the most important thing—the map!"

"Right!" Lila said, excitement bubbling within her as she approached the bandit. "We won the battle, so we get the map!"

Blaze grinned widely and presented the tattered parchment. "Indeed, you have proven yourselves worthy! The Eternal Flame awaits!"

With the map now in hand, Alarion felt a surge of determination. "This is it! We're one step closer to our goal."

Lila leaned close; her voice warm with encouragement. "Together, we can do anything."

As they stood there, the sun dipped below the horizon, casting a warm glow over their adventure. Alarion looked at Lila, his heart swelling with gratitude and excitement. "Ready for the next part of our journey?"

"Always!" she replied, her smile radiant.

And so, with the map guiding them and their spirits high, they set off into the night, leaving behind the chaos of battle and stepping boldly into the adventures that awaited. The journey to the Eternal Flame was far from over, but with each step, they grew stronger together, laughter and love lighting their way.

Song: *"Chasing the Flame"*
(Verse 1)

Through the woods, we roam and play,
With laughter brightening every day.
Facing foes, we stand so tall,
With friendship's fire, we'll never fall.
(Chorus)
We're chasing the flame, through the dark of night,
With every heartbeat, we ignite the light.
Together we rise, hand in hand,
With courage and love, we'll make our stand.
(Verse 2)
In the face of danger, we won't despair,
With jokes and laughter, we'll conquer our fear.
From shadowy figures to brightening skies,
With every battle, our spirits rise.
(Chorus)
We're chasing the flame, through the dark of night,
With every heartbeat, we ignite the light.
Together we rise, hand in hand,
With courage and love, we'll make our stand.
(Bridge)
So, bring on the challenges, bring on the fight,
With humor and magic, we'll shine so bright.
Through every twist and turn, we'll find our way,
With love as our guide, we'll seize the day.
(Chorus)
We're chasing the flame, through the dark of night,
With every heartbeat, we ignite the light.
Together we rise, hand in hand,
With courage and love, we'll make our stand.

As the echoes of their laughter faded into the evening air, Alarion, Lila, and Blaze moved forward, ready for whatever awaited them next. The journey was just beginning, but with humor, love, and unyielding determination, they would face it all together.

Chapter 11: A Test of Loyalty

Alarion must choose between a tempting offer from a shady ally and his loyalty to Lila. The humor in their banter makes the choice even harder, blending romance with the stakes of betrayal.

The sun hung high in the sky as Alarion and Lila made their way through the vibrant trails of the Whispering Woods. The air was thick with the sweet scent of blooming flowers, and the songs of birds accompanied their every step. Lila skipped ahead, her laughter ringing through the trees, while Alarion admired the way the sunlight danced through the leaves, casting playful shadows on the forest floor.

"Come on, slowpoke! You're not going to let a few roots trip you up, are you?" Lila teased, turning back to Alarion with a grin that could melt the hardest of hearts.

"Slowpoke? I prefer to think of myself as 'strategically pacing,'" Alarion replied with a dramatic flourish, pausing to adjust the imaginary crown on his head. "After all, a hero must maintain his regal poise!"

"Oh really? Is that why you tripped over that twig back there?" Lila giggled, pointing to where he had stumbled moments before.

Alarion feigned shock, placing a hand over his heart. "It was a conspiracy! The twig was plotting against me!"

Just as their laughter echoed through the woods, a figure emerged from the shadows—shady and mysterious, clad in dark robes that fluttered like smoke. His name was Zarek, a rogue known for his cunning and ability to sway hearts with persuasive offers.

"Well, well, if it isn't the gallant Alarion and the lovely Lila!" he crooned, a sly smile curling on his lips.

"What do you want, Zarek?" Alarion asked, stepping protectively in front of Lila. He didn't trust the rogue, and for good reason.

"Oh, nothing much. Just a little business proposition," Zarek replied, his voice dripping with charm. "I have information that could lead you straight to the Eternal Flame, but it comes with a price."

"What kind of price?" Lila asked, her brow furrowing. She felt an unsettling chill in the air.

"Just a small token of loyalty," Zarek continued, his eyes glinting with mischief. "Join forces with me, and I'll reveal the secrets of the flame. Together, we can rule the realm!"

Alarion's heart raced at the thought of betrayal. "And what would that mean for Lila? Would she be part of your plans, too?"

Zarek waved a dismissive hand. "Ah, the lovely Lila can come along for the ride—unless she's in your way, of course."

"Over my dead body!" Lila exclaimed fists clenched at her sides. "You think I'd ever side with someone like you?"

"Very feisty," Zarek chuckled, clearly entertained. "But think about it, Alarion. With my resources and your talents, you could achieve greatness! The Eternal Flame could be yours to control! Think of the power!"

Alarion felt the weight of the decision hanging heavy in the air. He looked at Lila, her face a mixture of determination and concern. "What do you think?"

"I think we should tell him to take his offer and shove it!" she declared. "Power without loyalty isn't worth anything!"

Zarek sighed dramatically, as if he were a character in a play. "How dull! But fine, let's make this interesting. How about a little wager?"

"A wager?" Alarion raised an eyebrow. "What do you propose?"

"If you can best me in a test of loyalty—filled with humor, riddles, and perhaps a little magic—I'll give you the information you seek. But if you lose, you'll have to consider my offer seriously," Zarek said, a wicked smile plastered on his face.

Lila and Alarion exchanged wary glances. "Fine," Alarion said, steeling his resolve. "But if you try anything funny, I won't hesitate to burn you to a crisp."

Zarek clapped his hands together, excitement sparkling in his eyes. "Oh, this is going to be fun! Let's begin!"

The First Challenge: Riddles of the Heart

Zarek conjured a swirl of shimmering mist, transforming it into a swirling backdrop of colors. "For the first challenge, I will ask you a riddle. Answer it correctly, and you prove your loyalty to each other!"

"Bring it on," Alarion said, standing tall beside Lila.

"Here it goes: I speak without a mouth and hear without ears. I have no body, but I come alive with the wind. What am I?"

Alarion pondered, and after a moment, Lila exclaimed, "An echo!"

"Correct!" Zarek nodded, feigning disappointment. "But that was too easy. Now, let's see how loyal you really are. For the next challenge, I'll need a little song!"

"A song?" Lila raised an eyebrow. "What kind of song?"

"A romantic one, of course! Sing me something that showcases your bond!" Zarek exclaimed, a mischievous grin spreading across his face.

"Alright, Alarion. I'll start," Lila said, ready to take the challenge head-on. With a twinkle in her eye, she began to sing a sweet, playful melody.

Song: "Two Hearts as One"
(Verse 1)

In this world of magic, we stand side by side,
Through laughter and trials, our love will abide.
With every adventure, with every leap,
Together we soar, our promises we keep.
(Chorus)
Two hearts as one, we'll dance through the night,
With love as our guide, we'll shine ever bright.
No shadows can break what we hold so dear,
In the warmth of your smile, I find my way clear.
(Verse 2)
Through storms and through battles, we'll never lose hope,
With friendship and laughter, together we cope.
In the heart of the forest, beneath the moon's glow,
With each step we take, our love will only grow.
(Chorus)
Two hearts as one, we'll dance through the night,
With love as our guide, we'll shine ever bright.
No shadows can break what we hold so dear,
In the warmth of your smile, I find my way clear.
(Bridge)
So, here's to the journey, to the stories we share,
With every new challenge, I'll always be there.
Hand in hand we'll wander, wherever it leads,
With laughter and love, we'll fulfill all our needs.
(Chorus)
Two hearts as one, we'll dance through the night,
With love as our guide, we'll shine ever bright.
No shadows can break what we hold so dear,
In the warmth of your smile, I find my way clear.

The final note hung in the air, soft and sweet, echoing through the forest like a gentle breeze. Zarek looked momentarily taken aback, as if he didn't quite expect such a heartfelt performance. "Very touching! But let's see if you can make me laugh with a funny song!"

Alarion, quick on his feet, began to improvise. "Alright, here goes!"

Song: "The Silly Song of Alarion"
(Verse 1)
There once was a knight who rode on a goat,
Who thought he could fly, but fell off and wrote,
A poem about dragons, all fiery and grand,
But he tripped on his sword and fell in the sand!
(Chorus)
Oh, silly knight, with a heart so bold,
With dreams of adventure, or so I'm told.
But riding a goat? Oh, what a sight!
With laughter and joy, we'll dance through the night!
(Verse 2)
He tried to impress a fair maiden so bright,
With tales of his battles, how he fought with all might.
But he slipped on a banana, and fell with a crash,
Now he just tells stories while eating some trash!
(Chorus)
Oh, silly knight, with a heart so bold,
With dreams of adventure, or so I'm told.
But riding a goat? Oh, what a sight!
With laughter and joy, we'll dance through the night!

Alarion's playful antics had everyone laughing, including Zarek, who struggled to contain his amusement. "Very good! But now for the final test—let's see how you handle a battle!"

The Final Challenge: Battle of Wits and Humor

Zarek snapped his fingers, and suddenly, shadowy figures emerged from the forest, cloaked in darkness. "These are your opponents! Defeat them with wit and teamwork, or you'll have to consider my offer!"

Alarion and Lila exchanged determined glances. "Let's show them what we've got!" Alarion said, conjuring flames around his hands.

The shadowy figures lunged at them, but Alarion and Lila moved in perfect harmony. Lila created shimmering barriers to protect them, while Alarion unleashed bursts of magical fire that sent the shadows reeling.

"Here's a riddle for you!" Lila shouted, directing her energy toward one of the attackers. "What has keys but can't open locks?"

"Um... a piano?" the figure stuttered, confused.

"Correct! Now get out of our way!" Lila commanded, her eyes shining with determination.

Alarion turned to another shadowy figure, flames dancing in his palm. "What do you call a fake noodle?" he quipped.

"Um... I don't know?" the figure replied, visibly baffled.

"An impasta!" Alarion laughed, and with that, he unleashed a fireball that sent the figure tumbling backward.

As the final shadowy figure fled in defeat, Zarek clapped his hands together, his smile wide and genuine. "Impressive! You've proven your loyalty to each other!"

The Choice

With the shadows dispersed, Zarek stepped forward, his expression shifting. "You've passed the test, but I must still offer my deal. What will it be, Alarion?"

Alarion glanced at Lila, who nodded firmly. "We'll find our own way to the Eternal Flame. We don't need you, Zarek."

Zarek raised an eyebrow but couldn't hide the respect in his gaze. "Very well, but remember, the offer stands." With that, he vanished into the mist, leaving Alarion and Lila standing together, stronger than ever.

A New Beginning

"Did you see that? We actually made it through!" Lila laughed, her eyes sparkling with joy. "I thought we'd be lost forever!"

"Never with you by my side," Alarion said, reaching for her hand. "I'll always choose loyalty over power."

As they walked together through the Whispering Woods, a sense of calm washed over them. The bond between them had only grown stronger through the trials they faced, and their laughter echoed through the trees, a melody of love and camaraderie.

And in the distance, the faint flicker of the Eternal Flame beckoned them onward, their hearts full of hope, humor, and a love that could withstand any test.

Chapter 12: The Flame Keeper

They encounter the ancient Flame Keeper, who offers cryptic advice about love and sacrifice. Alarion finds himself questioning what he's willing to give up for the Flame—and Lila.

The journey had led Alarion and Lila deep into the heart of the Ember Grove, a mystical forest filled with swirling colors and the scent of woodsmoke in the air. The trees glowed with an otherworldly light, their bark shimmering like embers, casting flickering shadows that danced around them. As they ventured further, the anticipation of finding the Eternal Flame filled their hearts with excitement and trepidation.

"This place feels magical, doesn't it?" Lila said, her eyes wide with wonder. She paused to touch the trunk of a tree that pulsed with warmth beneath her fingertips. "I can almost feel the Flame calling us."

Alarion smiled, his heart swelling with affection. "It's enchanting, just like you. But let's not forget we're not alone here. The Flame Keeper is said to be a tricky character."

"Tricky? That sounds delightful," Lila teased, winking at him. "I can handle a little trickiness. Just as long as he's not a raging fireball."

Just then, a flickering light appeared in the distance, growing brighter as they approached. It morphed into a figure—a tall, shadowy being wrapped in robes that seemed to be woven from flames and shadows. His face was obscured, but his presence radiated a warm glow.

"Welcome, travelers," the Flame Keeper said, his voice a melodic whisper that echoed through the grove. "You seek the Eternal Flame, but to obtain it, you must first understand the nature of love and sacrifice."

Alarion and Lila exchanged glances, intrigued. "What do you mean?" Alarion asked, stepping forward.

The Riddle of Love

The Flame Keeper raised a hand, and the air crackled with energy. "Love is like fire; it can warm you or consume you. To earn the Flame, you must answer this riddle:

I can be cracked, made, told, and played. What am I?"

Lila's brow furrowed in thought. "A joke?" she ventured, glancing at Alarion for support.

The Flame Keeper's laughter echoed through the grove, a sound that felt both warm and unsettling. "Correct! A joke can bring light into the darkest places. Now, tell me, what would you sacrifice for love?"

"Anything!" Alarion exclaimed, his voice filled with conviction. "I'd sacrifice my heart, my soul, even my favorite sword!"

Lila chuckled, shaking her head. "Not your favorite sword! That's going too far!"

The Flame Keeper tilted his head, amusement flickering in his fiery eyes. "You jest, but remember: true sacrifice often involves giving up what you hold dear. Are you willing to prove your loyalty?"

A Test of Sacrifice

As if summoned by the Flame Keeper's words, the air around them thickened, and shadowy figures emerged from the trees—malicious beings formed from darkness, their eyes glowing with menace.

"Defend your love!" the Flame Keeper cried, his voice echoing as he stepped back to observe the battle.

ALARION AND THE ETERNAL FLAME

"Lila, behind me!" Alarion shouted, drawing his sword as the shadows lunged. The forest erupted into chaos as Alarion swung his blade, illuminating the darkness with brilliant bursts of flame.

Lila conjured shimmering shields around them, deflecting the attacks of the shadowy figures. "Alarion, we can't let them separate us!" she yelled, focusing her energy on keeping them together.

With every swing of Alarion's sword and every incantation Lila whispered, they fought in perfect harmony, dodging and weaving through the onslaught. In the midst of the battle, Alarion felt a surge of determination. "Together!" he shouted, plunging his sword into the ground and summoning a wave of fire that swept through the shadows.

But just as victory seemed within reach, a shadowy figure broke through their defenses and seized Lila, dragging her backward. "Alarion!" she screamed, panic lacing her voice.

"Let her go!" Alarion roared, charging forward, but another figure intercepted him, striking with dark energy that sent him crashing to the ground.

The Turning Point

With Alarion momentarily dazed, Lila fought back against her captor, summoning all her strength. "You'll regret this!" she declared, conjuring a burst of light that temporarily blinded the shadow.

"Lila!" Alarion shouted, struggling to rise. "Just hold on!"

In a moment of clarity, he realized what he had to do. Summoning all his inner strength, he stood tall, focusing on the bond they shared. "I will sacrifice anything to save you, Lila!" he proclaimed. He closed his eyes and conjured the flames of love and determination that burned within him, pouring his energy into a single, powerful spell.

As Alarion's flames blazed to life, a dazzling light erupted around them, pushing back the shadows and engulfing the grove in a warm, radiant glow. The darkness hissed and recoiled, releasing Lila from its grasp.

With newfound strength, Alarion sprinted to Lila's side, their hands clasping tightly as they faced the remaining shadows together. "Now!" Lila shouted, and together they unleashed a wave of combined magic—a torrent of fire and light that sent the shadows fleeing into the depths of the woods.

A Moment of Reflection

As the last shadow dissipated, the Flame Keeper reappeared, his expression serious yet contemplative. "You have fought bravely, and your love has proven stronger than the darkness. But remember, love often requires sacrifice, not just in battle, but in life's choices."

"What do you mean?" Alarion asked, still catching his breath.

"Will you choose to put Lila's happiness before your own desires?" the Flame Keeper queried, his fiery eyes piercing through Alarion.

Lila looked up at Alarion, a mixture of admiration and fear in her gaze. "What do you think, Alarion?" she asked softly.

Alarion took a deep breath, weighing his thoughts. "I would do anything for you, Lila. But it's not just about what I want; it's about us, our dreams, and what we choose to pursue together.

I would give up my greatest ambitions if it meant you'd find happiness."

The Flame Keeper nodded, a hint of approval in his voice. "Love is a flame that grows brighter when nurtured. Your willingness to sacrifice for one another is the key to obtaining the Eternal Flame. It is not just a source of power, but a testament to the bond you share."

The Eternal Flame

With that, the Flame Keeper raised his arms, and a brilliant light erupted from the ground, forming a swirling column of fire. The Eternal Flame revealed itself, dancing majestically, colors shifting from deep crimson to vibrant gold.

"Take it," the Flame Keeper instructed, "and carry its warmth in your hearts. But remember, it is not merely a flame to be wielded; it is a responsibility. It will test your love, your resolve, and your willingness to sacrifice for one another."

Alarion stepped forward, gripping Lila's hand tightly. "Together," he said, and they approached the Eternal Flame. As they reached out, their fingers brushed against the warmth, and a wave of energy surged through them, binding their hearts in an unbreakable bond.

The Flame Keeper smiled, his form beginning to dissolve into the light. "Guard the flame, nurture your love, and may it guide you through the darkness ahead."

As the Flame Keeper vanished, Alarion and Lila stood side by side, the Eternal Flame flickering behind them, casting warmth and light into the Ember Grove. They exchanged glances filled with understanding, knowing that their journey was far from over but determined to face whatever challenges lay ahead—together.

"Ready for the next adventure?" Alarion asked, a grin breaking through his serious demeanor.

Lila smiled back, her eyes sparkling with excitement. "As long as we're together, I'm ready for anything."

And with that, they turned to face the path ahead, hand in hand, hearts ignited by the Eternal Flame and the unyielding power of their love.

Chapter 13: The Unexpected Ally

A strange creature named Blazewing, who's more helpful than he seems, joins their quest. His odd antics bring both laughter and wisdom, lightening the mood as they face darker challenges.

Alarion and Lila emerged from the Ember Grove, their hearts still racing from their encounter with the Flame Keeper. With the Eternal Flame safely in their possession, they were eager to continue their quest. However, they knew that the challenges ahead would require more than just their courage and love; they needed allies.

As they made their way along a winding path that twisted through a vibrant valley, Lila suddenly paused, her eyes wide with wonder. "What is that?" she pointed toward a glimmering creature perched atop a large rock.

Alarion squinted into the sunlight. "I'm not sure. It looks... unusual."

The creature, a small, dragon-like being with sparkling scales that shimmered in a spectrum of colors, flapped its wings. Its wings appeared to be made of flames, flickering as it moved. It opened its mouth to reveal a row of tiny, sharp teeth and let out a surprisingly high-pitched cackle.

"Hey there, travelers!" it shouted, bouncing on its perch. "I'm Blazewing! I couldn't help but overhear you're looking for adventure! Mind if I join?"

A Comedic Introduction

Alarion raised an eyebrow, sharing a skeptical glance with Lila. "And what exactly can you do, Blazewing?"

"Oh, I can breathe fire, fly, and give unsolicited advice!" Blazewing said proudly, puffing out his chest. "I also make a mean marshmallow! Here, watch!" He took a deep breath and shot a small flame into the air, igniting a nearby marshmallow hanging from a branch. It instantly toasted to perfection.

Lila giggled; her laughter contagious. "That's impressive! Can you also tell jokes?"

"Of course!" Blazewing said, rubbing his tiny claws together. "Why did the dragon cross the road? To get to the other side... to breathe fire!" He burst into laughter, his wings flapping joyously.

Alarion chuckled, feeling the tension from earlier dissipate. "Alright, you can come along. Just keep your fire-breathing to a minimum, okay?"

"Deal!" Blazewing soared into the air, performing a loop-de-loop before landing with a flourish beside them. "Now, what's the plan?"

An Uneasy Alliance

As the trio continued their journey, Blazewing's antics lightened the mood. He would occasionally break into a little dance, twirling and spinning, and Alarion and Lila couldn't help but join in, their laughter echoing through the valley.

"Hey, why don't we sing a song?" Blazewing suggested, his eyes sparkling with mischief. "I've got one in mind!" He cleared his throat dramatically.

"To the tune of 'Twinkle, Twinkle, Little Star':
Flicker, flicker, tiny flame,
Lighting up the world's old game.
When the shadows come to play,
Blazewing's here to save the day!
Flicker, flicker, tiny flame,
With my friends, I'll stake my claim!"

They all joined in, Lila and Alarion providing harmonies while Blazewing danced around them.

"Not too shabby for a little flame-breathing creature!" Alarion exclaimed, grinning widely.

"Wait until you see my fire dance!" Blazewing said, preparing to spin into another twirl.

But just then, the atmosphere shifted. The air became heavy, and the distant sound of clashing metal echoed through the valley. Alarion's smile faded. "What was that?"

A Shadowy Threat

Before anyone could answer, a group of armored figures appeared at the edge of the forest. They emerged silently, their eyes glowing with malice, ready to ambush.

"Get down!" Alarion shouted, pulling Lila behind a tree as Blazewing instinctively hid in the underbrush.

"What are they?" Lila whispered, her heart racing.

"Dusk Warriors," Alarion replied, his voice low. "They must have caught wind of our journey to the Eternal Flame."

The Dusk Warriors moved with eerie grace, their weapons glinting ominously. "We cannot let them reach the Flame!" one of them hissed, brandishing a wicked-looking sword.

"What do we do?" Lila asked, panic rising in her voice.

"I'll distract them," Alarion said firmly. "You find cover and get ready to help if I need you."

Blazewing suddenly burst out from his hiding place, flapping his wings in excitement. "Or I could cause a little chaos!"

"Chaos?" Alarion raised an eyebrow. "I don't know if that's a good idea—"

"Trust me!" Blazewing shouted, his fiery personality shining through. With a burst of energy, he zoomed straight toward the Dusk Warriors.

ALARION AND THE ETERNAL FLAME

"Hey, over here!" he yelled, drawing their attention. He twisted in the air, breathing a small jet of flame that singed the edges of their armor but did no real harm.

The Battle Begins

Alarion seized the moment, rushing toward the nearest warrior with his sword drawn. The warrior swung his sword, but Alarion dodged and retaliated with a swift strike. The clang of metal rang through the air, echoing in the valley as Lila joined in, using her magic to create barriers that blocked the warriors' advances.

Blazewing, meanwhile, darted between the warriors' feet, his tiny frame making him difficult to catch. "You'll have to be faster than that!" he taunted, breathing little puffs of fire that made the warriors jump.

"Stop that creature!" one of the warriors growled, lunging at Blazewing, but the agile dragon dodged easily.

"Nice try, but I'm not your snack!" Blazewing laughed, doing a flip in mid-air.

Alarion fought valiantly, dodging blows and parrying strikes as Lila continued to cast protective spells. Just as one of the Dusk Warriors prepared to strike Alarion from behind, Blazewing unleashed a burst of fire right in front of the warrior's face.

"Whoo! Hot stuff!" he shouted, grinning as the warrior stumbled backward.

Taking advantage of the moment, Alarion leaped forward and disarmed the distracted warrior with a swift kick. "Nice one, Blazewing!" he shouted, adrenaline coursing through him.

A Tactical Retreat

But the battle wasn't over. More Dusk Warriors emerged, closing in around them. Alarion and Lila exchanged worried glances.

"We need to retreat!" Lila urged; her voice urgent. "We can't take them all on!"

"Agreed!" Alarion shouted. "Blazewing, cover us!"

"On it!" Blazewing spun in the air, shooting bursts of flame to distract the warriors while Alarion and Lila maneuvered to the edge of the clearing.

They managed to break free, running deeper into the woods. "This way!" Lila cried, leading them down a narrow path lined with ancient trees.

As they reached a small clearing, they paused to catch their breath, panting heavily.

"Did we lose them?" Alarion asked, scanning their surroundings.

"Let's hope so," Lila said, looking at Blazewing with admiration. "That was impressive! I didn't know you had it in you."

Blazewing beamed, his eyes sparkling. "Just a typical Tuesday for Blazewing! You guys weren't too shabby either."

A New Bond

As they settled down to catch their breath, Alarion took a moment to appreciate his companions. "We make a pretty good team," he said, grinning.

"Of course! I'm fabulous!" Blazewing exclaimed, puffing out his chest again.

Lila laughed, the tension of the battle fading into the background. "What do we do now? We can't let those Dusk Warriors stop us from reaching the Eternal Flame."

"Right! We need a plan," Alarion said, determination sparking in his eyes. "But first, let's celebrate our victory over those shadows. Blazewing, how about that marshmallow trick of yours?"

"Oh, now you're speaking my language!" Blazewing said, darting off to gather some branches.

As they sat together, roasting marshmallows over a small fire Blazewing conjured, Lila couldn't help but smile. "You know, this might be the most unexpected adventure of my life."

Alarion chuckled, glancing at Blazewing, who was making overly dramatic faces as he tasted his perfectly toasted marshmallow. "Yeah, who knew we'd have a fire-breathing ally?"

Their laughter echoed through the woods as they shared stories and jokes, the bond between them growing stronger with each moment.

And as the stars twinkled overhead, casting their light upon the three unlikely friends, they knew that whatever challenges lay ahead, they would face them together, guided by the warmth of friendship, laughter, and the flickering light of the Eternal Flame.

Chapter 14: Trials of the Heart

Alarion faces his most challenging trial yet—his own emotions. A humorous love potion gone wrong leads to mixed signals and awkward confessions, testing the boundaries of their friendship.

The morning sun peeked through the lush trees of the Enchanted Forest, bathing everything in a golden glow. Alarion stretched and yawned, feeling the warmth on his face. It had been a few days since they had gained an unexpected ally in Blazewing, and he felt more optimistic about their quest for the Eternal Flame. But little did he know, today would bring a challenge unlike any he had faced before.

As Alarion joined Lila and Blazewing at their camp, he noticed Lila carefully mixing some herbs in a small pot. "What are you making?" he asked, leaning closer, intrigued.

"Just a little something I found in the ancient texts," Lila said with a mischievous smile. "It's supposed to enhance emotions, help people express their true feelings."

Alarion raised an eyebrow. "And by 'enhance emotions,' you mean...?"

"Love potions!" Blazewing interrupted, flapping his wings excitedly. "Ooh, this could be fun!

Or chaotic! Or both!"

"Love potions? Isn't that a bit risky?" Alarion said, scratching his head. "What if it backfires?"

Lila shrugged playfully. "What's the worst that could happen? Besides, it's just a little fun! You could use some excitement in your life, Alarion."

"Yeah! What's life without a little chaos?" Blazewing added, doing a little jig on the ground.

Against his better judgment, Alarion agreed, thinking it might be harmless enough. "Alright, but only if we're careful."

The Potion of Mixed Signals

After a few moments of chanting and waving their hands over the bubbling cauldron, Lila poured a few drops of the shimmering potion into three small vials. "Here you go!" she said, handing one to each of them. "Just a sip should do!"

"Bottoms up!" Blazewing shouted, and with that, they all downed their potions in unison.

At first, nothing happened. They laughed and chatted, enjoying their breakfast. But soon, Alarion began to feel a strange warmth in his chest, a giddiness that made him smile too widely. He glanced at Lila, who was laughing at one of Blazewing's silly jokes. The sunlight caught her hair, making it glow like spun gold, and suddenly, he found himself staring.

"Uh, Alarion?" Lila waved a hand in front of his face, snapping him out of his reverie. "You, okay?"

"Yeah! I mean, yes! I mean—" He stammered, his heart racing. "You're just... um... lovely today."

Lila blushed, her cheeks turning a rosy hue. "Thanks, I guess?"

Blazewing, noticing the sudden tension, decided to make things more interesting. "How about a song to lighten the mood? I've got just the thing!"

The Heartfelt Song
"To the tune of 'I'm a Little Teapot':
I'm a little Alarion, short and stout,
Here are my feelings, just let them out.

When I see Lila, my heart does race,
Oh, what a smile upon her face!
I'm a little Blazewing, full of glee,
Singing silly songs for you and me.
When emotions flare, just give a cheer,
Love is a dance that we hold dear!
I'm a little potion, bubbling bright,
Stirring up feelings, oh what a sight!
When hearts get tangled, don't you fret,
Love's just a potion we won't forget!"

As Blazewing danced around them, Alarion found himself caught up in the moment, laughter bubbling within him. But when he looked at Lila, her expression had turned serious.

"Alarion, do you really mean what you said?" she asked, her eyes searching his.

"Of course!" Alarion said quickly, but his heart raced as he realized what he had just admitted. The potion must be working its magic, or maybe it was the ambiance of the moment. "I mean, I think you're really amazing! You're so strong and kind, and..."

Suddenly, he was struck with the awkward realization that he was pouring out his heart in a way he never intended.

Lila's eyes widened, a mix of surprise and confusion on her face. "Alarion, I—"

Before she could finish, Blazewing interrupted, fluttering around them. "Whoa, hold up! Is this a moment? Are we witnessing a heartfelt confession?"

The Awkward Confession

"Wait, what?" Alarion's face turned beet red. "No! I mean, yes, but also no!"

Lila stifled a giggle, the tension between them shifting into something lighter. "You know, we're both a bit chaotic right now. Maybe we should just let this play out?"

"Let it play out?" Alarion exclaimed, his heart still racing. "What if we end up—"

"Being in love?" Blazewing added, his eyes twinkling with mischief.

"No! Yes! I mean—ugh!" Alarion threw his hands up in frustration, turning away from them both to gather his thoughts. "This is all a bit much!"

Lila, sensing his discomfort, took a step closer. "Alarion, whatever happens, we're still friends. Just know that you're important to me."

"Important?" Alarion echoed, feeling the weight of her words. "You're more than important. You're—"

Suddenly, the ground shook beneath them. They looked at each other in alarm, and Alarion's romantic turmoil was abruptly interrupted by a new threat.

The Battle Begins

From the depths of the forest, a group of dark figures emerged, shrouded in shadows. The Dusk Warriors had returned, their eyes glinting maliciously. "You thought you could escape us, didn't you?" one of them growled, stepping forward with a menacing sneer.

"Quick, we need to defend ourselves!" Lila said, pulling out her wand, her previous confusion forgotten in the face of danger.

Alarion unsheathed his sword, heart pounding for a different reason now. "Let's show them what we're made of!"

"Time to light things up!" Blazewing shouted, charging at the warriors with fiery enthusiasm.

"Fire! Fire! Who wants to play?"

The Fight of Their Lives

The battle erupted with a flurry of clashing swords and sparks of magic. Alarion fought valiantly, his movements fluid and determined. He took down one warrior after another, the rhythm of combat igniting his courage.

Lila flung her magic with precision, creating barriers that protected Alarion and Blazewing. "Stay close! I'll handle the rest!" she called out.

Blazewing zipped around, breathing tiny flames at the warriors. "Can't catch me, you dark dullards!" he taunted, his antics distracting the enemies just long enough for Alarion to strike.

Alarion couldn't help but admire Lila's strength and bravery as they fought side by side. Each time their eyes met, a spark of unspoken feelings danced between them, heightened by the chaos around them.

Just as it seemed they were gaining the upper hand, one particularly tall warrior lunged at Alarion, swinging a heavy sword. Alarion sidestepped, but not before Lila threw a protective spell, sending a blast of energy that knocked the warrior off balance.

"Nice save!" Alarion shouted, heart racing not just from the fight, but from the connection they shared in that moment.

A Revelation

After an intense battle, the remaining warriors fled, retreating back into the shadows from which they came. Alarion, Lila, and Blazewing stood panting in the clearing, catching their breath and feeling the rush of victory.

"We did it!" Blazewing exclaimed, doing a little dance in celebration. "We're unstoppable!"

But as the adrenaline faded, Alarion turned to Lila, his heart still racing. "About what I said earlier..."

Lila stepped closer, her eyes searching his. "You don't have to say anything. The potion may have muddled our emotions, but I think we both know what's real."

"Yeah," Alarion replied softly, a smile breaking through the tension. "What I feel for you is real."

Lila smiled back, the lightness of their earlier banter returning. "So, what now?"

"Maybe we can be both friends and... something more?" Alarion suggested, his voice a mix of hope and uncertainty.

"Absolutely," Lila said, her eyes sparkling. "But let's keep the potions to a minimum, shall we?"

"Agreed," Alarion laughed, feeling the weight of his heart lighten.

"Let's celebrate our victory!" Blazewing chimed in. "I'll whip up some marshmallows, and we can have a victory feast!"

As they settled back down, the sun began to set, casting a warm glow over the Enchanted Forest. Alarion and Lila shared a glance filled with promise and adventure, knowing that whatever trials lay ahead, they would face them together—with love, laughter, and chaos.

Chapter 15: Whispers of Flame

They discover an ancient prophecy that hints at a deeper connection between Alarion and the Eternal Flame. Romance blossoms amid the chaos, but can it withstand the heat?

The sun had barely dipped below the horizon when Alarion, Lila, and Blazewing found themselves standing before the entrance of the Crystal Cave. The walls shimmered with luminescent stones, casting a soft, ethereal glow. Legend had it that within these depths lay not only treasures but also ancient secrets waiting to be unveiled.

"Are you ready for this?" Alarion asked, glancing at Lila. There was a flicker of excitement and apprehension in her eyes, and he couldn't help but feel a rush of emotions swelling within him.

"Ready as I'll ever be," Lila replied, her voice steady, but a slight tremor betrayed her nerves. "Let's see what the prophecy has in store for us."

"Or what kind of weird creature will pop out and scare us," Blazewing chimed in with a laugh, flapping his wings enthusiastically. "I'm always ready for a good scare!"

As they ventured deeper into the cave, the air became thicker, charged with an ancient energy that made Alarion's skin tingle. The cave walls seemed to whisper, secrets echoing off the stone, enticing them forward.

The Prophecy Revealed

At the heart of the cave, they discovered an altar adorned with flickering candles and strange symbols etched into the stone. Lila approached it, brushing her fingers over the inscriptions.

"These markings tell a story," She said, her eyes lighting up with curiosity. "It's a prophecy about the Eternal Flame!"

"What does it say?" Alarion leaned closer, his heart racing. "It speaks of a bond forged in flame," Lila read aloud. "When the Chosen One embraces the Eternal Flame, a guardian shall rise from the ashes, destined to unite love and magic against the darkness."

"Sounds epic," Blazewing said, doing a little spin in the air. "But what does that mean for us?"

Lila turned to Alarion; her expression serious yet filled with wonder. "I think... it means you might be more connected to the Eternal Flame than we realized. There's a deeper purpose to our quest."

Alarion swallowed hard. "A guardian? Me?" His mind raced with possibilities, but beneath it all was the warmth of Lila's presence, a reminder of what was truly important.

"Yeah! You're the chosen one! You've got this!" Blazewing cheered, but Alarion could sense an underlying gravity to their situation.

A Heartfelt Song

Feeling the weight of the moment, Lila picked up a nearby candle, holding it aloft as if it were a torch.

"Let's sing a little song to lighten the mood!"
To the tune of "You Are My Sunshine":
You are my hero, my brave knight true,
The Flame's connection, I feel it too.
When darkness rises, we will stand strong,
With love beside us, we can't go wrong.
When shadows creep in, and troubles arise,
I'll stand with you, and together we'll rise.
With every battle, our hearts entwine,
Forever and always, you will be mine.
So, here's to the flame that lights up our way,

In the heart of the chaos, we'll find our way.
With laughter and courage, we'll break every chain,
Together we'll conquer, our love will remain!

As they sang, the air around them shimmered, the flames flickering in time with their voices, wrapping them in a warm embrace. Lila looked at Alarion, a playful glimmer in her eyes. "You know, if you do become a guardian, I expect a cool costume."

"Maybe a cape? I could definitely pull off a cape," Alarion joked, feeling lighter despite the gravity of their discovery.

"Definitely a cape," Lila agreed, her smile infectious. "And maybe a crown!"

Suddenly, the ground shook beneath them, and the cave erupted with an ominous roar.

The Darkness Unleashed

Emerging from the shadows was a figure draped in darkness, cloaked and menacing. The air grew colder as the dark warrior approached, his eyes burning with malice. "You dare seek the Eternal Flame?" he sneered, his voice echoing off the cave walls. "You'll never succeed!"

"Who are you?" Alarion shouted, stepping forward to protect Lila.

"I am Tharos, the Keeper of Shadows," the figure proclaimed, his voice dripping with disdain. "You think you can unite love and magic? You're a fool!"

Blazewing fluttered nervously. "Maybe we should've brought a bigger snack for him?"

"Enough of this banter!" Tharos roared, raising his hand to summon a wave of dark energy.

"Prepare to meet your end!"

The Battle Begins

In an instant, Alarion drew his sword, its blade gleaming in the dim light. "We won't back down!" he declared, charging at Tharos.

The clash of metal rang through the cave as their swords met, sparks flying.

Lila joined the fray, her magic swirling around her as she cast spells to shield Alarion and counter Tharos's attacks. "Stay focused, Alarion! We can't let him distract us!"

"Right! But it's hard when he's so... dark and brooding!" Alarion quipped, dodging another of Tharos's strikes.

As they fought, Alarion felt the connection to the prophecy strengthen within him. With every swing of his sword, he recalled Lila's words: "A bond forged in flame." That bond surged with power, fueling his resolve.

Blazewing darted around, breathing fire at Tharos. "Hey, shadow dude! Ever heard of a little thing called light?"

"Silence, pest!" Tharos shouted, swiping his hand and sending a shockwave toward Blazewing, who narrowly avoided it.

The Turning Point

Just when it seemed they were outmatched, Alarion felt a rush of energy. The cave pulsed with magic, and he realized that the Eternal Flame must be reacting to their struggle. "Lila! I think the Flame is responding! We have to channel it!"

"Right! Focus on the connection!" Lila shouted, raising her wand to channel her magic toward Alarion.

As their energies intertwined, a brilliant light enveloped them, creating a barrier against Tharos's dark magic. "No!" the Keeper of Shadows shouted, his face contorting with rage.

With a united front, Alarion and Lila unleashed a surge of light, causing the darkness to recoil. "Together!" Alarion called, and with one final, combined effort, they launched a powerful beam of light toward Tharos.

The dark warrior was engulfed in the brilliance, his form disintegrating into shadows as he howled in defeat. The cave trembled, the whispers of ancient spirits echoing in celebration.

Love Amid Chaos

As the dust settled and the light faded, Alarion turned to Lila, panting but exhilarated. "We did it! We actually did it!"

"Yeah, and we looked good doing it," Lila replied, a playful smile on her face.

"Just think of all the stories we'll tell!" Blazewing chirped, circling around them. "I mean, who doesn't want to hear about the epic battle against the Keeper of Shadows?"

"Not to mention the part where you were nearly fried!" Alarion joked, trying to lighten the mood.

Lila stepped closer, her expression softening. "You were amazing, Alarion. I couldn't have done it without you."

"You were incredible too," Alarion said, feeling the warmth of her praise wrap around him like a blanket. "I think the prophecy really means something. We're stronger together."

As they stood in the shimmering light of the cave, the connection between them deepened, a bond forged in both laughter and chaos.

"We should keep moving toward the Eternal Flame," Lila said, her voice steady yet filled with anticipation. "We're closer than ever."

"Agreed," Alarion replied, feeling the flutter of excitement in his chest. "But first... I think we deserve a moment."

A Moment of Connection

Lila looked at him, and the air around them thickened with unspoken words. "Alarion, about everything we've been through—"

Before she could finish, Blazewing swooped in dramatically, interrupting, "I demand a song to celebrate our victory! To the tune of 'We Are the Champions'!"

"Blazewing, not now!" Alarion exclaimed, but the little creature was already on a roll.

To the tune of
"We Are the Champions":

We are the heroes, my dear Lila,
Fighting through shadows, we shall never die.
We've faced the darkness, together we'll rise,
With love as our armor, we'll light up the skies!
You are my partner, the Flame is our guide,
With laughter and magic, we'll take it in stride.
Together we conquered, in the heart of the night,
With hearts intertwined, we'll continue the fight!

As Blazewing sang, Lila laughed, the tension melting away. Alarion couldn't help but join in, his heart light as they embraced the absurdity of the moment.

"Alright, Blazewing, you win!" Alarion chuckled. "But you owe us a really good marshmallow feast later!"

As the echoes of their laughter faded, Alarion felt a sense of calm wash over him. They had faced darkness together, and amidst the chaos, love had blossomed like a flower in the fire.

The journey ahead would be perilous, but with Lila by his side and a bond forged in flame, they would face whatever challenges lay ahead.

With renewed determination, they pressed forward, ready to uncover the secrets of the Eternal Flame, their hearts united and their spirits unbreakable. The whispers of flame guided their path, igniting a love that would burn brighter than any darkness they might encounter.

Chapter 16: The Inferno Maze

Alarion and Lila navigate a maze of flames that tests their courage and trust in one another. Their light-hearted banter keeps spirits high, even as danger lurks around every corner.

Alarion and Lila stood at the entrance of the Inferno Maze, a labyrinth of flickering flames that danced ominously in the twilight. The heat radiated from the walls, causing beads of sweat to form on Alarion's brow. "This looks... safe," he quipped, glancing sideways at Lila.

"Safe? This is exciting! Look at the fire!" Lila replied, her eyes sparkling with mischief. "It's like nature's own light show! We can have a little fun in here!"

"You mean like playing 'Dodge the Fireball'?" Alarion joked, raising an eyebrow. "I thought we were here to save the realm, not audition for a circus."

Lila laughed, and the sound echoed through the entrance. "Come on, Mr. Hero! Where's your sense of adventure? Besides, if we make it out, we'll have some wild stories to tell!"

With a resigned grin, Alarion stepped forward, stepping into the maze. The walls of flames shifted, creating an ever-changing path. "Alright, let's see if we can navigate this fiery maze without getting singed!"

The First Challenge

As they moved deeper into the maze, the flames flickered and flared, creating shadows that danced ominously around them. Alarion pulled out his sword, its blade glowing with a faint light. "I'll lead the way. If anything jumps out, you can throw fireballs at it," he said, trying to sound brave.

"Perfect! I've always wanted to be a fire-throwing sorceress," Lila replied playfully, twirling her wand. "Just make sure you don't get burnt."

Suddenly, a wall of flames surged up ahead, cutting off their path. "Oh great, just what we needed—a fiery dead end!" Alarion exclaimed, frustration creeping into his voice.

Lila stepped closer to the flames, a determined look on her face. "Maybe we can find a way through. I think I can channel my magic to create a protective barrier."

"Or we could just turn around and find another way," Alarion suggested, scratching his head.

"Where's your sense of adventure?" Lila teased, nudging him playfully. "I thought you were up for a little challenge."

"Alright, fine! Let's go for it!" Alarion exclaimed, rolling up his sleeves. "But if I get scorched, you owe me a healing potion."

The Barrier Spell

As Lila raised her wand, the flames began to writhe, reacting to her magic. "Here goes nothing!" she declared.

Steps for the spell: Focus your energy:

Lila closed her eyes, envisioning the flames bending to her will.

Draw a protective circle:

With a swift motion, she traced a circle in the air with her wand, the tip glowing brightly.

Channel your intention:

"By fire and flame, let this barrier remain!" she chanted, her voice steady and strong.

A shimmering barrier of light formed between them and the raging flames, creating a safe passage. "It worked!" Alarion exclaimed, his eyes wide with admiration. "You're amazing!"

"Of course! I'm a fire sorceress, remember?" Lila winked, pushing through the barrier as it dissolved behind them.

As they navigated the next turn, the walls of flames roared to life, and Alarion couldn't help but joke, "At this rate, we'll need marshmallows for a real campfire!"

"Only if you're willing to roast them!" Lila shot back, her laughter mingling with the sound of crackling flames.

The Hidden Enemy

Just then, a figure emerged from the shadows—a dark-cloaked stranger with eyes that glowed like embers. "You dare to trespass in the Inferno Maze?" he sneered, drawing a wicked-looking dagger.

"Uh-oh, looks like we're not alone!" Alarion said, instinctively stepping in front of Lila. "What do you want, flamey?"

The stranger laughed, a chilling sound. "I seek the Eternal Flame for myself! You'll not leave this maze alive!"

"Oh please," Lila retorted, brandishing her wand. "You really think you can take us down? We just survived a fiery dead end!"

Alarion positioned himself beside her, gripping his sword tightly. "Yeah, we're kind of a big deal. You know, destined to save the world and all that."

The Fight Begins

With a roar, the stranger lunged at them, dagger aimed for Alarion's heart. Alarion quickly sidestepped, deflecting the blow with his sword. "Lila, now!" he shouted.

"Fireball coming right up!" Lila responded, raising her wand. "Fireball!" A burst of flames erupted from her wand, striking the stranger in the chest and sending him staggering backward.

"Is that all you've got?" he sneered, brushing off the flames. "You'll have to do better than that!"

"Okay, but we weren't really warmed up yet," Alarion quipped, dodging another swipe of the dagger. "How about we turn up the heat?"

With their banter fueling their courage, Lila and Alarion launched into action, dodging the stranger's strikes while countering with their own magic and swordplay.

"Just like a dance, right?" Lila said, her eyes gleaming with excitement. "Step left, parry, spin!"

"I never signed up for dancing in a maze of fire!" Alarion laughed, executing a well-timed kick that sent the stranger reeling.

The Turning Point

As the fight intensified, Lila noticed something glimmering behind the stranger—a small shard of the Eternal Flame embedded in the stone wall. "Alarion! The shard! It's behind him!"

"Got it!" Alarion shouted, leaping forward to distract the stranger. "Hey, fire dude! You want a piece of this?"

The stranger turned, glaring at Alarion, giving Lila the opening she needed. "Now, let's see how you like this!" She thrust her wand forward, channeling her magic with all her might. "Inferno Shield!"

A wall of fire erupted around the stranger, trapping him momentarily. "What? No!" he yelled, panic in his eyes.

"Now, Alarion!" Lila called, her voice echoing in the fiery maze.

Alarion dashed toward the glimmering shard, grasping it in his hand. As he did, the flames around them surged with energy, intertwining with his own.

The Final Confrontation

With the shard in his grasp, Alarion felt a rush of warmth course through him. "Lila, together!" he shouted, holding the shard high.

Lila joined him, her wand aimed at the stranger. "We're not letting you take the Eternal Flame!"

They combined their powers, the light from the shard merging with Lila's magic to create a brilliant beam that shot toward the stranger. "No! This can't be happening!" he screamed, caught in the light's embrace.

The blast of energy engulfed the stranger, who staggered back, disappearing into the flames as they enveloped him. The heat dissipated, leaving only a faint echo of his cries behind.

Love in the Flames

As the last remnants of danger faded, Alarion and Lila stood together, breathless and exhilarated. "Did we just... win?" Alarion asked, disbelief dancing in his voice.

"I think we did! Together!" Lila exclaimed, her face aglow with triumph.

"I couldn't have done it without you," Alarion said, turning to her. The warmth of their victory surged through him, intertwining with the warmth he felt for her.

"Yeah, but let's be real—you were pretty amazing too!" Lila beamed; her laughter infectious. "You know, if this hero business doesn't work out, we could start a duo act—Fire and Sword!"

"Fire and Sword, huh? Sounds like a catchy name!" Alarion replied, chuckling.

As they made their way through the maze, Alarion felt a sense of calm enveloping him. The flames around them, once daunting, now felt like a protective embrace. "I think we make a pretty good team," he said softly.

"Agreed," Lila smiled, her eyes sparkling like the flames. "And I'm looking forward to more adventures together."

Alarion's heart raced, and he felt a warmth spread within him. "Me too, Lila. You make every moment worth it."

As they finally emerged from the maze, the sun began to rise on the horizon, bathing the world in golden light. The Inferno Maze was behind them, but ahead lay the promise of more adventures, more challenges, and perhaps a deeper connection that was just beginning to spark between them.

Together, they took a step forward, ready to face whatever awaited them, hand in hand. The path to the Eternal Flame was still long, but with each step, their bond grew stronger, fueled by laughter, love, and a shared destiny that would guide them through even the darkest of challenges.

Chapter 17: The Shadow Enemy

An enigmatic shadowy figure threatens their quest, casting doubt on Alarion's abilities. Lila's unwavering support becomes his guiding light, sparking deeper feelings between them.

The sun hung low in the sky, casting long shadows across the path Alarion and Lila traversed. They were on their way to find the next clue that would lead them to the Eternal Flame when an ominous chill enveloped the air. Alarion shivered, glancing sideways at Lila. "Do you feel that?" he asked, concern lacing his voice.

Lila stopped, her brow furrowing. "Yeah, it's like the warmth of the sun just... vanished." She looked around, her instincts sharpening. "Something's not right."

Suddenly, a shadow flickered across the path in front of them, drawing their attention. From the darkness emerged a figure cloaked in swirling black, his eyes glowing like embers in the night. "So, the little heroes have come to play," he sneered, a voice smooth and dripping with malice. "I am the Shadow Enemy, and your quest ends here."

The Threatening Presence

Alarion stepped forward, trying to mask his fear with bravado. "We're not afraid of you! We've faced tougher challenges than some overgrown shadow!"

"Overgrown?" the shadow figure chuckled darkly. "You underestimate me, boy. I'm the darkness that haunts your dreams, the doubt that lurks in your heart."

Alarion's confidence wavered. He had faced fire-breathing beasts and treacherous mazes, but this shadow invoked a different kind of fear—one that gnawed at his insecurities. "What do you know about me?" he demanded, trying to sound defiant.

"Enough to know that you doubt yourself, Alarion," the Shadow Enemy replied, stepping closer. "Your powers are weak, and you'll never wield the Eternal Flame."

"Hey!" Lila interjected, stepping protectively in front of Alarion. "You don't know him! He's more powerful than you think!"

The shadow figure chuckled again, his laugh echoing ominously in the clearing. "And what will you do, little sorceress? Cast a spell and hope for the best? Your support is but a flicker against my darkness."

The Power of Doubt

"Don't listen to him, Alarion," Lila said firmly, placing a reassuring hand on his shoulder. "You're brave, and you've come this far. We can do this together!"

"Together..." Alarion murmured, feeling a flicker of hope ignite within him. But the shadow seemed to sense his wavering spirit and intensified his presence.

"Can you hear that, Alarion? All your failures, all the moments you felt inadequate? They're all whispering to you now, aren't they?" the Shadow Enemy taunted, weaving between the trees, causing the shadows to dance ominously.

"You think you can just get into my head?" Alarion shot back, clenching his fists. "You're wrong!"

Lila's unwavering support felt like a light piercing through the darkness surrounding them. "Alarion, focus on the light! Remember the victories we've shared and how far you've come! You are stronger than this shadow!"

The Battle Begins

With newfound resolve, Alarion drew his sword, its blade shimmering with a hint of light. "You want a fight? Let's give you one!" he declared, stepping forward with confidence.

"Foolish boy," the Shadow Enemy sneered. "You think light can defeat darkness? Let's see how long you last!"

As the shadow lunged at them, Alarion quickly swung his sword, the blade cutting through the darkness with a brilliant flash. "Now, Lila!" he shouted, readying himself for the next move.

"Fireball!" Lila shouted, raising her wand. Steps for the spell: Gather energy: Lila closed her eyes, channeling her magic deep within.

Draw the fire: With a swift motion, she traced a circle in the air, igniting the flames around her.

Release the spell: "By the spark of hope, let fire grow!" she chanted, sending a brilliant fireball toward the shadow.

The fireball collided with the shadow, illuminating the clearing. The Shadow Enemy hissed in fury, momentarily retreating. "You think you can defeat me with mere tricks?" he spat, gathering darkness around him.

"Tricks? No, these are skills we've honed together!" Alarion replied, charging forward with renewed confidence. "We're stronger together!"

A Moment of Doubt

But even as he fought, the Shadow Enemy's words echoed in Alarion's mind, casting seeds of doubt. He found himself hesitating as the shadow retaliated with tendrils of darkness, wrapping around Alarion's feet. "You're not good enough," it whispered. "You'll always be in Lila's shadow."

"Shut up!" Alarion yelled, struggling against the binds. "I am not my doubts!"

Lila, sensing his turmoil, stepped closer. "Alarion, listen to me! You're brave and capable. Remember when you saved the villagers from that raging beast? You can do this!"

"I... I can do this," Alarion repeated, the light of her faith brightening the darkness around him. Summoning all his strength, he swung his sword, slicing through the tendrils. "I will not let you win!"

The Turning Tide

Rejuvenated by Lila's words, Alarion charged toward the shadow. "This ends now!" he shouted, raising his sword high. Lila joined him, channeling her magic as they launched a combined attack. "Together!" they cried in unison.

"Together!" Lila echoed, casting another fireball that spiraled toward the Shadow Enemy, merging with Alarion's sword strike.

The resulting explosion of light and fire illuminated the entire clearing, and for a moment, it felt as though hope had triumphed over despair. The Shadow Enemy screamed in fury as the light engulfed him, dissipating the darkness.

The Aftermath

As the light faded, the shadow figure crumbled into the ground, leaving behind nothing but a faint echo of his malevolence. Alarion and Lila stood in the clearing, panting and exhilarated.

"Did we... did we win?" Alarion asked, incredulity washing over him.

"Definitely!" Lila exclaimed, bouncing with excitement. "We did it together!"

Alarion turned to her, his heart swelling with gratitude and something deeper. "I couldn't have done it without you, Lila. You really are my guiding light."

Lila smiled, her cheeks turning a shade of pink. "And you're more powerful than you give yourself credit for, Alarion. I knew you had it in you."

As they caught their breath, a light breeze danced through the clearing, carrying with it the sweet scent of blooming flowers. For a moment, everything felt right in the world.

A Moment of Connection

"Hey," Alarion began, his voice softer now, "I know we still have challenges ahead, but I really appreciate everything you've done for me. You make me feel stronger than I ever thought possible."

Lila's gaze met his, and the connection between them felt palpable. "And you inspire me, Alarion. I believe in you, and I believe in us."

"Us?" Alarion echoed, his heart racing. "What do you mean by that?"

"Just that... we're a team," Lila replied, her voice steady despite the fluttering in her stomach. "I want to be by your side, not just as a friend but... more."

Alarion felt a rush of warmth at her words. "I want that too, Lila. You mean so much to me."

In that moment, the air around them thickened with unspoken emotions. They leaned closer, their hearts racing as the world around them faded away, leaving just the two of them, bathed in the light of their triumph and newfound connection.

But before their lips could meet, a distant rumble interrupted the moment. "Ugh, always with the interruptions!" Lila exclaimed, stepping back with a playful pout.

"Guess the universe has other plans," Alarion chuckled, trying to regain his composure. "But we'll have our moment, don't worry."

The Journey Continues

As they resumed their journey, hand in hand, the challenges they faced felt lighter, the path ahead brighter. Though shadows still loomed on the horizon, together they would conquer whatever lay in wait.

"Next stop: the Eternal Flame!" Alarion declared, a newfound determination fueling his steps. Lila smiled brightly beside him, ready to face the world—and all its shadows—together.

As they ventured onward, the bond between them grew, fortified by shared trials and the unbreakable light of their companionship. Little did they know, greater challenges awaited them, but with hearts entwined, they were ready to face anything that came their way.

Chapter 18: Heart of the Flame

As they reach the heart of the mountain, the challenges intensify. Alarion must confront his fears and insecurities, while Lila offers humorous pep talks that lighten the mood.

The towering peak of Mount Ignis loomed ahead, its jagged edges kissed by the wisps of clouds. Alarion and Lila stood at the base, staring up at the imposing structure. "Are you ready for this?" Lila asked, her eyes sparkling with excitement, even as trepidation danced in the corners of her expression.

"Ready as I'll ever be," Alarion replied, forcing a smile. But inside, he felt a storm of nerves brewing. He had come so far, yet the idea of facing the heart of the mountain—rumored to be where the Eternal Flame resided—filled him with a sense of dread. "Just... what if I mess up?"

Lila grinned; her usual light-heartedness infectious. "Alarion, if you mess up, we'll just blame it on that big scary mountain. It has a reputation for being cranky, you know?"

He couldn't help but chuckle at her antics. "You really think I could blame a mountain for my failures?"

"Why not? Mountains are known for being dramatic!" she replied, puffing out her chest and placing her hands on her hips. "I can just hear it now: 'Woe is me! Why can't I have a hero who doesn't trip over his own feet?'"

The Ascent

They began their ascent, and Lila continued with her playful commentary, weaving tales of the mountain's legendary grumpiness.

ALARION AND THE ETERNAL FLAME

"And don't forget about the rock trolls that guard this place. They're not known for their hospitality!"

Alarion smirked. "What if we meet a rock troll? Do we offer it cookies?"

"Only if we want to get squished!" Lila laughed, her voice echoing off the rocky walls. The sound of her laughter eased Alarion's anxiety as they climbed higher, facing steep inclines and rocky paths.

But as they neared the summit, the air grew heavier, thick with an unsettling tension. The challenges ahead were far from over. A sudden gust of wind swept through, sending a shiver down Alarion's spine. "Lila, something feels... off."

"Of course it does! We're approaching the Heart of the Flame. It's supposed to be dramatic!" she said, a hint of mischief in her voice. "But I promise, whatever's up there, we'll face it together."

Confronting Fears

Just as they reached a narrow ledge, a chilling voice echoed from the darkness ahead.

"Welcome, brave souls. Do you seek the Eternal Flame?"

Alarion's heart raced as a cloaked figure emerged from the shadows, eyes gleaming like molten gold. "I am the Guardian of the Flame. To pass, you must confront your deepest fears."

Alarion swallowed hard. "What do you mean?"

"Face your insecurities, and only then can you continue," the Guardian intoned ominously.

"Great," Alarion muttered under his breath, dread pooling in his stomach. "Just what I wanted—an existential crisis at a mountain summit."

"Don't worry, Alarion," Lila said, her voice steady. "You're stronger than you think! Just remember that time you faced that fire-breathing beast? You didn't back down then, and you won't back down now!"

As the Guardian raised his hand, shadows danced around Alarion, swirling and morphing into manifestations of his fears. He saw himself failing, losing Lila's trust, and not being able to wield the powers he desperately sought.

"Alarion, you're not good enough," the shadows whispered, echoing his insecurities. "You'll never be the hero you aspire to be."

The Battle Within

Just then, Lila stepped forward, determined. "You have to believe in yourself! You've come too far to let this shadow hold you back." She took a deep breath and began to sing, her voice ringing clear and sweet, as though the very air around them had come alive.

Song: "Believe in the Flame"
(To the tune of a whimsical, upbeat melody)
Verse 1:
In the heart of the mountain, where shadows play,
Fear may creep in, but we won't sway.
Together we stand, with hearts intertwined,
With courage and laughter, our path we will find.
Chorus:
Believe in the flame that flickers within,
With every challenge, we know we will win.
Hold tight to your dreams, let the light lead the way,
Together, forever, we won't go astray.
Verse 2:
The mountains may tremble, the rocks may fall,
But here at this moment, we're standing tall.
With every heartbeat, with every smile,
We'll conquer the shadows; we'll go that extra mile!
Chorus:
Believe in the flame that flickers within,
With every challenge, we know we will win.
Hold tight to your dreams, let the light lead the way,

Together, forever, we won't go astray.
Bridge:
*So, lift your head high, and take a deep breath,
With laughter and love, we'll dance past the death.
The shadows will tremble, the darkness will flee,
With love as our armor, we'll fight to be free!*
Final Chorus:
*Believe in the flame that flickers within,
With every challenge, we know we will win.
Hold tight to your dreams, let the light lead the way,
Together, forever, we won't go astray!*

The Shadows Retreat

As Lila's voice resonated through the air, the shadows flickered and began to retreat. Alarion felt a warmth spread through him, igniting the spark of courage that had been buried deep inside. "You're right, Lila," he shouted over the echoes of doubt. "I won't let my fears control me!"

Fueled by newfound determination, he drew his sword and charged toward the shadows. "I am more than my doubts!" he declared, slicing through the manifestations of his insecurities.

With each swing of his sword, the shadows shrieked and faded, unraveling the Guardian's power over him. Alarion felt the weight of his fears lifting, replaced by a sense of clarity and strength.

A Sudden Threat

But just as he thought they had triumphed, the Guardian stepped forward, a flicker of annoyance crossing his face. "You may have defeated the shadows, but your trials are far from over. To truly prove your worth, you must face my final test."

Before Alarion could respond, the ground shook, and a pack of shadowy creatures emerged from the darkness, their eyes glowing menacingly. "Looks like we have company!" Lila exclaimed, brandishing her wand. "Time for a little teamwork!"

The Battle for the Flame

Alarion and Lila sprang into action, dodging the creatures as they lunged at them. "You handle the left, and I'll take the right!" Alarion shouted, adrenaline coursing through his veins.

Lila nodded; determination etched on her face. "Fireball, go!" she cried, sending a wave of flames towards the nearest creature, which yelped and disintegrated into a wisp of smoke.

Alarion fought fiercely, his sword dancing in the air as he struck at the advancing creatures. "We've got this, Lila!" he encouraged, adrenaline fueling his movements. "Together, we're unstoppable!"

As they battled side by side, their laughter and encouragement echoed through the mountain. Lila's humor brought levity even in the heat of combat. "Did you know they say these shadow creatures are afraid of... tickles?" she yelled playfully, dodging a swing from one of the beasts.

"Tickles?" Alarion raised an eyebrow, surprised. "Is that true?"

"Absolutely! But we'll have to save that for later!" she laughed, dodging another creature.

The Final Blow

Just as it seemed the shadows would overwhelm them, Alarion remembered Lila's song.

"Believe in the flame," he whispered, a spark igniting in his heart. He raised his sword high, channeling all the power within him. "With the light of our friendship, I banish you!"

With a fierce cry, Alarion swung his sword, releasing a wave of brilliant light that engulfed the remaining creatures. They shrieked and faded into nothingness, leaving the Guardian alone, his expression a mix of surprise and admiration.

Victory and New Realizations

"You've passed the final trial," the Guardian said, his voice now tinged with respect. "You have faced your fears, fought bravely, and proved your worth. The Eternal Flame awaits you at the heart of the mountain."

Alarion turned to Lila, their eyes shining with exhilaration. "We did it! I couldn't have done it without you!"

Lila grinned; her cheeks flushed with victory. "And I couldn't have done it without your bravery! Together, we're unstoppable!"

As they made their way toward the heart of the mountain, Alarion felt lighter, the shadows of doubt that once lingered in his mind dissipating with each step.

"Alarion," Lila began, glancing at him. "About what we said earlier..."

"About us?" he prompted, his heart racing.

"Yeah, I think... I think we're more than friends now, don't you?" she replied, her voice softening.

"I definitely think so," he replied, a warmth blooming in his chest. "After everything we've faced, I can't imagine my journey without you."

Lila smiled brightly, her eyes sparkling with affection. "Then let's take on whatever comes next—together."

With renewed strength, they continued toward the heart of the mountain, ready to face the next chapter of their adventure, armed with laughter, love, and the courage to conquer whatever challenges awaited them.

Chapter 19: A Rival's Return

The jealous fire mage returns, seeking revenge. Alarion must outwit him in a comical showdown that highlights both their strengths and weaknesses, further complicating the love triangle.

As Alarion and Lila emerged from the fiery depths of Mount Ignis, their hearts still racing from the challenges they had faced, a sense of accomplishment washed over them. The air was crisp, carrying the faint scent of ash and victory. However, the moment of respite was short-lived; the sun was barely setting when a familiar figure appeared on the horizon, backlit by the golden rays.

"Just when you thought it was safe to bask in your glory..." Alarion muttered, squinting against the light.

"Is that who I think it is?" Lila asked her tone a mix of excitement and dread.

"Unless we're being attacked by an angry hedgehog, that would be Ignis," Alarion replied, rolling his eyes. Ignis, the flamboyant fire mage, had a reputation for his theatrics and fiery temper, and he wasn't one to take defeat lightly.

As Ignis approached, his vibrant robes flowed dramatically in the breeze, and his eyes sparkled with an intensity that could rival a blazing bonfire. "Ah, Alarion! How delightful to see you again!" he called out, his voice dripping with sarcasm. "And Lila, lovely as ever. I see you've survived your little escapade in the mountain. How quaint!"

The Jealous Mage

"What do you want, Ignis?" Alarion asked, crossing his arms, feeling a mix of annoyance and amusement.

"I come not for petty revenge but to reclaim my honor!" Ignis declared, dramatically raising his hands as flames flickered to life around him. "You may have bested me before, but today, I challenge you to a duel of wits and fire!"

"A duel?" Lila exclaimed; her eyes wide. "You mean, like a real battle?"

"Indeed! But fear not, I promise to keep it entertaining. A bit of theatrics never hurt anyone," Ignis replied, a wicked grin spreading across his face.

Alarion glanced at Lila, who shrugged, her expression a mixture of curiosity and concern. "I suppose we could use a little fun," she said, trying to lighten the mood.

With a sigh, Alarion stepped forward, "Alright, Ignis. But let's keep it... friendly?"

"Friendly?" Ignis chuckled, flames dancing between his fingers. "Oh, Alarion, you sweet summer child. This will be anything but friendly!"

The Showdown Begins

With a snap of his fingers, Ignis conjured a ring of fire around them, creating a makeshift arena. "Welcome to the Arena of Flame! May the best mage win!" he proclaimed, striking a dramatic pose.

"More like the arena of ridiculousness," Alarion muttered under his breath. He raised his sword, its blade gleaming in the sunlight. "What are the rules?"

"Simple!" Ignis said, tossing a ball of fire into the air. "We'll take turns casting spells and trying to outwit each other. The first one to crack under pressure loses!"

Lila stepped up, trying to regain some control. "And no burning each other to a crisp, okay?

We don't want the forest to catch fire!"

"Agreed," Ignis said, although the mischievous glint in his eyes suggested he might not adhere to the rules.

The First Round

The duel began, and Alarion took a deep breath, focusing on his magic. "I'll go first!" he declared, summoning a gust of wind that swept through the arena, swirling around Ignis playfully.

"Wind? Really?" Ignis scoffed, raising an eyebrow as he effortlessly deflected the breeze with a flick of his wrist. "Allow me to show you what true fire magic looks like!" He threw a fireball that lit up the sky, but instead of aiming it at Alarion, he created a dazzling display of sparks and flames, swirling into the shape of a phoenix.

Lila clapped her hands, caught between admiration and the absurdity of the situation. "That's beautiful!"

"Thanks, but it doesn't win the duel!" Alarion retorted, shaking his head as he prepared for his next move. "Here goes nothing!"

The Unexpected Twist

With a flick of his sword, he summoned a wave of water from a nearby stream, aiming to douse Ignis's flames. The water splashed harmlessly against the ring of fire, creating steam that hung in the air. Ignis, however, was prepared. He laughed heartily, conjuring a wall of fire that evaporated the water before it could touch him.

"Not bad, Alarion! But you'll need more than that!" Ignis said, leaning back confidently.

Feeling the pressure, Alarion thought of his next move. "Okay, I've got an idea." He glanced at Lila, who offered him an encouraging smile. "I'll turn the heat up a notch!"

The Battle of Wits

"I challenge you to a song duel!" Alarion declared, surprising everyone. "Let's see whose magic can inspire more than just flames!"

Ignis raised an eyebrow, clearly intrigued. "A song duel? How quaint! What are the rules?"

"We'll take turns singing lines, and whoever fails to keep up loses," Alarion explained, feeling the thrill of the challenge.

"Alright, I'm in," Ignis said, grinning. "But be prepared to lose!"

As Alarion began to sing, he chose a lighthearted melody, hoping to showcase his playful side:

Song: "Flames and Laughter"
(To a cheerful, upbeat tune)
Verse 1:
In the land of fire, where shadows dance,
With laughter and magic, we'll take our chance.
Fires may flicker, but spirits ignite,
With humor and courage, we'll set the night bright!
Chorus:
Flames and laughter, a duo so grand,
With sparks in our hearts, together we stand.
Ignite the night with joy and delight,
In the arena of flames, we'll shine so bright!
Verse 2:
So, bring on the heat, I won't back down,
With fire and wit, we'll take this crown.
You may be a mage, but I'm not afraid,
With laughter as armor, our friendship is made!
Chorus:
Flames and laughter, a duo so grand,
With sparks in our hearts, together we stand.
Ignite the night with joy and delight,
In the arena of flames, we'll shine so bright!
The Rivalry Intensifies

With every verse, Alarion poured his heart into the song, and Lila joined in for the chorus, her voice blending beautifully with his. Ignis watched, a mixture of admiration and annoyance flickering across his features.

"Alright, my turn!" Ignis exclaimed, stepping forward with a dramatic flair. He ignited a ring of flames around him, using it to accentuate his performance as he sang:

Verse 3:
You think you're clever with your flames of fun,
But watch as I burn brighter than the sun!
My fire is fierce, and my heart is true,
In this duel of magic, I'll always outdo you!
Chorus:
Flames and laughter, let the sparks fly,
In the heat of the moment, we'll reach for the sky!
Ignite the night with joy and delight,
In the arena of flames, I'll set it alight!

The Climax of Comedy

As Ignis's flames crackled, Alarion couldn't help but laugh at the sheer ridiculousness of the situation. "You really think that's enough to win?" he challenged, leaning into the playful rivalry. "Alright, let's turn this into a real battle of wits!"

With that, they began tossing playful jabs at each other, mixing lyrics and lighthearted insults:

Verse 4:
Ignis, oh Ignis, your flames are so bright,
But without any brains, you're a sad, lonely sight!
With every spark, you try to impress,
But your jokes are as dry as a desert, I guess!
Chorus:
Flames and laughter, a duo so grand,
With sparks in our hearts, together we stand.
Ignite the night with joy and delight,
In the arena of flames, we'll shine so bright!

The Final Showdown

As the song continued, the atmosphere transformed from one of rivalry to camaraderie, filled with laughter and light. Even Ignis found himself chuckling amidst the playful banter.

Suddenly, the ground shook beneath them, and dark clouds rolled in, casting a shadow over the arena. The playful banter faded as all eyes turned to the sky. "What is happening?" Lila asked, concern etched on her face.

From the depths of the shadows, a new threat emerged—figures cloaked in darkness, wielding dark magic. "Looks like your little show is over, mages!" one of them sneered, their voice cold and ominous.

Alarion's heart raced. "More hidden enemies?" he exclaimed, pulling his sword free. "What do they want?"

The Alliance

"We're not here for you!" one of the shadowy figures hissed. "We're here for the Eternal Flame!"

"Ignis, we need to work together!" Alarion shouted, his instincts kicking in. "Let's show them what we've got!"

"Agreed!" Ignis replied, his earlier rivalry forgotten in the face of danger. "But remember, no burning each other, okay?"

"Only if you don't get in my way!" Alarion quipped, grinning.

With a united front, Alarion and Ignis combined their powers, creating a dazzling display of fire and wind. Alarion summoned a whirlwind while Ignis unleashed a barrage of fireballs, the two elements intertwining and sending sparks flying in all directions.

The Final Battle

As the dark figures approached, Alarion felt a surge of adrenaline. "Lila, stay back!" he yelled, thrusting his sword toward the shadows. "Ignis, let's take them down!"

In a flurry of motion, they fought side by side, dodging attacks and retaliating with their combined magic. Flames danced and howled as Alarion and Ignis took turns launching their attacks, igniting the air with humor and camaraderie.

"Not bad for a rival!" Ignis shouted as he sent a wave of fire crashing into one of the shadowy figures.

"Likewise, fire mage! Just try to keep up!" Alarion called back, ducking under an incoming attack.

As the battle raged, laughter and playful banter filled the air, providing a lighthearted contrast to the chaos around them. Each time one of them landed a blow, they exchanged triumphant grins, solidifying their newfound alliance.

The Victory Dance

With a final combined spell—a swirling vortex of wind and flames—the last of the shadowy figures was vanquished, dissolving into a cloud of dark mist. The arena fell silent, the only sounds being their heavy breaths and the crackle of fading flames.

"We did it!" Lila cheered, rushing over to hug both Alarion and Ignis. "That was amazing!"

"Don't get used to this, Ignis," Alarion warned, a smirk on his face. "I still plan to outwit you next time!"

"I look forward to it, Alarion," Ignis replied, extending his hand. "A worthy opponent deserves respect."

They shook hands, the rivalry transforming into a reluctant friendship, one grounded in mutual respect and laughter.

The Heart of the Flame

As the sun dipped below the horizon, casting a warm glow over the arena, Alarion felt a sense of belonging wash over him. The earlier tension melted away, replaced by the camaraderie forged in battle.

"Now, who's up for some celebratory ice cream?" Lila suggested, her eyes sparkling with mischief.

"I think we all deserve a treat after that," Ignis agreed, grinning widely.

"Only if it's not on fire," Alarion quipped, earning laughter from both of them as they walked together, ready to take on whatever the next adventure had in store.

Thus, amidst laughter, flames, and newfound friendships, they ventured toward the horizon, their hearts ignited by the adventures yet to come.

Chapter 20: The Eternal Flame's Guardian

They finally meet the guardian of the Eternal Flame, who challenges Alarion to prove his worth through a series of trials filled with humorous twists and unexpected lessons about love.

As the trio—Alarion, Lila, and Ignis—set out on the path toward the fabled Eternal Flame, excitement buzzed in the air. Each step seemed to hum with energy, promising adventure and discovery. The trees whispered secrets, and the breeze carried a playful tune, hinting at the delightful trials ahead.

"Do you really think we'll meet the guardian of the Eternal Flame?" Lila asked, her eyes shining with curiosity.

"Of course! But I hear he has a rather peculiar sense of humor," Alarion replied, smirking. "I mean, how else would you guard something so magnificent?"

Ignis chuckled, his flamboyant robes billowing as he walked. "I can't wait to see what kind of tests he has in store. Maybe a fire-eating contest? Or a riddle that involves juggling flaming swords?"

Just then, as if summoned by their chatter, the forest opened up to reveal a clearing. At the center stood a majestic pedestal, crowned by the shimmering Eternal Flame, a swirling vortex of light and warmth. But perched next to it was a peculiar figure: the Guardian of the Flame, a stout man with a twinkle in his eye, wearing a robe made of vibrant flames and an oversized feathered hat that bounced with every movement.

"Ah, travelers! Welcome, welcome!" the Guardian boomed, his voice like the crackle of firewood. "I am Pyran, the Eternal Flame's Guardian. To prove your worth, you must each pass my trials. But be warned—my tests are not for the faint-hearted!"

The First Trial: The Dance of Flames

Pyran clapped his hands, summoning an array of dancing flames that twirled in mid-air. "For your first trial, you must perform the Dance of Flames! It's a whimsical dance that embodies the spirit of love and joy."

"Dance?" Alarion repeated, raising an eyebrow. "I didn't sign up for a dance-off!"

Lila nudged him, a playful grin on her face. "Come on, it'll be fun! Besides, how hard can it be?"

With a dramatic flourish, Pyran instructed them. "Follow my lead! The steps are simple: twirl, clap, and leap. Let the flames guide you!"

Alarion sighed but nodded. As Pyran began to dance, the flames flickered around him, swirling in rhythm to an upbeat melody.

Song: "Dance of Flames"
(To a lively, cheerful tune)
Verse 1:
In the circle of light, where the flames take flight,
Let your heart be your guide, dance with all your might.
Twirl to the left, clap your hands with glee,
Join the Dance of Flames, come and dance with me!
Chorus:
Dance, dance, oh feel the heat,
Let the rhythm guide your feet!
In the heart of love, let the sparks ignite,
Join the Dance of Flames, we'll shine so bright!
Verse 2:
Now leap to the right, let the fire twirl,

With laughter and joy, let your spirit unfurl.
Together we'll shine, with the warmth in our hearts,
In this dance of love, a masterpiece of art!
Chorus:
Dance, dance, oh feel the heat,
Let the rhythm guide your feet!
In the heart of love, let the sparks ignite,
Join the Dance of Flames, we'll shine so bright!

Lila started off with a graceful twirl, and Alarion, with an exaggerated sigh, followed her lead. He stumbled, tripped over his own feet, and nearly collided with Ignis, who was laughing so hard he almost fell over.

"Come on, Alarion! You've got to feel the rhythm!" Ignis yelled, doing an impromptu spin that sent flames spiraling into the air.

As they danced, the laughter became infectious. Alarion, embracing the absurdity of it all, twirled with more flair. Lila's eyes sparkled with joy as she joined in, her laughter mingling with the crackling flames.

"See? You're a natural!" Lila shouted, clapping along.

"Just don't tell anyone about my incredible dance skills," Alarion quipped, leaping into a half-hearted spin that sent sparks flying.

The Second Trial: The Riddle of Hearts

As the final chorus echoed into silence, Pyran applauded, his face beaming. "Bravo! You have passed the first trial! But now, let's test your wit with the Riddle of Hearts."

"What's a riddle without some good ol' fashioned humor?" Pyran grinned. "Here's the riddle: I can fly without wings; I can cry without eyes. Whenever I go, darkness flies. What am I?"

Alarion and Lila exchanged glances, furrowing their brows. Ignis, however, was deep in thought, stroking his imaginary beard.

"Hmm... could it be... a cloud?" Lila suggested, frowning.

"Too gloomy!" Ignis replied, shaking his head. "A firefly? No... too bright!"

Alarion sighed, feeling the pressure. "Wait! What about... laughter?" he proposed, his face lighting up with realization.

"Laughter?" Pyran echoed, his eyes gleaming. "Interesting answer, but not quite right!"

Lila nodded, thinking aloud. "What else flies? What about... time?"

"Bingo!" Pyran exclaimed. "Time flies, and it brings both laughter and tears! You have solved the riddle!"

The Unexpected Interruption

Just as they celebrated, a loud rustle erupted from the bushes nearby. The trio turned, eyes wide, as shadowy figures emerged, cloaked in darkness, their intentions clearly sinister.

"Looks like you're not the only ones looking for the Eternal Flame," one of the figures sneered, stepping forward.

"Great, just when things were getting fun!" Alarion muttered, reaching for his sword.

"I don't like the look of these guys," Lila said, her tone serious. "We need to stick together!"

The dark figures, armed with twisted staffs, approached menacingly, eyes glinting with malice. Pyran stepped back, eyes narrowing. "Looks like we have unwanted guests!"

The Battle: Flames vs. Shadows

Without warning, the cloaked figures charged, dark energy crackling around them. Alarion, fueled by a surge of adrenaline, shouted, "We can't let them take the Flame!"

With a flick of his wrist, he summoned a blast of wind, pushing back one of the shadowy figures. Ignis countered with a volley of fireballs, lighting up the clearing with bursts of flame.

Lila, channeling her magic, created a barrier of light to protect them. "Focus on their leader!" she yelled. "We need to take him down!"

The battle intensified as Alarion and Ignis fought back-to-back, laughter and banter mingling with the sounds of clashing magic. "You know, this is not how I imagined a magical quest would go!" Alarion shouted, dodging an attack.

"Just keep dancing, my friend!" Ignis quipped, unleashing a fiery spin that sent one of the attackers flying.

"Dancing? I thought we left that behind!" Alarion retorted, summoning a whirlwind that tossed another figure aside.

As the chaos erupted, Alarion noticed the leader lingering at the back, trying to rally his forces. "I've got an idea!" he said, winking at Ignis. "Let's give them a show!"

The Grand Finale

With a swift motion, Alarion began to hum the tune from their earlier dance. Ignis caught on, joining in with a fiery flourish. "Let's combine our powers!"

Pyran raised his hands, conjuring swirling flames around them. "Dance, my friends! Show them the true power of love and laughter!"

They launched into an improvised dance number, spinning and twirling as flames and wind wove together in a dazzling display.

Song: "United in Dance"
(To an energetic, triumphant tune)
Verse 1:
In the heart of battle, we find our way,
With laughter and love, we're here to stay.
Join the dance, let the magic ignite,
Together we stand, ready to fight!
Chorus:
Dance, dance, let the flames rise high,

With courage and joy, we'll touch the sky!
In the heat of battle, let the music play,
United in dance, we'll save the day!
Verse 2:
So come on, my friends, let the laughter soar,
With flames all around, we'll settle the score.
In this grand display, let our spirits be free,
Together we shine, just wait and see!
Chorus:
Dance, dance, let the flames rise high,
With courage and joy, we'll touch the sky!
In the heat of battle, let the music play,
United in dance, we'll save the day!

The dark figures were momentarily stunned, caught off guard by the sheer absurdity of the situation. But as the energy surged, they tried to counter, launching dark spells at the trio.

With laughter echoing around them, Alarion and Ignis combined their magic, creating a whirlwind of fire and light that engulfed the attackers.

"Dance, my friends!" Lila cried out, her voice ringing clear. "Let love guide our magic!"

The overwhelming power of joy and friendship erupted in a final blaze, engulfing the dark figures. They cried out, fading into wisps of shadow, while the clearing sparkled with warmth and light.

The Aftermath

As the echoes of battle faded, the trio stood panting, their laughter still hanging in the air. Pyran, eyes twinkling, approached them. "Well done! You've proven your worth not just in strength, but in unity and joy. The Eternal Flame is yours!"

With a flourish, he gestured toward the swirling light atop the pedestal. Alarion, Lila, and Ignis approached the Eternal Flame, hearts swelling with accomplishment.

Alarion turned to his friends, a wide grin on his face. "Who knew battles could be so… delightful?"

"I'll take laughter over gloom any day," Lila replied, her eyes shining brightly.

Ignis nodded, his fiery demeanor still sparkling with energy. "Here's to more dance battles in the future!"

The Flame's Gift

As they reached the Eternal Flame, it pulsed warmly, casting a golden glow around them. Pyran's voice filled the air. "Remember, the Eternal Flame symbolizes not just power but the love and laughter that fuel it. Carry this with you as you embark on your next adventures."

Alarion nodded, feeling a deep connection with the flame. "We will, Pyran. Thank you for the trials and the laughter!"

With the flame now safely in their hearts, the trio turned to each other, ready for whatever awaited them next. The bonds of friendship strengthened through trials and laughter, they set forth into the horizon, their spirits ablaze with joy and anticipation.

And in that magical moment, they knew that love, laughter, and a little dancing were the true treasures of their adventure.

Chapter 21: Flames of Reflection

In a moment of quiet, Alarion reflects on his journey and feelings for Lila. A light-hearted but touching conversation reveals deeper truths about their bond.

As Alarion, Lila, and Ignis walked away from the clearing, the warm glow of the Eternal Flame still flickering in their minds, they found themselves at the edge of a serene lake. The water mirrored the twilight sky, casting a magical aura around them. A gentle breeze rustled the leaves of nearby trees, and the chirping of crickets provided a calming soundtrack to the evening.

"Wow, this place is beautiful," Lila said, her eyes sparkling as she took in the scenery. "I could get lost in this moment forever."

Alarion smiled, feeling a warmth spread through him that was more than just the lingering effects of the Eternal Flame. "Yeah, it's stunning. Sometimes, it's nice to take a break from all the chaos and just... reflect."

Ignis, ever the jester, interrupted with a playful grin. "Reflect? Are you about to wax poetic on love and adventure? Because I have a feeling this could get mushy."

"Maybe I am!" Alarion shot back, a playful smirk on his face. "What's wrong with a little sentimentality, Ignis?"

"Nothing at all, my brooding friend! Just as long as you don't start serenading us with your love ballads!" Ignis laughed, doing an exaggerated impression of Alarion clutching his heart and singing to the moon.

Lila couldn't help but chuckle, but beneath the laughter, there was a weight to Alarion's thoughts. He looked at Lila, who was watching the reflections on the water, her expression softening.

"I've been thinking," he began hesitantly, "about our journey together and... well, about us."

Lila turned to him; her eyes full of curiosity. "What do you mean? What are you thinking?"

Alarion took a deep breath, feeling a mix of nervousness and excitement. "It's just that... we've been through so much together. The battles, the laughter, the dancing—" he waved a hand dramatically as if conducting an orchestra, "and through it all, I've realized something important."

"What's that?" Lila asked, her voice gentle, encouraging him to continue.

"It's that you mean a lot to me, Lila," he confessed, his cheeks warming slightly. "And not just as a friend. I think I'm starting to feel something deeper."

A Light-Hearted Conversation

Before Lila could respond, Ignis burst into song, dramatically posing as if he were on stage.

Song: "Reflections of the Heart"
(To a light-hearted, cheerful tune)
Verse 1:
In the stillness of the night, by the lake so bright,
We find the truths we hide, in the soft moonlight.
With laughter and love, we share our dreams,
In this dance of hearts, nothing's as it seems!
Chorus:
Oh, reflections of the heart, let your colors show,
In the waters of love, let the feelings flow!
With every laugh and sigh, our spirits soar,
Together we'll shine, forevermore!

Verse 2:
So, tell me your secrets, don't keep them inside,
In this magical moment, there's nowhere to hide.
With every step we take, let's embrace the night,
In the flames of our hearts, everything feels right!
Chorus:
Oh, reflections of the heart, let your colors show,
In the waters of love, let the feelings flow!
With every laugh and sigh, our spirits soar,
Together we'll shine, forevermore!

Alarion laughed, caught off guard by Ignis's impromptu performance. "Ignis, this isn't the time for a musical number!"

"Isn't it?" Ignis quipped, a mischievous glint in his eyes. "I mean, it's the perfect setting! Besides, every great love story needs a good soundtrack!"

Lila joined in, her laughter blending with Ignis's song. "He has a point, Alarion. What better way to reflect on feelings than with a grand musical moment?"

"Fine, fine!" Alarion relented, feigning annoyance but unable to hide his smile. "But if we're doing this, I get to join in!"

With newfound enthusiasm, Alarion jumped in, singing the next lines.

Verse 3:
In the heart of adventure, where our spirits ignite,
We'll face every challenge, together we'll fight!
With laughter and love, we'll take on the night,
In the flames of reflection, our hearts burn bright!

The three of them laughed and danced by the water's edge, Ignis striking poses and Lila twirling in delight. The moment was filled with joy, a beautiful reminder of their bond amid the seriousness of their quest.

A Shift in the Atmosphere

However, as the laughter faded, Alarion felt the weight of his earlier words return. The playful atmosphere shifted, and he turned to Lila, his expression serious. "But really, Lila, I want to know what you think about all this."

Lila hesitated, her eyes searching his. "I've felt it too, you know. This connection between us—it's more than friendship. But... it's scary, Alarion. What if things change?"

"Change is part of life," Alarion replied softly, his gaze unwavering. "But it doesn't have to be a bad thing. I believe we can face whatever comes our way together."

At that moment, a flicker of darkness darted through the trees, catching Alarion's attention. He narrowed his eyes. "Did you see that?"

Before Lila could respond, shadowy figures emerged from the treeline once again, cloaked and menacing, their eyes glinting in the fading light.

"Not again!" Ignis exclaimed, his humor vanishing as he readied his staff. "Why can't they just leave us alone?"

Alarion stepped in front of Lila, protective instincts kicking in. "Stay back! We can handle this!"

The Battle: Shadows of Doubt

As the cloaked figures closed in, Alarion raised his sword, flames igniting along the blade. Lila summoned her light magic, creating a barrier between them and the encroaching darkness.

"Let's show them we won't back down!" Alarion shouted, rallying his friends.

The figures lunged at them, and chaos erupted as Alarion, Lila, and Ignis sprang into action. Alarion swung his sword, slicing through the shadows, while Lila's light magic illuminated the battlefield.

"Remember the Dance of Flames!" Lila yelled, channeling her energy into a dazzling display of light that temporarily blinded their attackers.

"Ignis, now!" Alarion shouted, knowing the flamboyant mage was preparing a fiery counterattack.

With a flourish, Ignis unleashed a torrent of fireballs, sending the cloaked figures reeling. "They'll learn not to mess with us!"

Just when they thought they had the upper hand, a figure lunged at Lila, its dark hands reaching for her. Alarion felt a surge of panic. "Lila!"

The Turning Point

In a moment of instinct, Alarion dashed forward, blocking the attack with his sword. The impact sent vibrations through him, but he stood firm. "You won't touch her!" he declared, determination fueling his every word.

With renewed vigor, Lila summoned her light, casting a radiant spell that enveloped Alarion. "Together!" she shouted, and with a surge of magic, they created a barrier of light and fire that exploded outward, pushing the dark figures back.

The shadows hissed, retreating into the darkness as Alarion and Lila stood united, their energies intertwining. Ignis joined them, a triumphant grin on his face. "That's how you do it!"

Breathing heavily, Alarion glanced at Lila, feeling a mix of adrenaline and relief. "Are you okay?"

Lila nodded, her eyes sparkling with determination. "Yeah, thanks to you!"

Reflection Amid the Flames

As the last of the dark figures faded, the tension dissipated, replaced by a sense of victory. Alarion turned to Lila, his heart racing for reasons beyond the battle. "I know we're in the middle of a dangerous journey, but I want you to know that whatever happens, I'm here for you."

Lila's smile returned, a mixture of warmth and mischief in her eyes. "And I'm here for you, Alarion. Through battles, laughter, and... everything in between."

"I guess it's a good thing I'm not afraid of a little change," Alarion said, his grin widening.

As they shared a moment of understanding, the moon cast a silvery glow on the lake, reflecting the depth of their bond. The flames of the Eternal Flame flickered softly in the distance, a reminder of their triumph and the journey still ahead.

In that tranquil moment, surrounded by the remnants of their adventure, Alarion knew that whatever challenges lay before them, their love and friendship would guide them through. And as the stars twinkled above, he felt ready to face whatever fate had in store, one dance step at a time.

Chapter 22: The Betrayal

An unexpected betrayal shakes Alarion's confidence, leaving him doubting everything he's fought for. Lila's unwavering support shines through, rekindling his spirit with both humor and warmth.

The sun hung low in the sky, casting a golden hue over the enchanted forest as Alarion, Lila, and Ignis made their way back from the lake. Their spirits were high, filled with laughter and light-hearted banter after the battle with the dark figures. Yet, unbeknownst to them, shadows lingered in the heart of the woods, whispering secrets that would soon unravel their bond.

As they approached their camp, a strange tension hung in the air, an unsettling feeling that sent a shiver down Alarion's spine. He exchanged glances with Lila, who raised an eyebrow. "You feel that too, don't you?"

"Yeah," Alarion replied, his instincts on high alert. "Something doesn't feel right."

Ignis, oblivious to the unease, shrugged it off with a grin. "Maybe it's just the aftereffects of all that magical singing we did earlier! I mean, I could have used a few more fireballs!"

Before Alarion could respond, a figure stepped out from behind a tree—a familiar face that made his heart sink. It was Kael, the fire mage who had previously sought revenge. His eyes gleamed with a mixture of mischief and malice, and Alarion felt a knot tighten in his stomach.

"Ah, Alarion! You've been quite busy, haven't you?" Kael sneered, arms crossed and a smirk plastered on his face. "It's adorable to see you still clinging to that flame of hope. But I'm afraid it's time for a little... extinguishing."

"What do you want, Kael?" Alarion demanded, stepping forward defensively.

Kael chuckled, his voice dripping with sarcasm. "Oh, nothing much. Just a friendly little reminder that I'm still around. And this time, I've got something special planned for you!"

An Unexpected Twist

Before Alarion could react, a group of shadowy figures emerged behind Kael, their cloaks billowing like smoke in the wind. The betrayal hit Alarion like a cold wave, freezing him in place. "You've allied with them?" he said incredulously, turning to Lila, who stood beside him, her expression a mix of concern and anger.

"I knew you were weak," Kael taunted, pointing a finger at Alarion. "All that talk about friendship and love—pathetic! The real power lies in betrayal."

With a sudden roar, one of the shadowy figures lunged at Alarion, but Lila was quicker. "No! You won't touch him!" She cast a bright shield of light that enveloped Alarion, blocking the attack.

"Lila, stay back!" Alarion shouted, his heart pounding as he instinctively drew his sword, flames igniting along the blade. He had fought bravely before, but this was different; doubt crept in, and he wondered if they could really overcome this challenge.

A Fight with Shadows

"Time to see what you're made of!" Kael cackled, summoning fire from his hands, the heat radiating from him like a furnace. "Let's dance!"

The battle erupted as the shadowy figures advanced, merging with Kael's fiery magic. Alarion swung his sword, deflecting an attack while Lila shot beams of light at their assailants. Ignis joined the fray, launching fireballs with glee. "Just like old times, huh? Except this time, the stakes are higher!" he shouted, cracking jokes even amid the chaos.

"Stakes? More like a barbecue!" Alarion quipped back, trying to keep his spirits up despite the gnawing fear that gripped him.

Lila, radiant and fierce, fought valiantly beside Alarion, her determination palpable. "We can do this, Alarion! Don't let him get to you!"

Kael retaliated with a fiery blast, forcing Alarion to dodge. "You think you're strong? Look at you! You're just a puppet, dancing for Lila's affection!"

"Hey!" Lila yelled; her voice fierce. "Don't talk about him like that! He's more than just a puppet; he's my friend, and I won't let you hurt him!"

As the battle intensified, Alarion felt a surge of confidence from Lila's words. He wouldn't let doubt consume him. With a renewed sense of purpose, he charged at Kael, swinging his sword with precision.

The Song of Resilience

Amidst the clashing magic and flames, Lila began to sing, her voice cutting through the chaos like a beacon of hope. She infused her magic into the melody, creating a protective aura around them.

Song: "Flames of Resilience"
(To an upbeat, empowering tune)
Verse 1:
In the heart of the fire, we stand as one,
Through shadows and doubts, we'll rise with the sun.
With laughter and love, we'll break every chain,
Together we'll shine, through joy and through pain!
Chorus:
Oh, flames of resilience, burn bright in the night,
With courage and laughter, we'll conquer this fight!

Hand in hand we'll soar, no fear in our hearts,
In the flames of our love, a new journey starts!
Verse 2:
With every step forward, we'll face what we fear,
In this dance of resilience, we'll hold each other near.
Through battles we'll laugh, through struggles, we'll sing,
In the fire of our spirits, together we'll bring!
Chorus:
Oh, flames of resilience, burn bright in the night,
With courage and laughter, we'll conquer this fight!
Hand in hand we'll soar, no fear in our hearts,
In the flames of our love, a new journey starts!

As Lila sang, the light around them intensified, creating a barrier that pushed back the shadows. Alarion felt invincible, the music rekindling his spirit and drowning out the betrayal he had just faced.

With one last surge of energy, he charged at Kael. "This ends now!" Alarion shouted, swinging his sword with all his might.

The Turning Tide

In a brilliant clash of fire and magic, Alarion's flames collided with Kael's, creating a shockwave that sent both of them staggering. But Alarion, fueled by the love and support of his friends, stood tall. He could see the fear creeping into Kael's eyes.

"Lila, now!" he yelled, and together, they unleashed a wave of light that enveloped Kael, forcing him back. "You're not strong enough to break us!"

Kael, realizing he was losing, shouted in frustration, "This isn't over, Alarion! I will return, and when I do, you won't be so lucky!"

With that, he retreated, the shadowy figures dispersing into the forest, leaving behind a stillness that felt heavy with the weight of what had just transpired.

Rebuilding the Trust

Breathing heavily, Alarion turned to Lila and Ignis, who stood at his side, relief washing over their faces. "I can't believe that just happened," Alarion said, the adrenaline still coursing through him. "I didn't expect Kael to turn on us like that."

Lila placed a hand on his arm, her gaze steady and warm. "You can't let his words get to you, Alarion. You're stronger than you think, and you have us by your side."

"I know," Alarion replied, his voice wavering slightly. "But he made me doubt everything I fought for. I thought we were stronger than that."

"You are," Ignis chimed in, his usual jovial tone returning. "We all are. And remember, sometimes betrayal isn't about the actions of others but about how we choose to respond. You stood your ground, and we fought together!"

Lila smiled, her eyes shining. "You reminded me why we fight—because we believe in each other. No betrayal can change that."

As the sun dipped below the horizon, casting a brilliant array of colors across the sky, Alarion felt a warmth in his chest. The betrayal had shaken him, but the love and support from Lila and Ignis rekindled the flame of hope within him.

"Thanks, you two," Alarion said, feeling grateful. "I don't know what I'd do without you."

"Probably get into more trouble," Ignis teased, winking. "Now, how about we celebrate our victory with some food? I'm starving!"

As they walked back to their camp, laughter echoed through the forest, the warmth of friendship wrapping around them like a protective cloak. Together, they would face whatever challenges lay ahead, stronger and more united than ever.

Chapter 23: A Love Rekindled

Amidst the chaos, Alarion and Lila share a tender moment that reignites their romance. With laughter and light-hearted teasing, they confront their feelings head-on.

The sun rose softly over the enchanted forest, its golden rays filtering through the leaves, illuminating the remnants of the chaotic battle from the previous evening. Alarion sat on a log, absently twirling his sword, still reflecting on the whirlwind of emotions that had taken place. Beside him, Lila meticulously arranged the campfire, her movements fluid and graceful.

"You know," Alarion began, breaking the comfortable silence, "for a moment back there, I thought we were toast."

Lila turned to him, a playful smile dancing on her lips. "With the way you were swinging that sword, I thought you were trying to serve up a feast instead of fighting!"

Alarion chuckled, shaking his head. "Maybe I should just stick to cooking! At least that way, I can burn things on purpose."

"Only if you plan to burn the toast again!" Lila laughed, her laughter infectious, filling the air with warmth.

A Tender Moment

As they settled into their usual banter, the earlier tension began to fade. Alarion watched Lila, her hair catching the morning light like spun gold, and he felt a familiar warmth blooming in his chest—a feeling that had flickered in and out during their tumultuous journey.

"Hey, Lila," he said softly, trying to find the right words amidst the playful atmosphere. "About last night... I—"

"Don't worry," Lila interrupted gently, her eyes reflecting understanding. "I know how you felt. Kael's words were meant to hurt, but we won. And we're still here."

Alarion took a deep breath, realizing how much he valued her support. "It's just that when he attacked, I felt so... lost. I thought I might lose you."

Lila stepped closer; her expression serious yet tender. "You won't lose me. Not now, not ever." She reached out, her fingers brushing against his. "We're in this together, remember?"

Feeling emboldened by her reassurance, Alarion's heart raced. "You're right. And I want to be honest with you about my feelings."

The Song of Hearts

At that moment, Lila's playful nature resurfaced, and she grinned. "Oh, is this where you break into a song? Because I'd love to hear your melodious voice! You know, the one that scares away the enemies."

Alarion laughed, shaking his head. "I think I'll leave the singing to you. But if I must..." He cleared his throat dramatically, launching into a playful melody:

Song: "Flames of Our Hearts"
(To a light, whimsical tune)
Verse 1:
In the morning light, where our laughter glows,
Through shadows and battles, our love only grows.
With every adventure, side by side we stand,
In this wild journey, I'll take your hand!
Chorus:
Oh, flames of our hearts, burning bright like the sun,
Through laughter and tears, we're together as one.
In the dance of our fate, let the magic unfurl,

With you by my side, I can conquer the world!
Verse 2:
So, here's to the moments, both silly and sweet,
In the chaos of magic, my heart skips a beat.
With every new dawn, I'll cherish the start,
In the flames of our love, you'll always be in my heart!
Chorus:
Oh, flames of our hearts, burning bright like the sun,
Through laughter and tears, we're together as one.
In the dance of our fate, let the magic unfurl,
With you by my side, I can conquer the world!

Lila clapped her hands in delight, her eyes sparkling with mischief. "You really should consider a career in music! Or at least as a bard—your singing would distract the enemies while I take them down!"

"Ha! Maybe that's my secret plan," Alarion joked, puffing out his chest. "While they're busy laughing, I can sneak up behind them!"

Lila giggled, and the playful atmosphere hung between them, wrapping around them like a warm blanket. But underneath the humor, Alarion felt a shift—a deeper connection weaving through their laughter.

Confronting the Feelings

"Alarion," Lila said suddenly, her voice softening. "You know I've always cared about you, right? Like... really cared?"

"Of course," he replied, his heart pounding. "But I want to be more than friends. I want to fight beside you, not just in battles but in everything. I want to know what this is between us."

With that, Alarion stepped closer, his gaze locking onto hers. The moment hung thick in the air, anticipation crackling like magic. Lila's cheeks flushed a delicate pink, her laughter fading as sincerity filled the space between them.

"I want that too," she confessed, her voice barely above a whisper. "I've felt it for a while now, but I was afraid... afraid that the battles would pull us apart."

Alarion brushed a strand of hair behind her ear, his fingers lingering on her soft skin. "We're stronger together. I know that now."

Just as they leaned closer, preparing to bridge the gap that had lingered between them for far too long, a sudden noise interrupted—the rustling of leaves and a soft cackle echoed nearby.

A Battle with Shadows

"Ah, not again!" Alarion exclaimed, his playful moment with Lila shattered. He instinctively drew his sword, flames igniting along the blade. Lila quickly summoned her magic, ready to defend.

"More shadows?" she asked, her brow furrowed in concern.

"Seems like our romantic moment will have to wait!" Alarion said, grinning despite the seriousness of the situation.

From the underbrush emerged the same shadowy figures that had joined Kael in their previous battle. This time, however, they seemed more aggressive, their eyes glowing with malice as they advanced.

"Looks like someone's not happy we defeated their master," Lila said, readying herself.

"Let's show them how we do things together!" Alarion shouted, raising his sword. "For our love and for victory!"

The battle commenced, Alarion and Lila fighting side by side, their movements synchronized like a well-rehearsed dance. Alarion swung his sword with precision while Lila cast bursts of light, illuminating the darkness that surrounded them.

"Hey, how about a little light show?" Lila teased, creating a dazzling display of sparkles that momentarily blinded the nearest shadow.

"Perfect timing!" Alarion shouted, taking advantage of their confusion to strike. "I'm starting to see why you're my partner in crime!"

With each strike, they not only fought against the shadows but also supported one another, their bond strengthening with every blow. Lila ducked as one shadow lunged at her, and Alarion quickly intervened, blocking the attack with his flaming sword. "I've got your back!" he said, grinning through the sweat and chaos.

"Thanks! I knew I could count on you!" Lila replied, her heart swelling with appreciation.

The Turning Tide

As the battle raged on, Alarion and Lila found themselves in a rhythm, each movement echoing the affection they had only recently acknowledged. They were no longer just fighting for survival but for each other, a realization that infused their actions with renewed determination.

"Let's finish this!" Alarion declared, and with a nod from Lila, they combined their magic. Alarion called forth a wave of fire while Lila amplified it with her light, creating a dazzling inferno that surged toward the shadows.

"Together!" they shouted, and the combined magic erupted in a radiant explosion, illuminating the entire clearing.

The shadows writhed and shrieked as the flames consumed them, vanishing into wisps of smoke. As silence fell over the forest once more, Alarion and Lila stood victorious, panting and breathless.

A Moment of Connection

"Wow, we really did that!" Lila exclaimed; her eyes wide with excitement.

"Together," Alarion echoed, his heart pounding with pride and relief.

As they took a moment to catch their breath, the weight of the battle slowly faded. They stood close, the tension from before resurfacing, but this time with a different energy.

"Alarion," Lila began, her voice gentle, "I want to make this official. What we have... it's special. You mean so much to me."

He stepped closer, his heart racing. "I feel the same way. I want to explore this together, wherever it takes us."

Lila smiled, her eyes shimmering with unshed tears of joy. "Then let's do it. Let's make this an adventure!"

As if on cue, the forest around them seemed to echo their words, the leaves rustling in agreement. They both leaned in, and this time, they closed the distance, their lips meeting in a soft, lingering kiss that felt like the culmination of everything they had fought for.

At that moment, beneath the sun-drenched canopy, Alarion and Lila found their love rekindled, a flame that burned brighter than ever amidst the shadows of their past battles. They knew challenges would lie ahead, but together, they were ready to face anything, their hearts intertwined like the magic that bound their souls.

Chapter 24: The Final Battle Begins

The shadowy figure reveals their true identity, setting the stage for an epic showdown. Alarion and Lila must use their combined strengths and quick wit to outsmart this formidable foe.

The dawn broke over the horizon, casting an ethereal glow over the enchanted forest where Alarion and Lila had set up camp. Birds chirped cheerily, as if unaware of the impending confrontation that loomed ahead. However, Alarion felt the tension in the air, thick with anticipation.

"Today feels different," he muttered, pacing around the campsite. "I can feel it in my bones."

Lila, who was busy packing their supplies, glanced over at him with a smirk. "You mean you can feel the pancakes I burnt for breakfast? Because those are definitely not going to make it to the final battle."

"Those were... well, they were an experiment," Alarion replied defensively, a grin spreading across his face. "Let's call them 'charcoal delights.'"

"More like charcoal nightmares," she teased, her eyes sparkling with laughter.

Suddenly, the playful atmosphere shifted as a chill ran down Alarion's spine. "We should be on guard. I sense something—"

Before he could finish, the air crackled with dark energy, and from the shadows emerged a figure cloaked in black, their face hidden beneath a hood. As the figure stepped forward, an unsettling familiarity washed over Alarion.

ALARION AND THE ETERNAL FLAME

"Kael?" Alarion gasped, recognizing the form of his former friend. "How did you survive?"

Kael's laughter echoed through the clearing; a sound twisted with malice. "Oh, Alarion, you naive fool. You thought defeating me would be that simple? I've evolved, learned to harness the very shadows you seek to dispel."

The Revelation

As Kael removed his hood, revealing his gaunt, hollow eyes and a sinister smile, Alarion's heart sank. "You've become something else entirely," he said, anger and sadness swirling within him. "This isn't who you were."

Kael stepped closer, a dark aura emanating from him. "Who I was is irrelevant. I now control the darkness, and it has given me power beyond your imagination." He gestured to the shadows around him, which twisted and writhed like serpents. "And soon, I will control you both!"

Lila stepped forward, her magic glowing brightly in her hands. "We won't let that happen, Kael. You may have power, but you've lost your humanity."

Kael's eyes narrowed, fury radiating from him. "Let's see if your bond can withstand the darkness I've summoned."

The Song of Battle

As the atmosphere thickened with tension, Alarion felt a sudden surge of inspiration. "We need a plan, Lila. And maybe a song to rally our spirits!" He took a deep breath, his voice rising to fill the air.

Song: "Shadows We Fight"
(A battle anthem)
Intro:
In the heart of the night, when shadows arise,
With courage and hope, we'll shatter the skies.
Together we stand, with our hearts intertwined,
Against the darkness, our spirits combined!

Verse 1:
We've traveled through trials, faced monsters and fears,
With laughter and love, we've conquered our tears.
Through flames and through shadows, we'll fight to the end,
In this battle for the light, together we'll stand!
Chorus:
Oh, shadows we fight, together as one,
With love as our armor, we'll rise with the sun.
In the heat of the moment, we'll never back down,
With laughter and magic, we'll wear victory's crown!

As Alarion's voice rang out, Lila joined in, her melodic tone harmonizing beautifully with his.

Verse 2:
When the darkness encroaches, and hope feels so far,
With each other beside us, we'll reach for the stars.
For love is our weapon, our hearts are our guide,
In this final showdown, we'll turn the tide!
Chorus:
Oh, shadows we fight, together as one,
With love as our armor, we'll rise with the sun.
In the heat of the moment, we'll never back down,
With laughter and magic, we'll wear victory's crown!
Outro:
So here we stand tall, against all that we fear,
With laughter and love, we'll persevere!
The shadows may linger, but we'll chase them away,
For together, my love, we'll win this day!

The Clash of Powers

As their song echoed through the clearing, Alarion felt renewed strength coursing through him. The shadows around Kael writhed in anger, but Alarion and Lila stood resolute, their bond shining brighter than the darkness.

"Enough!" Kael roared, unleashing a wave of shadows that crashed toward them like a tidal wave.

"Lila, now!" Alarion shouted, raising his sword.

Lila focused her energy, and with a flick of her wrist, a barrier of light erupted around them, clashing with the darkness. "We can do this together!"

They fought with synchronized precision, Alarion deflecting blows while Lila shot bursts of light to counter Kael's shadows.

But Kael was relentless. "You think you can defeat me? I've got a few tricks up my sleeve!" He conjured shadowy tendrils that lashed out at them.

"Let's outsmart him!" Lila exclaimed, dodging a strike. "We need to find his weakness!"

The Strategy

"Right!" Alarion replied, ducking another attack. "We know he draws power from the shadows. If we can light them up, he'll weaken!"

As Kael unleashed another dark wave, Alarion and Lila combined their powers. "Now!" they shouted in unison, unleashing a blast of light that illuminated the shadows. The tendrils recoiled, and Kael staggered back, eyes wide with shock.

"No! This can't be!" he screamed, the shadows around him flickering.

"Your darkness has no hold over us, Kael!" Alarion declared, charging forward. "We're not alone in this fight!"

Lila joined him, their powers merging in a brilliant display of light. Together, they pressed forward, pushing Kael deeper into the shadows.

The Final Confrontation

As they advanced, Kael's anger twisted into desperation. "You think this is over? I will not be defeated!"

With a final surge of power, he summoned a storm of darkness that spiraled around him. "You will regret crossing me!"

Alarion and Lila stood their ground, determination etched on their faces. "We'll never regret fighting for what's right!" Lila shouted, and with that, they unleashed a combined attack of light, their powers exploding in a dazzling display.

"Shadows be gone!" they cried together, the light enveloping Kael completely.

In an eruption of brilliance, the shadows imploded, and Kael's form was consumed by the radiant light. As the darkness dispersed, Alarion and Lila fell to their knees, panting but triumphant.

A New Dawn

As the dust settled, the forest began to shimmer with life once more. The birds resumed their songs, and the sun broke through the trees, casting golden rays upon the clearing.

"We did it!" Lila exclaimed, her voice a mix of joy and disbelief.

Alarion turned to her, his heart swelling with pride. "We fought together and prevailed. I couldn't have done it without you."

Lila smiled brightly, her eyes sparkling with admiration. "We're a team. I always knew we'd make it through."

As they stood amidst the remnants of the battle, Alarion felt a warmth spread through him, a sense of love and camaraderie that transcended their fight. They had faced their darkest fears and emerged victorious; their bond stronger than ever.

A Love Unbroken

"Hey," Alarion said, breaking the comfortable silence. "You know, after all this chaos, I think we deserve a proper celebration."

"Like pancakes?" Lila teased, raising an eyebrow.

"Only if you promise not to burn them this time!" Alarion laughed, taking her hand.

As they walked back towards their campsite, Lila squeezed his hand. "You know, this is just the beginning. We've got many adventures ahead of us."

Alarion nodded, his heart racing at the thought. "Together, we can conquer anything."

And as they moved forward, hand in hand, the forest glowed with the promise of new beginnings and unbreakable bonds—a love rekindled amidst the shadows of their past.

Chapter 25: The Heart of the Storm

In the heat of battle, Alarion faces his fears and insecurities. With Lila's encouragement, he finds the strength to embrace his destiny, leading to a powerful but humorous confrontation.

The sun hung high in the sky, casting a bright light over the landscape. However, the tranquil setting belied the storm brewing on the horizon. Alarion stood at the edge of a cliff, gazing at the dark clouds swirling ominously above. He could feel the tension in the air—heavy and charged, like the calm before a thunderstorm.

"Lila, I don't know if I can do this," he confessed, running a hand through his hair as his eyes darted back and forth, scanning the ominous sky. "What if I'm not strong enough?"

Lila, standing beside him with her unwavering confidence, placed a reassuring hand on his shoulder. "Alarion, you've faced so many challenges already. This is just another one. Remember what we've been through together? You can do this!"

Her encouragement filled him with warmth, but doubt still lingered like a shadow. "But what if I fail? What if I can't protect you?"

The Calm Before the Storm

As the clouds drew closer, a soft rumble of thunder echoed in the distance. Lila laughed lightly, trying to break the tension. "If it helps, you can think of it like a really bad hair day! Just remember to keep your cool, and don't let the storm mess up your fabulous hairstyle!"

Alarion chuckled, imagining himself as a heroic figure with wind-blown hair in a dramatic pose, only to be interrupted by Lila's laughter. "Okay, fine! But really, you'll look good no matter what!"

"Right," he replied with a smirk. "Good hair, strong heart. Got it."

As the first raindrops began to fall, Lila stepped closer to Alarion, her expression turning serious. "You have to face your fears, Alarion. It's the only way we can push through this storm and confront whatever is waiting for us."

"I know. But what if my fears are more powerful than I am?" he admitted, his voice barely above a whisper.

Lila tilted his chin up, forcing him to meet her gaze. "You're stronger than your fears. Just remember that you have me by your side. We'll face whatever comes together."

The Heart of the Storm

Just then, a powerful gust of wind swept through the cliffside, howling like a banshee. The dark clouds roared louder, and suddenly, a figure appeared within the storm. A shadowy warrior, clad in armor, stepped out of the swirling tempest, their eyes glinting with menace.

"Fools!" the shadowy warrior taunted, their voice booming like thunder. "You think you can challenge the heart of the storm? I am Tempest, the harbinger of chaos! You're nothing but a spark in the wind!"

"Tempest?" Lila exclaimed, narrowing her eyes. "I thought that was just a fancy name for a thunderstorm!"

"You don't know what you're dealing with!" Tempest shouted, raising a hand to summon a bolt of lightning that crackled through the air.

"Right!" Alarion shouted back, stepping forward with newfound determination. "And we're not afraid of a little rain and lightning! This is just another challenge, right? Just like... um... that time I tried to impress you with my cooking!"

Lila burst out laughing, her laughter ringing like music amidst the chaos. "Oh, that was definitely a storm of its own! You almost set the kitchen on fire!"

"That's the spirit!" Alarion said, gathering his courage. "And besides, you've had your share of battles too! Remember that time you nearly lost your wand to that overly affectionate kitten?"

"Oh, don't remind me!" she giggled, her eyes sparkling with mischief. "It was like fighting a furry tornado! But look at us now! We can take on anything!"

The Showdown

With laughter still echoing between them, Alarion took a deep breath and turned to Tempest. "You may think you can intimidate us, but we won't back down! We're here to reclaim the heart of the storm!"

Tempest let out a booming laugh that reverberated through the cliffs. "You think humor can save you? Let's see if you can withstand my storm!"

With a swift motion, Tempest sent a wave of lightning arcing toward Alarion and Lila.

"Lila!" Alarion yelled, extending his hand. "Now!"

Lila concentrated, her magic flaring brightly as she summoned a protective barrier. The lightning struck, creating a brilliant explosion of light and energy, but the barrier held firm, crackling and shimmering.

"We've got this!" Lila shouted; her spirit unyielding.

As the dust settled, Tempest looked slightly taken aback. "Impressive, but you'll need more than that to defeat me!"

The Song of Unity

With adrenaline surging through his veins, Alarion felt the spark of inspiration rise within him once again. "Lila, let's sing! We need our song to harness our power!"

"Right! I've got your back!" she replied, ready to join him.

Song: "Storm of Courage"
(A rallying anthem)
Intro:
In the heart of the storm, where shadows play,
We'll rise up strong, we'll light the way!
With laughter and love, we'll stand our ground,
In the tempest of fear, our courage is found!
Verse 1:
The thunder may roar, the lightning may strike,
But together we'll shine, our hearts full of light.
With each step we take, we'll banish the dark,
United we fight, igniting the spark!
Chorus:
So here we stand tall, against all we fear,
With love in our hearts, we'll persevere!
In the eye of the storm, we'll find our way,
With laughter and magic, we'll seize the day!

Alarion and Lila sang together, their voices melding into a powerful harmony that echoed through the air. The storm rumbled, as if reacting to their determination.

Verse 2:
Tempests may rise, but we'll never back down,
With strength in our hearts, we'll claim the crown.
The shadows may linger, but we'll chase them away,
For together, my love, we'll win this day!

As they sang, the storm around them began to shift. Lightning arced away from them, and the winds howled less fiercely.

The Climactic Battle

Tempest, realizing the power of their united front, roared in anger. "You think your little song can defeat me? I am chaos incarnate!"

"Chaos has met its match!" Alarion shouted, his confidence growing with each note. "We are the heart of the storm!"

As they finished the song, they unleashed a torrent of light that burst forth from their hands, forming a radiant beam that surged toward Tempest.

"No!" Tempest yelled, the shadows around them flickering wildly as the light engulfed him. The warrior struggled against the power, but the radiant energy overwhelmed the darkness. With one final burst, Tempest dissipated into the storm, leaving nothing but a whisper in the wind.

A New Dawn

As the storm began to clear, sunlight broke through the clouds, illuminating the landscape with a warm glow. Alarion and Lila stood side by side, panting but victorious.

"We did it!" Lila exclaimed, throwing her arms around Alarion in an exuberant embrace. "You faced your fears and embraced your destiny!"

"I couldn't have done it without you," he replied, his heart swelling with pride and affection. "You were my strength."

As they pulled apart, Lila's eyes sparkled with warmth. "And you were mine. Together, we can face anything!"

"Next up, let's find a cozy place to celebrate! I'll even promise not to cook this time," Alarion joked, and they both burst into laughter.

With the storm behind them and the sun shining bright, they set off together, ready to embrace whatever adventures awaited them. Their bond was stronger than any tempest, and with love and laughter as their guide, they knew they could conquer the world.

Chapter 26: The Power of Unity

Alarion and Lila must unite their powers to face the shadowy enemy. Their playful banter and budding romance strengthen their resolve, reminding them of what they fight for.

The dawn broke with a spectacular display of colors painting the sky, a vivid reminder of hope after the tumultuous storm. Alarion and Lila stood side by side on the edge of the cliff, gazing at the horizon. The remnants of the storm hung in the air like a faded dream, but deep within, they both knew a new challenge awaited them.

"Do you think we finally get a break?" Lila asked, squinting at the bright light ahead.

Alarion chuckled, his usual playful spirit surfacing again. "If by 'break' you mean facing another shadowy enemy, then yes, we're definitely getting that! It's like a recurring nightmare that keeps coming back."

"Oh great, just what I wanted," she replied, rolling her eyes dramatically. "Nothing says romance like fighting dark forces, right?"

"Hey, it's what we do best! It's either this or I make us dinner again, and I think we both know how that turned out last time!" Alarion replied, a mischievous glint in his eye.

Lila laughed, recalling the chaotic kitchen incident where Alarion's attempt to impress her had nearly resulted in setting fire to the curtains. "Fine, let's save the dinner drama for later. First, we need to figure out how to face this shadowy menace. It's only a matter of time before they come looking for us."

Gathering Their Strength

The air suddenly felt charged, a tingling sensation flowing through them as they turned to face the approaching shadows. Out of the mist, two shadowy figures emerged, cloaked in darkness and wielding eerie weapons. The atmosphere thickened with tension as Alarion and Lila prepared to confront them.

"What do we know about them?" Lila whispered, her eyes narrowing.

"Not much," Alarion replied, trying to keep his voice steady. "But they don't look friendly. How about we start with a plan?"

"Sounds like a great idea," Lila said, a hint of determination igniting in her gaze. "Let's distract them with our incredible charm, then hit them with the magic!"

"Charm? Did you forget who you're talking to? I'm basically a master of charisma!" Alarion said, puffing out his chest in mock pride.

"Right, Mr. Charisma. Let's see you work your magic then!" she teased, smirking at him.

"Challenge accepted!" Alarion replied, stepping forward. "Hey, you shadowy figures! Do you even lift? I mean, look at those arms! They're as skinny as twigs!"

The shadowy figures paused; their expression unreadable. Lila couldn't help but burst out laughing at Alarion's audacity. "You think they'll be impressed by your... um, insightful commentary?"

"Just wait!" he winked. "They'll be so distracted; they won't know what hit them!"

The Battle Begins

Alarion and Lila joined hands, feeling the warmth of their connection fuel their resolve. As the shadowy figures regained their composure, Alarion shouted, "Prepare to face the power of unity!"

The figures lunged at them, weapons raised, but Lila quickly conjured a protective barrier, shimmering with light. "You'll have to do better than that!" she said playfully.

As the shadows struck against the barrier, Alarion shouted, "Okay, Lila, let's combine our powers!"

"On it! Let's channel our magic!" she replied, her face lighting up with excitement.

Together, they summoned their energies, feeling the electric current flow between them. The air around them crackled as they began to sing a song that echoed their unity and strength.

Song: "Together We Stand"
(An anthem of their bond)
Intro:
In the heart of the storm, where shadows creep,
Together we stand, our promise we keep!
With laughter and love, we'll light the way,
United in strength, we won't go astray!
Verse 1:
When the darkness descends, and the shadows loom,
We'll shine like the stars, breaking through the gloom!
With courage ablaze, and hearts open wide,
Side by side, we'll take on the tide!
Chorus:
So here we are, ready to fight,
With the power of love, we'll conquer the night!
In unity, we'll rise, with no fear in our hearts,
Together we stand, we won't fall apart!

As they sang, beams of light burst forth from their joined hands, creating a dazzling display that enveloped them. The shadows hesitated, their forms flickering under the intensity of Alarion and Lila's combined magic.

Verse 2:

Though the path may be rough, and the journey long,
With laughter as our shield, we'll carry on strong!
Through trials we've faced, and battles we've won,
Together we'll shine, like the dawn of the sun!

With each note, the shadows grew weaker, struggling against the waves of light. Alarion and Lila poured their hearts into the song, each lyric resonating with their unwavering bond.

Facing the Darkness

The shadowy figures, realizing they were losing ground, roared in frustration. "You think you can defeat us with a song? Pathetic!"

Alarion smirked, feeling empowered by Lila's presence. "It's not just the song. It's the connection we share that gives us strength! Together, we are unstoppable!"

With a final surge of energy, they launched their combined light toward the shadows. "Together we stand!" they shouted, their voices intertwining as their magic clashed against the darkness.

The shadows screamed, a sound that echoed through the air, as they were engulfed by the brilliance. In an explosion of light, the shadowy figures disintegrated, leaving nothing but remnants of darkness in the air.

The Aftermath

As the echoes of their song faded, Alarion and Lila stood, breathless but victorious. They exchanged glances, laughter bubbling up between them.

"We did it!" Lila exclaimed, her face glowing with exhilaration. "I can't believe you actually managed to distract them!"

"I knew my charm would win the day!" Alarion grinned, his heart racing. "And your magic was incredible!"

"Let's not forget your witty banter—it really did the trick!" she said, shaking her head with amusement. "We make a great team!"

"Yes, we do!" he replied, his expression softening. "And I couldn't have asked for a better partner in this crazy adventure."

They took a moment, the air around them charged with the aftermath of their triumph. Lila stepped closer, her eyes shining. "You know, I really admire how you handle fear and still manage to crack jokes in the middle of chaos."

Alarion chuckled. "Well, someone has to keep the mood light, right? Plus, I'm just trying to impress you!"

"Oh, you definitely have my attention!" she said, grinning, her heart swelling. "Now, let's see what else awaits us on this wild journey!"

With renewed energy and a deeper bond, Alarion and Lila continued their adventure, side by side, ready to face whatever challenges awaited them. The power of their unity shone brightly, illuminating the path ahead.

Chapter 27: A Dance of Flames

During the climactic battle, Alarion's powers ignite in a spectacular display. Lila's clever tactics help turn the tide, blending romance and humor in the heat of the moment.

The battlefield lay before Alarion and Lila like a canvas splattered with colors of chaos. Shadows writhed and flickered in the dim light, a dance of darkness that threatened to engulf everything in its path. Yet, amid the turmoil, an unexpected spark ignited between the two of them, a radiant fire fueled by love, laughter, and the thrill of the fight.

Alarion took a deep breath, feeling the warmth of magic coursing through his veins. "This feels like one of those epic movies, doesn't it?" he quipped, flashing Lila a grin. "You know, the kind where the hero saves the day and gets the girl."

Lila rolled her eyes, a smile playing on her lips. "You do realize we're in the middle of a battle, right? But if you insist on being the hero, I'm definitely getting the popcorn for the sequel!"

"Perfect! I'll have my fan club ready, too!" Alarion laughed, adjusting his grip on his staff as a shadowy figure lunged at them.

As the figure approached, Lila flicked her wrist, summoning a shield of shimmering light that deflected the shadow's attack. "Your turn, Mr. Hero! Show me what you've got!"

The Battle Ignites

With a cheeky salute, Alarion leaped forward, his powers igniting in a brilliant display of flames. The fire danced around him, swirling in vibrant reds and oranges, casting flickering shadows across the battlefield. "Prepare for a fiery performance!" he shouted, channeling the magic into a spectacular fireball that surged toward the enemy.

The fireball exploded upon contact, sending sparks flying and illuminating the darkness around them. But just as the smoke cleared, more shadows emerged, relentless in their pursuit.

"Okay, time for a little strategic maneuvering," Lila said, her eyes narrowing as she scanned the battlefield. "I'll distract them while you gather your flames. Think of it as our very own dance of chaos!"

"Is that your battle strategy? Because it sounds like a plan!" Alarion winked, exhilaration bubbling within him.

The Dance Begins

As Lila dashed forward, weaving between the shadows, she called out, "Hey, you overgrown puddles of darkness! Why don't you try to catch me?" Her playful taunts echoed through the battlefield, drawing the shadows toward her.

Alarion watched in awe as Lila executed her clever tactics with agility and grace, leading the enemies into a chaotic chase. With every step, she flipped and twirled, evoking laughter even in the direst of moments.

Song: "Dance of Flames"
(A celebration of their bond amid battle)
Intro:
When the shadows surround us, and hope seems far away,
We'll light up the darkness, and together we'll play!
With laughter and love, we'll ignite the night,
In this dance of flames, we'll stand and fight!
Verse 1:
Alarion twirls, with fire in his hands,
While Lila's laughter spreads across the lands!
With every step forward, they rise and they shine,
Two hearts ignited, perfectly aligned!

As Alarion joined the rhythm of the battle, he summoned more flames, each burst reflecting the light of their connection. He twirled and spun, creating a dazzling display of fire that surrounded them like a protective aura.

Chorus:
In this dance of flames, we'll rise and we'll soar,
With laughter as our armor, we'll settle the score!
Together we'll conquer, together we'll stand,
In this wild adventure, hand in hand!

Turning the Tide

With the shadows now fully engaged with Lila's antics, Alarion seized the moment. "Ready to turn up the heat?" he called out, his heart racing as he felt the connection between them intensify.

"Always! Let's show them what we've got!" Lila shouted, determination sparking in her eyes.

They combined their powers, Alarion channeling the flames while Lila amplified them with her magic. The flames roared to life, swirling around them like a vortex, igniting everything in a spectacular display of light and energy.

Verse 2:
As the shadows retreat, and the darkness takes flight,
We'll dance through the chaos, igniting the night!
With every heartbeat, our powers align,

In this dance of flames, our love will shine! The shadows recoiled, unprepared for the onslaught of their united magic. Alarion and Lila moved together, a seamless choreography of fire and light, battling the encroaching darkness with humor and heart.

Chorus:
In this dance of flames, we'll rise and we'll soar,
With laughter as our armor, we'll settle the score!
Together we'll conquer, together we'll stand,
In this wild adventure, hand in hand!

The Final Confrontation

Just as they thought they had the upper hand, a colossal shadow materialized, towering over them with glowing red eyes. "Foolish mortals! You think you can defeat me with your little tricks?" it bellowed, its voice reverberating through the ground.

"Oh, we're just getting started!" Alarion shouted, determination filling his voice.

"Dance with us!" Lila added, winking at Alarion. "Let's show this dark giant how it's done!"

They spun into action, Alarion summoning flames that spiraled into the air, while Lila created a dazzling array of light that surrounded the shadow like a halo. Together, they executed a magnificent display of magic, illuminating the battlefield in a blaze of color.

Outro:
In this dance of flames, our spirits will rise,
With love as our weapon, we'll claim the prize!
Together we'll shine, as the night fades away,
In this dance of flames, we'll live for today!

Embracing Destiny

With one final, united push, they launched their combined magic at the towering shadow, engulfing it in a whirlwind of fire and light. The darkness shrieked and twisted, fighting against the force of their connection, but it was no match for the flames fueled by their love.

As the shadow disintegrated, Alarion and Lila collapsed to the ground, breathless and exhilarated. "Did we really just do that?" Alarion panted, looking at Lila with wide eyes.

"I think we did!" she laughed, her heart racing. "We made quite the fiery team!"

"Let's keep dancing through life, shall we?" he suggested, reaching out for her hand.

"Absolutely! Just maybe with fewer shadowy enemies' next time?" Lila replied, a mischievous glint in her eye.

Hand in hand, they rose, ready to face whatever awaited them next. With the echoes of their laughter resonating in the air, they stepped forward, fueled by the flames of their love and the promise of adventure that lay ahead.

Chapter 28: The Eternal Flame Unleashed

Alarion finally unlocks the power of the Eternal Flame, leading to a breathtaking transformation. However, the responsibility weighs heavily on his shoulders, leading to comical moments of doubt.

The air crackled with anticipation as Alarion stood at the edge of the Sacred Fire Cavern, the legendary Eternal Flame flickering at its heart. Lila watched him with a mix of awe and concern, her eyes reflecting the radiant glow that emanated from the mystical fire.

"Are you ready for this?" she asked, her voice a blend of excitement and trepidation. "I mean, this is the Eternal Flame we're talking about. No pressure!"

Alarion chuckled nervously, scratching the back of his head. "You know, I was thinking of running away and joining a traveling circus instead. Maybe juggle flaming torches? How hard can that be?"

Lila rolled her eyes, trying to suppress a laugh. "Alarion, this is not the time for jokes! You're about to unlock the greatest power in the realm. Focus!"

With a deep breath, he stepped forward, feeling the warmth of the flame calling to him. It was a magnificent sight, the flame pulsating with vibrant colors, casting a hypnotic glow in the cavern. Yet, beneath the beauty lay an immense weight of responsibility.

The Unlocking of Power

As Alarion extended his hand towards the Eternal Flame, he felt its energy coursing through him. A brilliant light enveloped him, and the cavern resonated with an otherworldly hum.

Suddenly, his body surged with power, transforming him into a beacon of light.

Song: "Ignite the Eternal Flame"
(An anthem of discovery and empowerment)
Intro:
When the shadows loom and doubts arise,
We'll reach for the light, and break through the skies!
With the fire of courage, we'll stand up tall,
In the dance of the flame, we'll never fall!
Verse 1:
Alarion feels the heat, the magic so bright,
With Lila by his side, everything feels right!
Unlocking the power, a new journey begins,
Together they'll conquer, through thick and thin!

With each word, Alarion's confidence grew. The flame wrapped around him like a warm embrace, fueling his spirit. Lila clapped her hands, her face beaming with pride. "You're doing it! You're actually doing it!"

Chorus:
Ignite the Eternal Flame, let it shine, let it soar,
With laughter and love, we'll conquer the war!
Hand in hand, we'll face whatever comes our way,
With the fire in our hearts, we'll seize the day!

Doubts and Comedic Moments

Just as Alarion felt invincible, a sudden thought clouded his mind. "Wait, what if I mess this up? What if the Eternal Flame turns me into a giant marshmallow or something?" His voice trembled with mock fear.

ALARION AND THE ETERNAL FLAME

Lila burst into laughter, shaking her head. "Alarion, I highly doubt the flame has that capability. But if you do turn into a marshmallow, I'll be sure to roast you over the campfire!"

"Great! Because who wouldn't want to be a tasty treat?" he replied, grinning. "Do you think I'd be a s'more or just plain toasted?"

Just as they shared a laugh, the cave rumbled ominously. Shadows flickered, and the walls trembled. The transformation Alarion underwent began to attract hidden enemies—shadowy figures that lurked in the depths, sensing the awakening of the Eternal Flame's power.

The Shadows Emerge

Suddenly, a horde of dark figures burst into the cavern, their eyes glinting with malice. "Foolish mortals! You think you can wield the power of the Eternal Flame?" one of them hissed, stepping forward, cloaked in swirling darkness.

Alarion, feeling a mix of fear and exhilaration, straightened his back, summoning the newfound strength within him. "Well, you're about to find out!" he declared, raising his hand, now glowing with the light of the flame.

"Just remember, aim for the center!" Lila shouted, her voice echoing through the cavern. "And don't forget to look cool while doing it!"

With a deep breath, Alarion unleashed the flames, a torrent of brilliant fire spiraling toward the approaching shadows. They scattered, but the darkness regrouped quickly, circling around them with sinister intent.

A Battle of Flames and Shadows

Alarion danced around the cavern, igniting the flames with every movement, each spell casting colorful sparks that illuminated the darkness.

Verse 2:

The shadows surround, but fear won't stay,
With laughter and courage, we'll find a way!
Alarion stands tall, Lila by his side,
Together they'll fight, with love as their guide!

With Lila's clever tactics, they dodged and weaved, countering the shadows with bursts of light. "You're doing great!" she cheered, firing off her own spells that complemented Alarion's flames.

"Thanks! And you're not too shabby yourself! Maybe we should consider opening a magic show after this!" Alarion replied, dodging a swipe from a shadowy figure.

"Only if you promise to wear sparkly pants!" Lila retorted, chuckling as she sent another blast of light flying.

Chorus:
Ignite the Eternal Flame, let it shine, let it soar,
With laughter and love, we'll conquer the war!
Hand in hand, we'll face whatever comes our way,
With the fire in our hearts, we'll seize the day!

The Climax of the Battle

As the shadows converged, Alarion felt the weight of the Eternal Flame growing heavier, yet the laughter and love from Lila fueled his resolve. "I can't let them win! Not when we've come this far!"

With renewed determination, he focused on the heart of the Eternal Flame, channeling its energy. The flames erupted in a magnificent blaze, swirling around him, creating a protective shield that radiated warmth and light.

"Lila! Now!" he shouted, extending his hands toward her.

The Final Stand

With one last combined effort, they merged their magic, unleashing a powerful wave of light that surged through the cavern. The shadows screamed in defiance as the flames engulfed them, illuminating every corner with brilliant light.

Outro:

*In the heart of the flame, we'll always be strong,
With laughter and love, we'll right every wrong!
Together we'll rise, with the fire as our guide,
In this dance of destiny, we'll always abide!*

As the last of the shadows dissipated, silence fell over the cavern. The air was thick with a sense of victory and warmth, the Eternal Flame's glow illuminating their faces. Alarion and Lila stood side by side, panting but exhilarated.

"I think we just saved the day," Alarion said, a grin stretching across his face.

"And I think you just unlocked the Eternal Flame!" Lila replied, beaming with pride.

But then, with a mock-serious face, he added, "Just promise me one thing. If I ever turn into a giant marshmallow, you'll save me some graham crackers, okay?"

"Deal!" she laughed, squeezing his hand. "But for now, let's enjoy this moment. Together."

In that sacred cavern, beneath the glow of the Eternal Flame, they shared a heartwarming embrace, knowing that whatever challenges lay ahead, they would face them together, ignited by the eternal flames of love and laughter.

Chapter 29: The Price of Power

With great power comes great responsibility. Alarion grapples with the implications of wielding the Eternal Flame, leading to humorous but poignant conversations with Lila.

The aftermath of the battle in the Sacred Fire Cavern left Alarion and Lila basking in the glow of their victory, but a new weight hung in the air—one that wasn't just from the lingering warmth of the Eternal Flame. As they emerged from the cavern, a sense of uncertainty loomed over Alarion.

"So, how does it feel to be the wielder of the Eternal Flame?" Lila asked, her eyes sparkling with mischief as she walked beside him, the soft glow of the flame reflecting in her gaze.

"Honestly?" Alarion scratched his head, a sheepish grin on his face. "It feels like I just got handed the keys to a giant magical sports car without reading the manual. What if I accidentally set fire to my own eyebrows? Or worse, what if I turn a cute bunny into a fire-breathing monster?"

Lila burst into laughter, her melodic voice ringing out like a sweet song. "Well, you're definitely not a bunny, and I think you'd handle that situation like a pro. Just imagine it:
'Alarion, the flame-wielding bunny whisperer!'"

"Yeah, that sounds like a hit at the magic shows," he chuckled, but the mirth faded slightly as he continued. "But really, this power comes with a lot of responsibility. What if I make a mistake? What if I hurt someone?"

The Weight of Responsibility

Lila's laughter faded, replaced by a serious expression. "You're not alone in this, Alarion. We're in this together. Besides, power doesn't define who you are—it's how you choose to use it."

"Wise words from my amazing partner," he said, flashing her a grin that made her heart flutter. But then his expression turned contemplative. "But what if I let you down? What if I become some kind of overconfident fire lord and start burning things without thinking?"

She playfully nudged him with her elbow. "Alarion, you're not the type to go on a power trip. You're way too much of a goofball for that. Just remember to keep your feet on the ground and your heart in the right place."

Song: "Flames of Responsibility"
(A song about navigating power and responsibility)
Intro:
With power in hand, the weight feels so strong,
But with you by my side, I know where I belong.
Through laughter and trials, we'll find our way,
In the flames of responsibility, together we'll stay!
Verse 1:
Alarion stands tall, the flame in his heart,
But doubt creeps in, tearing him apart.
What if he stumbles? What if he falls?
With Lila beside him, he'll answer the calls!

"What if I try to impress you and accidentally start a forest fire? I can already see the headline: 'Alarion the Arsonist! Legendary Flame Wielder Turns Hero to Villain!'" he said, putting on a mock-serious face.

Lila laughed heartily, rolling her eyes. "Oh, please! If you start a forest fire, I'll be right there with a bucket of water and a hose, ready to put out your 'fiery' mistakes!"

The Unseen Threat

As they walked along the path toward their next destination, Alarion couldn't shake the feeling of being watched. The shadows that had emerged in the cavern were not entirely vanquished; they had retreated, but they were still lurking, plotting their revenge.

"Hey, do you feel that?" Alarion paused, scanning the treetops for any movement. "Like we're being... observed?"

Lila nodded; her playful demeanor replaced with cautious seriousness. "I feel it too. It's like the air is charged with tension. We should be on guard."

Suddenly, figures emerged from the forest—shadowy figures that had once cowered in the depths of the cavern. Their eyes glinted menacingly in the dim light, their forms shifting like smoke.

"Foolish mortals!" one of them hissed, stepping forward. "You think you've escaped us? The Eternal Flame will be your undoing!"

The Battle Resumes

"Great! Just when I thought it was safe to walk through the woods," Alarion muttered, summoning the flame to his hands. "What do you want, shadowy dudes? An autograph?"

Lila positioned herself beside him, readying her spells. "Focus, Alarion! We've handled worse. Together!"

Chorus:
In the flames of responsibility, we'll stand our ground,
With laughter and courage, victory will be found!
With the heart of the flame, we'll fight side by side,
In the fires of our love, we'll never have to hide!

With that, Alarion and Lila sprang into action, casting spells that lit up the night like fireworks.

Alarion unleashed bursts of flame, while Lila summoned shimmering shields of light that deflected the shadows' dark magic.

A Dance of Flames

As they fought, their movements synchronized in a dance of flames and magic, humor laced in their banter. "Do you think I can roast marshmallows with this flame?" Alarion joked as he dodged an attack, sending a burst of fire back at a shadowy figure.

"Only if you promise not to burn them to a crisp! We need some good snacks after this battle," Lila quipped, her laughter brightening the tension of the fight.

Verse 2:
With magic entwined, their hearts beat as one,
In the heat of the moment, they're having such fun!
No shadow can break them, together they'll shine,
With the flame of their love, they'll always be fine!

As the battle raged on, Alarion felt the power of the Eternal Flame surging within him, but so did the responsibility that came with it. He took a moment to breathe, allowing Lila to cover him as he strategized.

"Okay, I need to channel this properly," he said, focused on the flickering flames. "It's not just about throwing fire. It's about controlling it."

The Final Confrontation

The shadows closed in, their forms twisting and writhing. Alarion focused, his eyes narrowed as he sensed the heart of their darkness. With a deep breath, he unleashed a torrent of flame that erupted in a spiral, illuminating the forest around them.

"Now, Lila!" he shouted, and she stepped forward, combining her magic with his, creating a whirlwind of light and heat.

Together, they formed a radiant barrier that engulfed the shadowy figures, pushing back the darkness until it finally shattered into a million sparkles of light. The shadows dissipated, leaving nothing but a peaceful silence in their wake.

Outro:
In the flames of responsibility, we've learned to be strong,
With laughter and love, we'll always belong!
Together we'll rise, with the fire in our hearts,

In this dance of destiny, we'll never be apart!
A Moment of Reflection

With the battle won, Alarion and Lila took a moment to catch their breath. "That was intense!" Alarion exclaimed, a mixture of relief and exhilaration washing over him.

"Yeah, but we did it! We fought them off together," Lila said, her eyes sparkling with pride.

Alarion smiled, his heart swelling with affection. "You know, maybe the price of power isn't as daunting with you by my side. I'll always have your back, and you'll have mine."

"Absolutely! We're a team, forever," Lila replied, leaning closer. "And besides, who else would keep you from turning into a marshmallow?"

As they stood together under the glowing light of the Eternal Flame, Alarion realized that the true power didn't just lie in the magic he wielded, but in the bond he shared with Lila—one filled with laughter, love, and the strength to face whatever challenges lay ahead.

Chapter 30: Flames of Destiny

Alarion confronts the consequences of his choices, leading to a showdown that tests his resolve. Lila's unwavering belief in him provides the spark needed to overcome his challenges.

The sun hung low in the sky, casting golden hues over the realm as Alarion stood at the edge of the cliff, staring into the horizon. The wind whipped through his hair, carrying whispers of the past and echoes of the future. He could feel it—the weight of his choices pressing down like an anvil on his chest. The power of the Eternal Flame burned brightly within him, but with that power came the responsibility he had tried so hard to shoulder.

Lila approached; her footsteps light yet purposeful. "Hey, you look like you're about to duel with a dragon. What's going on in that head of yours?"

Alarion turned, forcing a smile that didn't quite reach his eyes. "Just... contemplating destiny and the flames it brings. You know, the usual dramatic stuff."

Lila rolled her eyes playfully. "You and your brooding! If you keep this up, you'll scare away the dragons before you even get the chance to duel one."

Her humor pierced the heaviness in the air, causing Alarion to chuckle. "Well, you're right about one thing—I'm definitely not ready to fight a dragon. I'm more of a 'run away screaming' type."

The Weight of Choices

But the truth weighed heavier than any dragon's fury. Alarion's recent choices had consequences, and he couldn't ignore them. "Lila,

I've done things... I've used the Flame without thinking. What if I hurt someone? What if I can't control it?"

Lila stepped closer, her gaze steady and reassuring. "You're not the same person who first wielded the Flame. You've grown. You've learned. And besides, if you ever lose control, I'll be right there with my magical hose to put out the fire!"

He laughed, grateful for her lighthearted spirit. "You really know how to lighten the mood, don't you?"

"Of course! It's my job as your partner in heroics!" She winked, then her tone grew serious. "But in all seriousness, Alarion, you need to believe in yourself. You've got this. Together, we can face whatever comes next."

Song: "Flames of Destiny"
(A song about confronting choices and embracing love)
Intro:
In the shadows of doubt, where fears reside,
I'll stand with you always, right by your side.
With the flame in our hearts, we'll conquer the night,
In the flames of destiny, we'll shine so bright!
Verse 1:
Choices weigh heavy, like anchors in the sea,
But with you beside me, I can finally be free.
We'll face the unknown, with courage as our guide,
In this journey together, there's nothing we can't abide!

Alarion felt the heat of Lila's unwavering belief spark something within him. It wasn't just the Eternal Flame that ignited; it was the fire of determination that flickered to life in his heart.

He nodded, feeling stronger. "You're right. Let's face this together."

Shadows from the Past

But as fate would have it, the shadows they had once battled resurfaced. Out of the corners of the woods, dark figures emerged, their eyes glinting like malevolent stars. The leader, a tall figure cloaked in darkness, stepped forward with a sneer. "You think you can hide from your past, Alarion? The consequences of your actions are here to collect!"

"Speak of the devil!" Alarion quipped, clenching his fists as flames flickered at his fingertips. "I was just thinking how you really know how to ruin a perfectly good day!"

Chorus:
In the flames of destiny, we'll rise and we'll fight,
With laughter and love, we'll chase away the night!
Through battles and trials, our bond will stay true,
In this dance of destiny, it's me and you!

The Showdown

Lila stepped up beside him, summoning her own magic. "We're not afraid of you or your shadows! We've faced worse than you!"

"Together," Alarion added, and the two prepared for the fight of their lives.

As the shadows lunged at them, Alarion unleashed a burst of fire, lighting up the darkness. The flames danced around him, creating a barrier of warmth and light. "Lila, now!"

With perfect synchronization, Lila conjured a shield of shimmering light, deflecting the dark magic that surged toward them. "Get ready for a little magic of my own!" she exclaimed, launching a volley of sparkling energy that cascaded through the air.

A Dance of Flames and Magic

The battle was fierce, but amid the chaos, Alarion found himself laughing, buoyed by Lila's fearless spirit. "You know, I never thought I'd enjoy fighting shadowy villains this much! It's like a dance party with fire!"

Lila laughed, casting spells that intertwined with Alarion's flames. "Just don't step on my toes, okay? This isn't a waltz!"

As they battled, Alarion felt the connection between them intensifying. The fire within him surged, igniting with every spell they cast. "Lila, I think I'm starting to understand the true power of this Flame—it's not just about wielding it; it's about the love and trust we share!"

The Climactic Moment

With a final surge of energy, Alarion conjured a massive ball of fire, channeling every ounce of his strength and love for Lila. "This is it! Let's end this together!"

Lila's eyes sparkled with determination. "Together!"

They launched the fiery orb toward the leader of the shadows, engulfing him in a brilliant explosion of light. The shadows screeched, their forms disintegrating into wisps of smoke as the darkness dissipated into the night.

Outro:

In the flames of destiny, we've conquered our fears,
With laughter and love, we've shed all our tears.
Together forever, through battles and strife,
In this dance of destiny, you're my love, my life!

Aftermath

As the echoes of battle faded into the night, Alarion and Lila stood together, breathless but triumphant. "We did it," Alarion marveled, wrapping an arm around her shoulder.

Lila grinned, her face glowing with pride. "Of course we did! I knew you had it in you. And look at us—still standing!"

"I guess you were right about the power of belief," he said, looking deeply into her eyes. "I couldn't have done it without you."

"Same here," she replied, leaning in for a soft kiss that felt like the warmth of the Eternal Flame itself.

As they embraced, Alarion realized that while destiny may come with its challenges and choices, the fire of their love would always guide them through the darkest of nights. Together, they would face whatever awaited them in the future, united by the flames of destiny.

Chapter 31: The Bonds of Love

In a touching moment, Alarion realizes that love is the true power behind the Eternal Flame. Their connection deepens as they prepare for the final confrontation.

The stars twinkled above the enchanted forest, illuminating the path Alarion and Lila walked. They had just emerged victorious from their latest battle, the thrill of their triumph still buzzing in the air around them. But as Alarion glanced at Lila, her expression turned thoughtful, a mix of joy and concern etched across her face.

"What's on your mind?" Alarion asked, curiosity piquing as he noticed the way she bit her lip, a habit he found endearing yet revealing of her inner turmoil.

"I just... I can't help but think about everything we've faced. The battles, the shadows, and the power of the Eternal Flame," Lila said, her voice softening. "Sometimes I wonder if the Flame is the true source of our strength or if it's something else."

Alarion chuckled, attempting to lighten the mood. "Well, if it's not the Flame, then I'm definitely not getting my money's worth out of this whole magical journey!"

But Lila didn't laugh. Instead, she turned to him, her eyes reflecting the moonlight. "No, really, Alarion. I think it's love. Love is what has fueled us through every challenge. It's the bonds we share, the laughter, the support—it's all of that that makes us stronger."

The Realization

As Lila spoke, Alarion felt a warmth unfurling in his chest. The truth of her words resonated deeply. He thought back to their shared moments—the playful banter, the late-night strategizing, the warm hugs after every narrow escape. "You're right," he said, his voice steady. "It's our connection that gives the Flame its power."

Song: "The Flame of Love"
(A song about love as the true source of strength)
Intro:
In the heart of the storm, when the shadows creep,
With you by my side, my heart starts to leap.
The Flame burns brighter with every embrace,
In this dance of love, we'll find our place.
Verse 1:
When darkness surrounds us, and the fear starts to grow,
Your laughter's my shield, it's the light in the glow.
With every challenge, together we stand,
In the warmth of your smile, I'll take your hand.

Lila's heart raced as Alarion began to sing, his voice a melody that seemed to harmonize with the very essence of their journey. She joined in, her laughter mingling with the lyrics, creating a beautiful symphony of love and unity.

Chorus:
Together we shine, like stars in the night,
With the Flame of Love, we'll soar to new heights.
In this world of magic, our bond is our might,
With you by my side, everything feels right!

Preparing for Confrontation

As their song filled the air, the weight of the impending confrontation with the shadowy figures loomed over them like a storm cloud. But with each note, they felt fortified, ready to face whatever lay ahead.

Alarion paused, looking into Lila's eyes. "You know, I've faced many foes, but nothing frightens me more than the thought of losing you."

"Not on my watch!" she exclaimed, playfully punching his arm. "Besides, I'll be right there with you, wielding my magic and possibly a frying pan if things get rough!"

They shared a laugh, the tension easing between them. But as they prepared for the final confrontation, the lighthearted banter morphed into a serious tone. Alarion took a deep breath, placing his hands on Lila's shoulders.

"We're ready. We just have to remember what we're fighting for," he said earnestly. "And what we have together."

Lila nodded, her heart swelling with determination. "Love is our greatest weapon. Let's go show them!"

The Final Confrontation

As they approached the edge of the forest, the dark figures awaited them, their eyes glinting with malice. The leader stepped forward, a twisted grin spreading across his face. "Ah, the heroes return! How quaint. Do you really think love can save you?"

"Actually, yes!" Lila shouted, stepping in front of Alarion. "Love is more powerful than you could ever understand!"

Verse 2:
With every heartbeat, our magic ignites,
In the face of our foes, we'll conquer the nights.
Together we stand, no fear in our eyes,
With the Flame of Love, we'll reach for the skies!

The dark leader sneered, raising his hands as shadows swirled around him. "Then let's test this so-called love!"

"Bring it on!" Alarion shouted, igniting the Eternal Flame within him. The air crackled with energy as the light surged around them, pushing back the darkness.

The Epic Battle

As the battle erupted, Alarion and Lila fought side by side, their movements synchronized like a well-rehearsed dance. Flames clashed against shadows, and magic sparkled through the air.

Lila sent bursts of energy toward the enemy, laughing as Alarion conjured up a protective shield. "Hey! Watch out for the shadows; they're sneaky little buggers!"

"Like a cat with a laser pointer!" Alarion retorted, deflecting a shadowy attack with a flick of his wrist.

Amid the chaos, they stole glances at each other, their connection deepening with every shared spell and laughter. "Remember, we're fighting for our love!" Lila called out, her confidence soaring.

Chorus:
Together we shine, like stars in the night,
With the Flame of Love, we'll soar to new heights.
In this world of magic, our bond is our might,
With you by my side, everything feels right!

The Final Stand

With their hearts and minds united, they surged forward, channeling the power of their love. Alarion gathered all his strength, flames bursting around him in a radiant display. "This ends now!"

Lila joined him, her energy intertwining with his. "Let's show them what love can do!"

As they unleashed their combined power, a brilliant wave of light surged forward, engulfing the dark leader and his minions. The shadows screeched, dissipating into nothingness, leaving only the light of the Eternal Flame.

The Aftermath

The battlefield fell silent. Alarion and Lila stood together, panting but triumphant. They had faced the darkness, and together, they had emerged victorious.

"Did you see that? We did it!" Lila exclaimed, jumping into Alarion's arms, and he spun her around, laughter spilling from them both.

Alarion set her down, looking deeply into her eyes. "We did it together. Our love was the true power behind the Flame."

"Exactly! And now we're unstoppable!" she grinned, a spark of mischief dancing in her eyes. "Next time, though, maybe let's take on a less dramatic foe—like a rogue cupcake or something?"

Alarion laughed, shaking his head in disbelief. "Only if you promise to wield the frying pan again!"

As they shared a tender moment, the light of the Eternal Flame flickered gently around them, a reminder of their bond and the journey they had shared. Together, they had forged a truly powerful love, and together they would face whatever destiny had in store.

Chapter 32: A Heart Divided

Alarion faces a moral dilemma, torn between personal desires and the greater good. Lila's light-hearted approach helps him navigate these tough choices with humor.

The moon hung low over the realm of Tiderune, casting a silver sheen over the landscape. Alarion stood atop a grassy hill, the cool breeze tousling his hair as he gazed at the horizon. In the distance lay the Valley of Decisions, a place rumored to hold the power to reveal one's true desires and moral dilemmas. Alarion felt the weight of his recent victories but also the burden of what was to come.

He was torn, caught between his personal desires and the greater good. Should he pursue the next adventure for personal glory, or should he help the villagers suffering under the oppressive rule of the Shadow King? The choice felt monumental, and his heart was divided.

Just then, Lila appeared beside him, her presence illuminating the darkness that had crept into his mind. "Hey, brooding hero!" she called out, playfully nudging his shoulder. "You look like you've just swallowed a portion of doom!"

Alarion sighed, turning to her. "It's just... I'm stuck. I want to help the villagers, but part of me craves the thrill of adventure. What if I let them down?"

Lila laughed, shaking her head. "You're a hero, Alarion! You're supposed to be torn between epic quests and saving the day. It's in the job description!"

The Dilemma

He chuckled, but the seriousness of the situation lingered. "What if I choose wrong? What if I let my desires cloud my judgment?"

"Ah, the classic 'hero in distress' dilemma!" she replied, her eyes sparkling. "Let's turn this into a song. Music always makes dilemmas easier, right?"

Song: "Heart of Choices"
(A whimsical take on navigating tough decisions)
Intro:
In the valley of decisions, where dreams collide,
With a heart full of wishes, and fate as my guide.
I stand at the crossroads, unsure where to go,
But I've got my friend here, to help me through the flow!
Verse 1:
Should I chase my desires, or answer the call?
To save those who struggle, or rise up and stand tall?
With every choice I ponder, my hearts in a twist,
But with laughter and friendship, I know I can't miss it!

Lila joined in, her voice bright and cheerful. The melody danced through the air like the twinkling stars above them.

Chorus:
So, I'll laugh in the face of confusion and doubt,
With my heart as my compass, I'll figure it out!
In the dance of decisions, we'll find our way through,
With love as our guide, there's nothing we can't do!

The Lighthearted Banter

As they sang, the tension began to melt away, replaced by the warmth of camaraderie. Alarion felt a spark of confidence reignite within him. "You know, if we write a song for every dilemma, we'll be the most famous duo in Tiderune!" he quipped, feigning a grandiose gesture.

ALARION AND THE ETERNAL FLAME

"Of course! I can see it now: 'Alarion and Lila: The Dynamic Dilemma Duo!'" she replied, breaking into a fit of giggles. "We'll have our own fan club of confused heroes!"

Alarion laughed, his heart feeling lighter. "As long as they bring snacks to our concerts, I'm in!"

A Shadow Approaches

Suddenly, the atmosphere shifted. A shadow loomed behind them, dark and foreboding. Lila sensed it first, her laughter fading as she squinted into the darkness. "Alarion, do you feel that?"

Before they could react, a figure emerged, cloaked in black. It was one of the Shadow King's minions, eyes glinting with malice. "The time for song and laughter is over, heroes!" he hissed. "You will not escape your fate!"

"Just when I thought this chapter couldn't get any more exciting," Alarion muttered, rolling his shoulders back. "Ready for some action, Lila?"

"Always! Let's show this shadow what we've got!" she replied, brandishing her wand with a playful flourish.

The Battle

The minion lunged at them, shadows swirling like a storm. Alarion ignited his Eternal Flame, flames bursting to life in response to the danger. "Lila, cover me!" he yelled, charging forward.

Lila nodded, summoning her own magic. "Get ready for a fireworks show!" she called, releasing a blast of energy that sent sparks flying. The shadows collided with their light, creating a dazzling display.

Verse 2:
In the heat of the battle, we're laughing and bold,
With magic and friendship, our story unfolds.
Together we're stronger, with hearts intertwined,
In the face of the shadows, our fears are maligned!

They danced around the minion, their movements fluid and harmonious. Alarion launched a fiery bolt while Lila struck with a flurry of glittering light. The shadows screamed, recoiling under their combined might.

A Moment of Clarity

Amidst the chaos, Alarion had an epiphany. "Lila, I know what I have to do!" he shouted, dodging an attack. "I can't let personal desires overshadow my duty!"

"Exactly!" she exclaimed, narrowly avoiding a strike. "The choice you make defines you, not just your powers!"

With renewed determination, Alarion focused on the minion, gathering the power of the Eternal Flame. "For the villagers! For Tiderune!" he roared, unleashing a torrent of flames that engulfed the dark figure.

The minion howled, the shadows dispersing into nothingness. Alarion and Lila stood victorious, breathing heavily, hearts racing.

The Aftermath

"We did it!" Alarion exclaimed, a mixture of relief and exhilaration washing over him. "I found my answer in the heat of battle!"

Lila grinned; her eyes sparkling. "See? Nothing like a little danger to help clarify your thoughts! Just think, we could have a whole album dedicated to 'facing our fears'!"

He chuckled, wrapping an arm around her shoulders. "I can already hear the ballads."

As they walked back toward the village, the weight of their earlier dilemma felt lighter. Alarion knew he had made the right choice—not only in the battle but in understanding that his heart could guide him through any struggle, especially with Lila by his side.

Outro:
So here in the valley, with laughter and light,

We face all our choices, ready to fight.
With love as our compass, we'll journey on true,
For together, dear Lila, there's nothing we can't do!

Hand in hand, they continued their journey, ready to face whatever awaited them, knowing that together, they could navigate any dilemma that came their way.

Chapter 33: The Last Stand

The final battle looms as Alarion, Lila, and their friends unite against the shadowy enemy. With courage, humor, and love, they face the ultimate test of strength and friendship.

The sun dipped below the horizon, painting the sky in hues of crimson and gold as Alarion stood at the edge of the Valley of Shadows. The air crackled with anticipation, and the weight of what lay ahead pressed heavily on his chest. The final battle against the Shadow King was at hand, and he could feel the gathering storm of dark forces.

Lila arrived beside him, her expression a mix of determination and excitement. "You ready for this, hero?" she teased, nudging him playfully. "Or do you need a snack to fuel that Eternal Flame of yours?"

"Funny you mention it," Alarion replied, grinning. "But I might need more than just snacks to face what's coming."

"Don't worry! We have our friends, and I brought some really good chocolate!" Lila exclaimed, producing a small pouch from her satchel. "It's enchanted, so it'll give us an extra boost!"

"Let's hope it works better than the last 'enchanted' snack you brought!" Alarion chuckled, remembering the incident with the Giggle berries that had made them laugh uncontrollably during an important negotiation with a magical creature.

The Gathering

They turned to see their friends approaching from the tree line: Fynn, the skilled archer, and Kira, the powerful sorceress, accompanied by a band of villagers rallying behind them, ready to fight for their home.

"Alarion! Lila!" Fynn called, adjusting his quiver of arrows. "We're ready to give those shadowy creeps a taste of their own medicine!"

Kira stepped forward, her eyes sparkling with magic. "We've trained hard for this moment. Together, we'll show the Shadow King that friendship is stronger than fear!"

Alarion felt a swell of pride and affection for his friends. "Then let's make this count! This is our last stand, and we're not backing down!"

The Plan

As the group huddled together, Lila pulled out her enchanted chocolate and distributed it. "One for each of us! It's time to channel our inner warriors!"

They munched on the chocolate, feeling a warm rush of energy. Alarion could sense the magic igniting within him, reinforcing his determination. "Okay, team, let's review the plan. We need to draw the Shadow King out of his lair and face him on open ground."

"Got it!" Fynn said, adjusting his bowstring. "I'll shoot the signal arrow when it's time. Then we surround him and unleash everything we've got!"

"Let's also keep the humor flowing," Lila added with a smirk. "A little laughter goes a long way, even in the face of danger!"

Song: "Stand as One"
(A rallying anthem for their final battle)
Intro:
In the heart of the shadows, where darkness takes its toll,
We stand together, united, with courage in our souls.
With laughter as our armor and friendship as our sword,
We'll fight for our freedom; we'll fight for our reward!
Verse 1:

The shadows gather closer, but we'll never lose our way,
With Alarion at the forefront, we'll light the dark of day.
Lila's spells will guide us, Fynn's arrows will take flight,
In this battle for our future, we'll rise up and ignite!

The friends joined in, their voices melding together in a harmonious blend of determination and spirit.

Chorus:
So, stand as one, together we'll fight,
In the face of the shadows, we'll shine so bright!
With love and laughter fueling our might,
In this last stand, we'll make it right!

The Showdown

As the last notes faded, the air grew still. They marched toward the Shadow King's lair, a crumbling castle shrouded in darkness. Alarion felt his heart race; this was it.

"Remember, we're in this together," he reminded them, glancing at each friend. "No matter what happens, we face it as a team!"

With a nod of agreement, Fynn stepped forward, releasing an arrow high into the sky. It exploded in a brilliant burst of color, illuminating the surrounding darkness.

From the shadows, the menacing figure of the Shadow King emerged, a cloak of darkness swirling around him. "Foolish mortals," he sneered, "you think you can challenge me?"

Lila took a step forward, her wand crackling with magic. "We don't just think; we know we can! You've underestimated the power of friendship!"

The Battle Begins

The Shadow King laughed, a chilling sound. "Let's see how powerful you truly are!" He summoned waves of shadowy minions that rushed toward the group.

"Here they come!" Alarion shouted, igniting the Eternal Flame around him. "Let's light them up!"

ALARION AND THE ETERNAL FLAME

With courage, the group charged into battle. Arrows flew, spells crackled, and the sounds of clashing magic filled the air. Alarion swung his flaming sword, cutting through the shadows while Lila danced around him, casting spells that left trails of sparkling light.

Verse 2:
In the chaos of battle, we fight side by side,
With laughter in our hearts, we'll turn the tide!
Together we'll conquer, together we'll stand,
With the flames of our spirits, we'll take back our land!

Kira unleashed a powerful wave of magic, sending a shockwave through the minions, scattering them like leaves in the wind. "Keep pushing forward!" she called, her voice strong and unwavering.

A Comical Twist

Just when it seemed like they were gaining the upper hand, the Shadow King unleashed a particularly nasty spell that sent Lila sprawling. "Oof! I didn't sign up for the ground-flying technique!" she quipped, shaking her head as she got back to her feet.

"Focus, Lila!" Alarion shouted, fighting back a grin. "We can't have you flying off too soon!"

"Too late! I'm already grounded!" she replied, determination shining in her eyes as she prepared to cast another spell.

As they battled, their playful banter kept spirits high amidst the chaos, proving that humor was indeed their greatest weapon.

The Final Confrontation

With shadows swirling around them, Alarion spotted the Shadow King preparing to unleash a devastating attack. "We need to combine our powers! Now!" he yelled.

The group quickly gathered, channeling their energies into a single spell, their hands linked together in solidarity. "For friendship, for Tiderune!" they shouted in unison.

The Shadow King laughed menacingly, but Alarion felt the warmth of the Eternal Flame pulsing within him, fueled by their connection. "Together!" he commanded, and they released their magic in a brilliant surge of light.

The Triumph of Light

The explosion of light collided with the dark forces, and for a moment, time stood still. The shadows writhed and twisted, and then—BOOM! The light burst forth, engulfing everything in its brilliance.

When the light faded, the Shadow King lay defeated, the darkness dissipating around him.

Cheers erupted from their friends and the gathered villagers.

"We did it! We actually did it!" Alarion exclaimed, his heart soaring.

Lila threw her arms around him. "I knew we could! And we did it with a little laughter and a lot of friendship!"

Celebrating Victory

As the sun rose, bathing the valley in golden light, the group celebrated their victory. Fynn and Kira led a round of laughter and cheers, recounting their hilarious moments during the battle.

"Let's not forget my amazing flying technique!" Lila teased, causing everyone to burst into laughter.

"I'd say it was more of a grounding technique," Alarion countered, playfully nudging her.

Outro:
So here in the dawn of a new day,
With laughter and love lighting our way,
We've fought through the shadows, and now we stand tall,
For in the heart of friendship, we've conquered it all!

With hearts full of hope and laughter ringing in their ears, Alarion, Lila, and their friends embraced the new dawn, ready for whatever adventures lay ahead, united by the bonds of love and friendship that would carry them through anything.

Chapter 34: The Echo of the Past

Old friends and foes return, complicating the battle. Alarion must reconcile his past as Lila helps him find the humor in their chaotic reunion.

The air was electric with tension as Alarion and Lila made their way to the Glimmering Grove, a serene forest that had once been a battleground for light and darkness. The birds chirped cheerily above, unaware of the emotional storm brewing in Alarion's heart. They were on their way to meet old friends who were supposed to help them in their ongoing struggle against the remnants of the Shadow King's forces.

However, Alarion couldn't shake the feeling that this gathering would be more complicated than expected. He turned to Lila, who was skipping ahead, her vibrant spirit as contagious as the blooming flowers around them.

"Hey, Lila," he called, slowing his pace. "You know, some of the folks we're meeting today are... well, let's just say they're from my less-than-stellar past."

Lila spun around, a mischievous grin on her face. "What, are you afraid they'll call you 'Alarion the Awkward' again? Because that's my favorite nickname for you!"

"Very funny," he replied, rolling his eyes. "But seriously, there are some people I'd rather not face again."

"Just think of it this way," Lila said, trying to lighten the mood. "If they give you a hard time, we can always challenge them to a dance-off! You know how terrible they are at dancing."

Alarion couldn't help but chuckle. "A dance-off? That's a brilliant plan, Lila."

As they entered the grove, the scene that awaited them was anything but serene. Old allies and rivals stood in a circle, each with expressions that ranged from excitement to outright confusion.

The Reunion

"Alarion! Lila!" shouted Fynn, waving enthusiastically from across the grove. "You made it!"

As they approached, Alarion noticed a few familiar faces. Among them was Rowan, his childhood friend turned rival, with a smirk that promised trouble. "Look who it is! Alarion the Awkward and his trusty sidekick, Lila the Lively!"

Lila raised an eyebrow, ready to retort, but Alarion held her back with a grin. "Nice to see you too, Rowan. Still wearing that same ridiculous outfit?"

Rowan's face darkened for a moment before he chuckled, brushing it off. "Well, at least I don't wear flowers in my hair!"

"Touché," Lila chimed in, plucking a flower from a nearby bush and tucking it into her own hair.

Alarion could feel the tension easing slightly as laughter filled the grove. They were joined by Mira, a once-foe who had now become a valuable ally, her aura a mix of intrigue and mischief. "You two haven't changed a bit! Still bickering like an old married couple, I see!"

"Married? Please, we're just friends," Lila said, winking at Alarion, who felt his face flush at the suggestion.

The Hidden Threat

As the banter continued, the mood shifted abruptly. A chilling wind swept through the grove, and Alarion sensed an unease settling over their group. "We need to focus," he said, trying to regain control. "We're here for a reason. The remnants of the Shadow King's forces are still out there, and we need to be prepared."

ALARION AND THE ETERNAL FLAME

Just then, a rustle came from the bushes, and a figure stepped out, cloaked in shadows. "Well, well, if it isn't the little heroes of Tiderune," hissed a voice that sent a shiver down Alarion's spine.

"Not you again!" Mira exclaimed, stepping forward defensively. It was Darius, a cunning foe who had been a thorn in their side before.

"Surprised to see me?" Darius sneered, his eyes glinting with malice. "I've come to settle some old scores."

Song: "Echoes of the Past"
(A song reflecting on their history and the bonds they share)
Intro:
In the shadows of our history, where echoes of laughter play,
We gather here as warriors, united in a brand-new way.
With humor and courage, we'll face what's coming fast,
For together we are stronger, and we'll break free from the past!
Verse 1:
Once we were just children, with dreams that danced in the light,
But shadows came to haunt us and turned our day to night.
Now we stand together, no more enemies at play,
With Lila by my side, we'll chase the darkness away!

Alarion felt the power of their shared history in the air as they sang, lifting spirits and reminding them of their purpose.

Chorus:
So let the echoes of the past guide us on our way,
We'll face the dark together, we'll shine through every fray!
With laughter as our armor, and love those lights our hearts,
In this battle for our future, we'll never fall apart!

The Battle with Darius

As the last notes of their song faded, Darius lunged forward, summoning shadows to his side. "You think you can sing your way out of this? You're fools!"

"Looks like he didn't get the memo about our dance-off!" Lila exclaimed, her wand glowing brightly. "Let's show him what we've got!"

With that, chaos erupted. Alarion charged forward, wielding the Eternal Flame, while Lila cast a flurry of sparkling spells that danced through the air like fireflies. Fynn and Mira took to the sides, launching arrows and magic from a distance, working together seamlessly.

"Let's give him a taste of what friendship really means!" Alarion shouted, his laughter mingling with the battle cries around him.

Darius summoned shadowy tendrils that lashed out, but Lila spun gracefully, dodging them with a light-hearted twirl. "Is that the best you can do? I've seen toddler shadows that pack more punch!"

Mira laughed, adding her own magic to the mix. "You might want to step up your game, Darius! We're here to have fun!"

The Humor in Chaos

As the battle raged on, Alarion realized that amidst the chaos, their camaraderie was shining brighter than ever. They were united, old wounds healing with laughter and love.

"Lila! Watch out!" he shouted, seeing a shadow dart toward her. In a split second, he dashed forward, shielded her, and felt the impact of Darius's attack as he pushed her out of the way.

"Thanks, hero," Lila said, a grin plastered on her face. "But next time, maybe let me handle my own shadows!"

"Just trying to protect my favorite flower," he replied, feeling a warmth spread through him that had nothing to do with the Eternal Flame.

The Climax

As the battle reached its peak, Alarion felt a surge of determination. He and Lila locked eyes,

a silent understanding passing between them. They were stronger together.

"Let's finish this!" Alarion shouted, raising his sword high. "For Tiderune! For friendship!"

With their powers combined, Alarion and Lila unleashed a final attack that illuminated the grove with an explosion of light. Darius cried out in frustration as the shadows disintegrated around him, leaving nothing but echoes of defeat.

The Aftermath

With Darius defeated and the remnants of the Shadow King scattered, the grove erupted in cheers. They had faced their past, both old friends and foes, and emerged victorious.

"Looks like we won that round!" Rowan said, clapping Alarion on the back.

"I'd say we won more than just a battle," Lila added, her eyes sparkling. "We've reconciled our past and come out stronger!"

As they celebrated, Alarion couldn't help but feel grateful. Lila was right; their connections had grown deeper, forged in the fires of adversity and laughter.

Outro:
So here in the light of a brand-new day,
We've conquered the shadows; we've paved our own way.
With laughter and our friendship, we'll face what's ahead,
For the echoes of our past are the stories we've spread!

As the sun set over the Glimmering Grove, Alarion, Lila, and their friends embraced the journey ahead, ready to face whatever challenges awaited them—together.

Chapter 35: The Price of Love

Sacrifices must be made in the final showdown. Alarion grapples with what he's willing to give up for love, leading to poignant moments interspersed with humor.

The sun hung low in the sky, casting a golden glow over the enchanted land of Tiderune as Alarion and Lila stood at the edge of the Crystal Canyon. The weight of their upcoming battle loomed heavy on their hearts. They were preparing for the final showdown against the Shadow King and his relentless army.

As they gazed into the canyon, the shimmering crystals reflected not only the light but also their own inner turmoil. Alarion turned to Lila, his heart racing. "Do you ever think about what we might have to sacrifice today?" he asked, his voice tinged with uncertainty.

"Only all the time," Lila replied, attempting to lighten the mood with a wink. "But remember, it's just a little sacrifice. I mean, what's love without a few dramatic moments, right?"

Alarion chuckled, his nerves easing slightly. "I suppose you're right. And I'm sure whatever happens, we'll face it together."

With a deep breath, Lila took Alarion's hand, her grip warm and reassuring. "Whatever we face, love is our strongest weapon," she said. "And if I have to face the Shadow King with a bouquet of flowers in one hand and a sword in the other, so be it!"

"Now that's the spirit!" Alarion laughed, envisioning Lila in a battle of flowers versus shadows.

The Calm Before the Storm

Before the chaos began, they gathered their friends—Fynn, Mira, and even Rowan, who had begrudgingly put aside his rivalry with Alarion for the moment. They shared a light meal, a last supper of sorts, filled with laughter and memories.

Fynn, ever the jokester, raised his cup. "To the bravest warriors in Tiderune! May our swords be sharp, our spells be powerful, and our jokes be as terrible as ever!"

Lila laughed. "If you don't stop with the puns, I might have to 'sword' you out of here!"

"Nice one, Lila!" Rowan added, his competitive spirit momentarily forgotten. "Just make sure to keep your eyes on the prize—our glorious victory!"

The Song: "For Love We Fight"
(A song embodying their camaraderie and resolve)
Intro:
In the heart of the battle, where shadows loom tall,
We stand here united; we won't let love fall.
With laughter as our armor, and hope as our guide,
Together we'll conquer, we'll turn the tide!
Verse 1:
When the darkness surrounds us, and fear takes its hold,
We'll raise up our voices, let our courage be bold.
For every sacrifice made, for every tear shed,
We'll fight for each other, with love as our thread!

Lila led the song, her voice ringing clear in the air, wrapping around them like a protective spell. Alarion couldn't help but feel uplifted by the strength in their words.

Chorus:
For love, we fight, through the shadows and pain,
Together we'll stand, through the sunshine and rain.
With hearts intertwined, and spirits so bright,
We'll battle the darkness, for love is our light!

The Showdown

As the last notes of their song faded into the crisp air, they prepared to face the Shadow King. The ground shook as dark clouds rolled in, and ominous laughter echoed through the canyon. Shadows materialized, revealing the menacing form of the Shadow King himself.

"Ah, the little heroes of Tiderune!" he sneered. "You think your love can save you? Sacrifices will be made today, and I intend to collect!"

With a flick of his wrist, he sent waves of shadowy figures surging toward them. Alarion felt a rush of adrenaline. "Stay together!" he shouted. "We can't let them divide us!"

Mira unleashed a torrent of magic, sending sparkling light flying toward the shadows. Fynn and Rowan joined forces, their attacks synchronized in a brilliant display of teamwork.

"Let's dance!" Fynn shouted, spinning dramatically to dodge an incoming attack. "Lila, you should take notes!"

Lila rolled her eyes, but she couldn't suppress her laughter. "I'd rather not take dance lessons from you, Fynn!"

As the battle escalated, Alarion found himself fighting side by side with Lila, their movements fluid and instinctual. With each spell cast and each strike delivered, they grew more in sync, their bond deepening in the heat of battle.

The Dilemma

But then came a moment that froze Alarion's heart. The Shadow King, sensing their connection, turned his attention to Lila. "Ah, sweet Lila," he taunted. "You're so full of light. How tragic it would be if something were to happen to you."

In that instant, Alarion felt a wave of fear wash over him. "Lila!" he shouted, rushing forward to shield her.

The Shadow King smirked, raising his hand. "Sacrifice is the price of love, Alarion. Choose wisely!"

With a sudden surge of power, he conjured a massive shadow creature, its form twisting and writhing as it lunged toward Lila. Alarion felt a spark ignite within him—the need to protect the one he loved. But at what cost?

The Turning Point

In that moment of chaos, Alarion glanced at Lila, her eyes filled with unwavering determination. "You know what to do, Alarion!" she urged. "We can't lose each other!"

Taking a deep breath, Alarion raised the Eternal Flame, feeling its warmth pulse through him. "I will give up anything for you, Lila!" he declared, knowing he would face whatever darkness came next.

The flames swirled around him, illuminating the shadows and revealing the hidden enemies lurking within. "Together!" he shouted, rallying his friends. "Let's end this once and for all!"

The Final Push

As Alarion and his friends united their powers, Lila's laughter rang through the chaos. "Time to show them what love can do!"

In a magnificent display of light and strength, they unleashed their combined magic. The canyon blazed with energy, casting away the shadows and revealing the truth within.

"Your darkness has no power here!" Alarion cried, charging forward with Lila by his side.

They fought with the strength of their love, dodging attacks and striking back with newfound courage. The shadows began to crumble, and Alarion felt the weight of his fears lifting.

The Aftermath

As the last of the shadows dissipated, the Shadow King let out a scream of defeat. Alarion and Lila stood side by side, breathless but triumphant.

"You did it!" Lila exclaimed, her eyes sparkling with pride. "We did it together!"

"Love is our greatest weapon," Alarion said, pulling her close. "I would sacrifice anything to protect you."

"And I'd do the same for you," Lila replied, her voice filled with warmth.

Outro:
So here in the aftermath, with shadows cast away,
We stand hand in hand, ready for a brand-new day.
For love is the light that guides us through the night,
In the price of love, we've discovered our might!

With the echoes of their battle behind them, Alarion and Lila looked toward the horizon, ready to embrace whatever challenges awaited, knowing that together, they could face anything—because love was the true magic of Tiderune.

Chapter 36: The Flame's Embrace

With the battle raging, Alarion taps into the true essence of the Eternal Flame. Lila's unwavering support fuels his resolve, culminating in a moment that transforms their relationship.

The battlefield stretched out before Alarion like a living tapestry woven with chaos and desperation. Shadows twisted and danced among the flickering lights of the Eternal Flame, casting eerie silhouettes across the terrain. The air crackled with tension, and the ground trembled underfoot as the forces of darkness surged forward, their intentions clear and malicious.

In the center of it all stood Alarion, his heart pounding like a war drum. He could feel the weight of the world on his shoulders, the fate of Tiderune hanging in the balance. Beside him, Lila's eyes sparkled with determination, a beacon of light in the swirling chaos.

"Are you ready for this?" Alarion asked, trying to mask the apprehension in his voice.

"With you? Always!" Lila replied, her smile radiant even amid the encroaching shadows. "Remember, love is our secret weapon!"

A Dance of Flames

As the dark figures approached, Alarion felt the flicker of the Eternal Flame within him, warm and inviting. He closed his eyes for a brief moment, drawing on its essence. The flame whispered to him, reminding him of their bond, of the laughter they had shared, and the love that ignited his very soul.

"Let's do this!" he shouted, raising his arms as the flame surged forth, engulfing him in a fiery embrace.

With newfound strength, Alarion summoned the flames, casting them outward like a protective barrier. The shadows recoiled as the bright fire illuminated their forms—terrifying creatures with hollow eyes and twisted features.

The Song: "Embers of Our Hearts"
(An anthem of courage, love, and togetherness)
Intro:
When the shadows creep in, and the world feels cold,
We stand as one, with a heart made bold.
Together we'll rise, through the smoke and the fire,
With the flame of our love, we'll lift ourselves higher!
Verse 1:
In the chaos around us, when fear grips the night,
We'll fight side by side, fueled by our light.
With every heartbeat, and every breath drawn,
Together, we're stronger, we'll carry on!

Lila joined in, her voice rising above the clamor. The melody flowed through them, igniting a fire in their hearts as they sang together.

Chorus:
Through the flames, through the shadows, we'll make our stand,
With the embers of our hearts, we'll take back our land.
In the heat of the battle, love conquers all,
With each other beside us, we'll never fall!

The Clash

As they sang, Alarion felt the power of the Eternal Flame surge within him, amplifying his resolve. He and Lila charged forward, their love manifesting as a force of nature. They danced through the chaos, weaving in and out of the fray, a whirlwind of flames and laughter.

Fynn and Mira joined them, launching spells and witty banter as they fought off the dark minions. "Do you think they'd rather be doing laundry than battling us?" Fynn shouted, narrowly dodging a swipe from a shadowy figure.

"Only if it involves cleaning up after you!" Mira shot back, sending a blast of light that sent several shadows tumbling.

Lila glanced at Alarion, their eyes locking with an unspoken understanding. "This is our moment, Alarion," she said, her voice steady amid the clamor. "We have to push forward!"

The Transformative Moment

As they pressed on, the shadows began to falter under their combined strength. But just when victory seemed within reach, the Shadow King emerged from the darkness, towering and ominous, his presence chilling the air.

"Foolish children," he hissed. "You think you can defeat me with mere flames? Sacrifice is the price of love, and you will learn it well!"

With a wave of his hand, he summoned a monstrous creature, a nightmarish beast formed from the very shadows themselves. Its eyes glowed with malice, and it roared as it lunged toward Alarion and Lila.

"Alarion!" Lila shouted, fear briefly flashing across her face. But then, she squared her shoulders. "We can do this! Together!"

In that instant, Alarion felt an overwhelming surge of love for her. It was more than just a spark; it was a raging fire. He tapped into the Eternal Flame, allowing it to envelop him completely.

"Lila, we need to merge our powers!" he called, his voice steady and resolute. "We can't let him win!"

With a nod, Lila stepped closer, their hands intertwined. "On three!"

"On three!" Alarion echoed.

The Climactic Union

"One... two... three!"

They channeled their energies into one massive blast of flame, a wave of pure love and determination that surged forward, colliding with the shadow beast. The world seemed to pause as their hearts beat in sync, and the flames danced together, forming a brilliant heart-shaped inferno that consumed the darkness.

The creature howled, but the power of their love burned brighter. As the flames licked at the edges of the shadows, they began to dissolve, leaving only light in their wake.

With one final push, they directed their combined flame toward the Shadow King himself. The ground shook, and the air crackled with energy. "This is for Tiderune!" Alarion declared, pouring every ounce of love and strength into the fire.

The Aftermath

As the light enveloped the Shadow King, his form began to flicker and fade. "No! This cannot be!" he screamed, his voice drowning in the blaze of the Eternal Flame.

Then, with a brilliant flash, the darkness was banished, leaving only silence in its wake. Alarion and Lila stood amidst the remnants of the battle, their hearts racing.

"Did we... did we do it?" Lila asked, breathless and wide-eyed.

Alarion pulled her close, their foreheads touching. "We did it. Together. I've never felt more alive than I do right now, with you by my side."

The Song Reprise: "Embers of Our Hearts"
(Celebrating their victory and love)
Outro:
With the shadows behind us, and light in our souls,
We've forged our destiny; we've made ourselves whole.
In the fire of our love, we found our way back,
Through the flame's embrace, we've stayed on track!

With their voices rising in harmony, they celebrated their victory, laughter mingling with the remnants of flames, igniting the dawn of a new era in Tiderune. At that moment, amid the wreckage of their battles and the warmth of their triumph, Alarion realized that love truly was the flame that guided them through the darkest of times.

Chapter 37: The Turning Tide

As the tide of battle turns, Alarion faces the final showdown with the shadowy enemy. The humorous banter between him and Lila keeps their spirits high amid the chaos.

The battlefield was a swirling mass of chaos, filled with the clang of metal, the crackle of magic, and the shouts of warriors. Alarion stood at the forefront, his heart racing as he surveyed the scene. The Eternal Flame had flickered and danced beside him, but it was Lila's laughter that truly fueled his courage.

"Hey, Alarion!" she shouted, dodging a wayward arrow with the agility of a nimble cat. "Do you think those shadows even have a clue about fashion? I mean, what is with that all-black ensemble? So last season!"

"Maybe they're just trying to blend in with the darkness!" Alarion shot back, a grin breaking across his face despite the tension in the air. "I can't wait to tell them they should consider some brighter colors. How about a nice sunshine yellow?"

Their banter flowed like a current, keeping their spirits buoyant even as the tide of battle shifted ominously. Shadows flickered and lunged, but the duo's humor turned their fear into laughter, creating a shield of joy around them.

The Song: "Light Up the Night"
(An anthem of resilience, love, and humor)
Intro:
When the night is dark and the shadows creep,
We'll laugh in the face of fear, not lose a beat.

With every joke and every smile, we'll fight with delight,
Together, dear Lila, we'll light up the night!
Verse 1:
They may come with their fangs and their terrible roars,
But our love is a weapon, it opens doors.
With every punchline, we'll send them away,
Shadows don't stand a chance when we play!

"Just think," Lila chimed in, her eyes sparkling, "if we beat them, we can tell everyone we fought off the 'Fashion Police' of the Underworld!"

Chorus:
So light up the night, let our laughter ring,
In this crazy battle, we're the lovebirds that sing!
With every quip and every jest, we'll soar and we'll fly,
Together forever, just you and I!

The Shifting Battle

As they sang, the shadows pressed in, and the air thickened with tension. Alarion felt the familiar warmth of the Eternal Flame radiating within him, urging him to harness its power.

He glanced at Lila, her unwavering smile kindling the fire of hope within him.

"Alright, my warrior muse!" he declared, thrusting his sword forward. "Let's show these creatures what real style looks like!"

With a shared look of determination, they charged into the fray. Alarion swung his sword, igniting flames that cascaded into the air like fireworks. Lila, wielding her staff, danced gracefully around him, casting spells of protection and light.

In the chaos, Alarion spotted a familiar figure in the distance—a shadowy form he recognized. It was the Shadow King, glaring down at them from his dark throne, plotting his next move. Alarion felt a surge of anger and determination. He wouldn't let fear rule his heart.

The Confrontation

"Hey, Shadow King!" Alarion shouted, waving his sword dramatically. "Is that the best you can do? I've seen more menacing looks from my Aunt Gertrude's cat!"

"Silence!" the Shadow King bellowed, his voice rumbling like thunder. "You think your humor can defeat me? I will plunge Tiderune into darkness!"

"Not if I have anything to say about it!" Lila shot back, her tone light but fierce. "Also, let's talk about your hair. It's like a storm cloud had a bad hair day!"

With that, they lunged forward, laughter and magic intertwining as they advanced against the oncoming tide of shadows. Each spell cast was infused with their humor, sending shockwaves through the ranks of their foes.

The Ultimate Showdown

The tide began to turn as Alarion and Lila reached the Shadow King. He loomed large, his eyes glimmering with rage. "You dare challenge me?"

"Absolutely!" Alarion replied, stepping forward with confidence. "But first, let's settle the score. Do you really think black is the new black? Because I've got news for you—it's SO over!"

The Shadow King growled, raising his hand to unleash a wave of darkness, but Alarion and Lila held firm, their hands united. The Eternal Flame flared, pushing back against the darkness.

The Final Song: "Light Up the Night"
(A powerful crescendo of love and courage)
Chorus:
So light up the night, let our laughter ring,
In this crazy battle, we're the lovebirds that sing!
With every quip and every jest, we'll soar and we'll fly,
Together forever, just you and I!
Bridge:
Through the storm, through the fight,

We'll rise again, shining bright.
With the flame of love, we'll never part,
Together, we conquer, heart to heart!
Outro:
As the shadows fall and the dawn breaks wide,
We'll dance in the light, with love as our guide.
With laughter as our armor, we'll face what's in sight,
In this battle of darkness, we'll light up the night!

The Turning of the Tide

With their voices rising in unison, the power of their love ignited the air around them. The shadows shrank back, trembling in the wake of Alarion and Lila's combined magic.

The Shadow King staggered, his darkness dissolving under the brilliance of the Eternal Flame. "This cannot be!" he roared, frustration lacing his voice.

"Oh, but it is!" Lila shouted, launching a final burst of light. "Love always wins!"

With one last surge of strength, Alarion and Lila merged their magic, sending a wave of radiant energy crashing into the Shadow King. The dark figure howled as he was consumed by the light, his form dissipating like mist in the morning sun.

The Victory

As silence fell across the battlefield, Alarion and Lila stood side by side, breathing heavily, their hands still clasped tightly. The shadows that had once loomed over them were gone, replaced by the warm glow of the Eternal Flame.

"We did it!" Alarion exclaimed, pulling Lila into a joyful embrace.

"Of course, we did!" she laughed, her eyes twinkling. "When have we ever failed to shine together?"

As they gazed into each other's eyes, the chaos of battle faded into the background, leaving only the warmth of their connection.

At that moment, surrounded by the remnants of battle, Alarion knew they could face anything together.

"Now," he said, still holding her close, "let's find some ice cream. I think we've earned it!"

And with laughter echoing through the battlefield, they began their journey back, hand in hand, ready to light up the world together, one joyful step at a time.

Chapter 38: The Power of Love

In a dramatic moment, Alarion realizes that love is his greatest weapon. His bond with Lila strengthens as they fight side by side, weaving humor and romance into their actions.

The battlefield stretched out before Alarion and Lila like a twisted tapestry of chaos. Shadows flickered among the trees, and the air buzzed with the energy of impending conflict. Alarion's heart raced—not just with the thrill of battle, but with the intoxicating presence of Lila by his side.

"Ready to show these dark forces what we're made of?" Lila grinned, her fingers twirling her staff like a baton. "Or should I start with a joke? I hear they hate laughter!"

"Only if you promise it's better than your last one!" Alarion shot back, winking at her. "What was it again? 'Why did the wizard break up with his girlfriend? She kept casting spells on his heart!'"

"Exactly!" she laughed, her eyes sparkling. "But hey, I've got a new one: 'Why did the scarecrow win an award?'"

"Why?" Alarion asked, feigning innocence.

"Because he was outstanding in his field!" She burst into giggles, and for a moment, the weight of the battle melted away, leaving only the warmth of their connection.

The Song: "Stronger Together"
(An anthem celebrating love, courage, and humor)
Intro:
In the darkest night, when the shadows creep,
We'll rise as one, our bond runs deep.

With laughter as our shield and love as our sword,
We'll face the storm, united, and adored!
Verse 1:
With every swing and every spell,
We fight for love, we'll never dwell.
Side by side, our hearts entwined,
In this dance of fate, our spirits aligned!

Alarion felt a surge of power coursing through him, ignited by Lila's laughter. Their bond was a force unlike any other, and he realized it was more potent than any magic he wielded.

The First Clash

Suddenly, a group of shadowy figures emerged from the trees, their eyes glinting like shards of glass. Alarion and Lila turned, ready to confront the encroaching darkness.

"Looks like we have company!" Alarion shouted, gripping his sword tightly. "I'll take the left; you handle the right?"

"Why not just ask them to leave? A friendly chat, perhaps?" Lila replied cheekily, raising her staff. "You know, 'Excuse me, gentlemen of darkness, but could you kindly vacate this area?'"

"Right! Because that's what they teach us in battle school!" Alarion laughed, dodging an incoming attack. "But if that fails, I'll use my backup plan: 'The Scarecrow Special!'"

As the first shadow lunged at him, Alarion stepped aside and struck with precision, the flame from his sword illuminating the dark. He felt Lila's magic swirl around him, empowering each move he made.

The Heart of the Battle

With each swing of their weapons, Alarion and Lila fought side by side, a seamless blend of humor and heroics.

"Did you see that?" Lila giggled after sending a shadow crashing into a tree. "I think I just gave him a splinter! Maybe he'll think twice before attacking again!"

"Good plan!" Alarion replied, parrying a blow. "Nothing says 'stay away' like a wood-related injury!"

The shadows pressed in, relentless and determined, but with each punchline and witty remark, Alarion felt his confidence soar. It was as if their humor acted as a barrier against despair, fortifying their resolve.

The Turning Point

The battle raged on, but Alarion suddenly spotted a particularly large shadowy figure—darker than the rest, with a twisted, mocking smile. It was the Dark Conjuror, the mastermind behind this invasion.

"There's the ringleader!" Alarion pointed. "I'll distract him, and you hit him with everything you've got!"

"Distract him? Oh, I can do that!" Lila said with a grin. "What's a shadow's favorite snack? Dark chocolate!"

"Great idea!" Alarion laughed, charging toward the Conjuror, who looked momentarily baffled.

Lila seized the opportunity. "Let me show you how I like my chocolate!" she shouted, unleashing a dazzling burst of magic that enveloped the Conjuror.

The Climactic Moment

The Dark Conjuror faltered, his shadows wavering as Lila's light flooded the battlefield. Alarion saw his chance. "Hey, Shadow King! Have you ever heard of the power of love?"

"What nonsense is this?" the Conjuror snarled, struggling against the radiant energy surrounding him.

"It's not nonsense; it's a fact!" Alarion yelled, charging forward with determination. "When love is our weapon, we are unstoppable!"

With Lila's magic intertwined with his sword, Alarion struck the Conjuror's dark heart, releasing a wave of light that banished the shadows from the land.

The Final Song: "Stronger Together"
(A triumphant celebration of their love and unity)
Chorus:
Together we rise, through laughter and tears,
With love in our hearts, we conquer our fears.
In this grand adventure, we'll dance and we'll sing,
With the power of love, we'll face anything!
Bridge:
No shadow can break us, no darkness can bind us,
For in our hearts, true magic we find.
With every battle, our bond only grows,
In this world of shadows, our light overflows!
Outro:
As the dawn breaks bright, we'll laugh in delight,
Hand in hand, we've won this fight.
With our love as our guide, we'll shine evermore,
Together forever, our hearts will soar!

The Aftermath

With the Dark Conjuror defeated, the battlefield erupted into light. The remaining shadows dissipated, leaving behind a serene calm.

"We did it!" Lila cheered, throwing her arms around Alarion.

He spun her around, their laughter ringing through the air. "All thanks to you and your terrible jokes! I think the shadows were so confused, they didn't know how to react!"

"Hey, if it works, it works!" she replied, her cheeks flushed with joy. "And you know, we make a pretty great team."

Alarion nodded, a warm glow of love filling his chest. "The best. Together, we can conquer anything—even the worst of puns!"

As they stood together, the sun breaking through the clouds, Alarion realized that love was indeed his greatest weapon. With Lila by his side, he could face any challenge that came their way.

Hand in hand, they turned toward the horizon, ready to embrace whatever adventures awaited them next, knowing that together, they were unstoppable.

Chapter 39: The Final Confrontation

The ultimate clash between light and darkness unfolds. Alarion's newfound confidence, supported by Lila, leads to a battle filled with both heart-stopping moments and humor.

The air was thick with tension as Alarion and Lila stood at the precipice of the battle that would determine the fate of their realm. Before them lay the Dark Fortress, a jagged silhouette against the backdrop of a stormy sky. Dark clouds swirled ominously above, and flashes of lightning illuminated the fortress, revealing the twisted shapes of lurking enemies.

"Ready for the grand finale?" Alarion asked, flashing Lila a confident grin.

"Only if you promise to keep your 'cool' under pressure!" she replied playfully, her eyes sparkling with mischief. "Remember the last time you got a bit too 'fired up'?"

"That was one time!" he protested, raising his hands defensively. "And the enemy deserved it. Who brings a flaming marshmallow to a sword fight?"

"Just promise not to roast any more foes, okay?" Lila laughed. "I'm more interested in what comes after our victory: a feast worthy of our legendary status!"

"Deal!" Alarion said, his heart swelling with affection for the spirited girl by his side. Together, they were ready to face the darkness head-on, with humor lighting their path.

The Song: "Light of Our Hearts"
(An anthem of love and bravery in the face of adversity)

Intro:
In the shadows where fear resides,
We stand united, side by side.
With laughter as our shield, and love as our guide,
We'll face the darkness, hearts open wide!
Verse 1:
When the night is long and the road is tough,
We'll shine like stars, our spirits enough.
With every challenge, we'll rise above,
With the power of friendship, the strength of our love!

"Here they come!" Alarion shouted, watching as shadowy figures emerged from the depths of the fortress. These weren't just the typical minions; these were the Dark Conjuror's elite—a group of mischief-makers with a penchant for chaos. Alarion and Lila exchanged glances, their hearts racing with excitement and anticipation.

The Clash of Forces

With a shared nod, they charged forward, Alarion leading the way with his sword ablaze. Lila followed closely, weaving her magic into a vibrant shield that flickered with light.

"Let's give them a taste of our power duo routine!" she called a cheeky grin on her face.

As they approached, one of the shadows lunged at Alarion, who sidestepped effortlessly. "You missed!" he taunted. "But don't worry, practice makes perfect!" He swung his sword, sending sparks flying as it clashed against the enemy.

"Why did you bring a shadow to a light fight?" Lila quipped as she unleashed a torrent of light magic, sending several shadows sprawling. "Because he thought it was a dark joke!"

"Good one!" Alarion laughed, feeling the weight of the world lift with every punchline they exchanged.

A Moment of Humor Amidst Chaos

As the battle intensified, Alarion found himself back-to-back with Lila, their synergy undeniable. She twirled and unleashed a wave of light that blinded the nearest foes. "You know, they really should've considered a career in shadow puppetry instead!" she joked.

"Right? They've got the right look for it!" Alarion grinned, dispatching another enemy with a swift move. Their playful banter kept their spirits high, even as the stakes rose.

Then, the ground trembled beneath them as the Dark Conjuror stepped forth, cloaked in swirling darkness. "You think your laughter can save you?" he sneered, his voice echoing like thunder. "Prepare to be extinguished!"

"Extinguished? Sounds like someone's a bit melodramatic!" Lila shot back, her confidence unwavering. "Do you need a thesaurus to find better words?"

"Enough!" he roared, raising his hands to unleash a wave of darkness. But Alarion stood firm, gathering his courage.

The Turning Point

"Together!" Alarion shouted, locking eyes with Lila. They joined forces, their energies intertwining like a beautiful dance.

"Time for the grand finale!" Lila exclaimed, her hands glowing with brilliant light.

"Let's show them the light of our hearts!" Alarion added, feeling the warmth of their bond strengthen.

Chorus:
We'll shine together, through shadows we'll run,
With laughter and love, we've already won.
In this battle of darkness, we'll find our way,
With the light of our hearts, we'll seize the day!

They unleashed a blinding burst of energy that surged toward the Dark Conjuror, illuminating the battlefield and sending a shockwave through the ranks of shadowy enemies.

"Is that all you've got?" Alarion shouted, his voice filled with determination.

"No!" the Conjuror screamed as the light engulfed him, pushing back against the darkness that had surrounded them for so long.

The Climax of Battle

The shadows writhed in pain, their forms flickering as if they were nothing more than wisps of smoke.

"Now, while he's distracted!" Lila urged, her eyes shining with excitement. "Let's finish this!"

With a powerful leap, Alarion charged at the Conjuror, sword drawn. "This is for everyone you've hurt!" he yelled, channeling all his love and resolve into a single blow.

The Conjuror's darkness clashed against Alarion's radiant light, and for a moment, it felt as though the entire world held its breath.

Then, with a surge of energy, Alarion's sword pierced through the darkness, and the Conjuror let out a final, echoing cry before exploding into a flurry of shimmering sparks.

The Aftermath

As silence descended upon the battlefield, Alarion and Lila stood together, panting but victorious. The shadows that had once threatened their world had been vanquished, and a new dawn began to break over the horizon.

"Did you see that?" Lila exclaimed, jumping up and down in excitement. "We totally rocked that fight!"

"We did!" Alarion agreed, unable to contain his laughter. "And your jokes—definitely part of the secret weapon!"

As the first rays of sunlight streamed across the landscape, illuminating their faces, they embraced each other, feeling the warmth of their triumph and love.

Outro:
With laughter as our armor, and love as our guide,
We conquered the darkness and stood side by side.

In this tale of magic, our bond we'll defend our,
Together forever, our hearts will transcend!

A New Beginning

Hand in hand, they walked away from the battlefield, ready to embrace whatever adventures awaited them next. They knew that as long as they had each other, they could face any challenge with a smile and a laugh.

And so, with hearts full of hope and love, Alarion and Lila ventured forward into their new chapter, where the power of love would always be their greatest ally.

Chapter 40: The Light of Hope

Alarion's determination shines as he faces the enemy, showcasing the power of unity and love. Their shared laughter becomes a beacon of hope amidst the darkness.

The final battle had ended, but the aftermath left Alarion and Lila standing on the brink of a new dawn. The air crackled with the remnants of magic, and the shadows that once haunted their realm had dissipated, leaving behind a promise of peace. As they surveyed the landscape, the sun began to rise, casting warm golden rays over the remnants of the Dark Fortress.

"Look at that," Lila said, her eyes wide with wonder. "It's beautiful."

"It's like the world is celebrating our victory," Alarion replied, a smile breaking across his face. "Though I'm pretty sure the flowers and trees didn't need to throw such a wild party." He pointed to a nearby tree that appeared to have sprouted confetti-like leaves, clearly a side effect of the magical battle.

"Just wait until the squirrels find it!" Lila laughed, imagining the woodland creatures throwing their own celebration.

Their laughter echoed through the quiet clearing, a refreshing sound that pushed away the remnants of fear that had lingered. But amid their lightheartedness, Alarion could feel a shift in the air, as if something unseen was still watching them.

"Do you think it's over?" Lila asked, her voice suddenly serious.

Alarion frowned, his instincts kicking in. "I don't know. We should stay alert. Sometimes darkness has a way of lurking in the corners, even after a victory."

The Song: "Shine On, Brave Hearts"
(A tribute to their love and unity in the face of uncertainty)
Intro:
In the shadows where darkness tried to creep,
We stood together, our hearts won't weep.
With laughter and light, we'll chase away fear,
Hand in hand, forever nearby!
Verse 1:
When the storm clouds gather and the night feels long,
We'll raise our voices, and sing our song.
With every challenge, we'll stand tall,
For love is the answer, it conquers all!

"Let's not let our guard down just yet," Alarion said, scanning the horizon. "We'll take one last look around. Who knows what we might find?"

Chorus:
Shine on, brave hearts, let your spirit ignite,
With courage and love, we'll conquer the night.
Through laughter and tears, we'll light up the way,
Together we'll stand, come what may!

As they walked through the remnants of the battlefield, Alarion felt a surge of hope swell within him. They had faced the darkness together and emerged victorious.

But just as he began to feel comfortable, a chilling wind swept through the clearing, sending shivers down their spines. The shadows shifted once again, and from the depths of the forest, a figure emerged—a familiar face cloaked in darkness.

"Not you again!" Alarion shouted, recognizing the former ally turned adversary, Elysia. "I thought we sent you packing!"

"Oh, darling Alarion, you really should know by now," Elysia purred, her voice smooth yet menacing. "Darkness never truly leaves; it merely waits for the opportune moment to strike!"

The Battle of Wits

Without missing a beat, Lila stepped forward. "You know, you really should consider a new career path. Maybe a life of knitting would suit you better? Less drama, more purls!"

Elysia narrowed her eyes. "Do you think your humor can save you? I am here to reclaim what is mine!"

"Your mind?" Alarion shot back. "Because last I checked, it was lost somewhere in the fog of your bad decisions!"

Verse 2:
With courage, we face the shadows that loom,
For together we shine, dispelling the gloom.
With laughter and magic, we're ready to fight,
With love as our armor, we'll bring forth the light!

"Is that all you've got?" Lila taunted, preparing her magic. "Come on, Elysia! We've faced armies together! You should have a better game plan than just lurking around!"

Elysia scowled, her frustration palpable. "You'll regret underestimating me!" With a flick of her wrist, she unleashed a wave of shadowy magic that curled like smoke toward Alarion and Lila.

The Power of Unity

"Now's our chance!" Alarion shouted, channeling the energy of the Eternal Flame within him.

"Together, Lila!"

They raised their hands, the light of their bond radiating outwards. The shadows recoiled as if burned by the intensity of their connection.

Chorus:
Shine on, brave hearts, let your spirit ignite,
With courage and love, we'll conquer the night.

Through laughter and tears, we'll light up the way,
Together we'll stand, come what may!

As the magic coursed through them, Alarion felt the weight of his love for Lila fueling him. "You may be powerful, Elysia, but love is the strongest magic of all!" He launched forward, their combined light blasting through the darkness toward Elysia.

With a brilliant flash, their light collided with the shadows, illuminating the forest and revealing hidden enemies lurking in the depths. The shadows trembled, and the once-confident Elysia faltered, taken aback by the strength of their unity.

A Moment of Realization

"Why fight against us?" Lila called out. "You could be part of something beautiful instead of hiding in the darkness!"

Elysia paused, uncertainty flickering across her face. "I... I thought power was all that mattered..."

"Power is nothing without love and friendship!" Alarion countered, stepping forward. "Join us! We can create a future together!"

In that moment, Elysia's facade cracked. "What if I can't?"

Outro:
With laughter and light, we'll chase away fear,
Hand in hand, forever near.
So, shine on, brave hearts, let your spirit ignite,
With love and laughter, we'll conquer the night!

The Turning Point

As the light enveloped her, Elysia felt the warmth of their love breaking through the icy shell she had built around her heart. "I...I don't know if I can change," she admitted, her voice trembling.

Lila stepped forward, reaching out a hand. "You don't have to do it alone. Together, we can find a way."

Elysia hesitated but then slowly took Lila's hand, and as she did, a ripple of light spread through the clearing, illuminating the path to redemption. The hidden enemies, realizing their leader's shift in allegiance, began to dissolve into the light.

A New Dawn

With Elysia joining their ranks, the shadows fled into the forest, defeated not just by magic, but by the bonds of friendship and love that had woven together during the fight.

"Looks like we did it," Alarion said, feeling a wave of relief wash over him.

"Of course we did!" Lila chimed; her smile radiant. "With a little humor and a lot of heart!"

Elysia stood at their side, transformed by their acceptance. "Thank you," she said softly, her eyes shining. "For believing in me when I didn't believe in myself."

As the sun fully rose, casting golden rays over the land, Alarion, Lila, and Elysia looked ahead, ready to embrace whatever new adventures awaited them.

Together, they had faced the darkness, laughed in the face of danger, and discovered the true light of hope that resided within unity and love. And in that moment, Alarion knew that no matter what challenges lay ahead, they would face them together, hand in hand, hearts intertwined, shining brighter than any darkness ever could.

Chapter 41: The Awakening Flame

With the enemy vanquished, the Eternal Flame awakens. Alarion and Lila reflect on their journey, realizing that their bond is stronger than ever, full of both love and humor.

The battlefield lay quiet, the echoes of laughter and courage still lingering in the air. Alarion and Lila stood hand in hand, gazing at the remnants of the Dark Fortress, now bathed in golden sunlight. The defeat of Elysia and her shadows had not only restored peace to their realm but also awakened something deep within the heart of the Eternal Flame that they had fought so hard to protect.

"It feels surreal, doesn't it?" Lila said, her voice barely above a whisper as she turned to Alarion. "We actually did it. We faced our fears, battled our enemies, and... lived to tell the tale!"

"Not just lived," Alarion replied, a grin breaking across his face. "We thrived! And you did that incredible thing with your magic at the end. I mean, where did that come from?"

Lila shrugged playfully, a twinkle in her eye. "Oh, you know. Just some light spell I picked up along the way. Nothing fancy." She pretended to wave her hands as if casting a spell, her fingers swirling through the air like a dancing flame.

The Song: "Eternal Flame"
(A celebration of their bond and journey together)
Intro:
In the ashes of the night, we found our way,
Through shadows and doubts, we dared to stay.
With laughter as our guide, and love as our song,

ALARION AND THE ETERNAL FLAME

We'll rise like the dawn, where we both belong!
Verse 1:
With every battle fought, we grew ever stronger,
Together we faced the storm, singing our song.
Through the darkness and the light, hand in hand we'll roam,
In the warmth of the flame, we've found our home!

Just as Alarion was about to respond, the ground beneath them began to tremble, a gentle vibration that pulsed like a heartbeat. Lila's eyes widened. "Alarion, what's happening?"

"I think it's the Eternal Flame!" he exclaimed, taking a step back as a soft glow erupted from the center of the battlefield. The ground split open, revealing a swirling vortex of light that rose into the sky, illuminating the entire realm.

A Sudden Shift

From the depths of the flame, a magnificent figure emerged, radiant and powerful. It was the Spirit of the Eternal Flame, her presence filling the air with warmth and peace. She looked at Alarion and Lila, her gaze filled with pride. "Brave hearts, you have awakened the true essence of the Eternal Flame through your courage and unity."

Alarion felt a surge of emotion. "We only did what was necessary! We fought for our home, our love, and each other!"

Chorus:
Eternal flame, forever bright,
In the darkest of times, you are our light.
Through laughter and love, we'll rise and we'll stand,
Together forever, hand in hand!

"Indeed, love is the strongest magic of all," the Spirit continued, her voice echoing like a gentle breeze. "It binds us, fuels us, and empowers us to face any darkness that may come."

Lila glanced at Alarion, her heart swelling with warmth. "She's right, you know. I couldn't have done it without you."

"Or without your magical spark!" Alarion winked, causing Lila to laugh. "You're the one who turned our fears into something beautiful."

The Unexpected Reunion

As they basked in the glow of the Eternal Flame, a sudden commotion erupted from the trees nearby. Alarion and Lila turned to see a group of familiar faces emerging—friends they thought had been lost in the chaos.

"Did someone order a hero's welcome?" shouted Finn, his arms wide open as he sprinted towards them. Behind him were Gwendolyn, Thorne, and even the wise old wizard, Eldrin, who had guided them on their journey.

"Where have you all been?" Lila exclaimed, rushing to embrace them.

"Just taking care of some business in the shadows," Thorne replied with a smirk. "But we heard the news and couldn't resist joining the victory parade!"

Verse 2:
From the ashes we rise, like the sun in the sky,
With friends by our side, we'll always fly high.
Through trials and laughter, we're never alone,
In the heart of the flame, we've all found our home!

"Together, we are stronger," Gwendolyn added, her eyes sparkling with determination. "With the Eternal Flame awakened, we can ensure that darkness never returns."

A New Dawn

The Spirit of the Eternal Flame smiled at the gathering of friends. "Your bond is a testament to the power of unity. With the light of your love and laughter, you will protect this realm and inspire those who come after."

Alarion felt the warmth of her words wrap around him like a comforting blanket. "What do we do now?" he asked, glancing at his friends and Lila.

The Spirit raised her hands, and the flame pulsed gently. "Continue your journey. Explore the lands, share your stories, and let your love shine like the Eternal Flame. The world is vast, and many need to hear your tale."

Chorus:
Eternal flame, forever bright,
In the darkest of times, you are our light.
Through laughter and love, we'll rise and we'll stand,
Together forever, hand in hand!

The Final Embrace

As the sun dipped lower in the sky, Alarion turned to Lila, his heart racing. "Are you ready for this?"

"Ready for anything," she replied, squeezing his hand. "As long as we're together."

With laughter echoing in the air and the Spirit of the Eternal Flame watching over them, Alarion and Lila shared a tender kiss, the warmth of their love igniting the spark of hope that would guide them through every adventure to come.

The Outro:
So, let's light the way, with laughter and cheer,
For the flame of our love will always be nearby.
With friends by our side, and courage in hand,
We'll conquer the world, as we make our stand!

As the Eternal Flame flickered around them, Alarion knew that they had not only vanquished their enemies but had also discovered the true strength of their bond. Together, they would face whatever awaited them, knowing that love would always light the path ahead.

Chapter 42: A New Beginning

With the Flame restored, Alarion must decide what to do next. Lila's quirky suggestions lead to a humorous yet heartfelt conversation about their future together.

The glow of the Eternal Flame danced across the horizon as Alarion and Lila stood atop the hill overlooking the valley. The echoes of laughter and victory still lingered in the air, a reminder of the battle they had fought together. But now, with peace restored and the warmth of the flame enveloping them, the question lingered: what came next?

"Okay, let's think about our next adventure," Lila said, her eyes sparkling with mischief. "How about we start a traveling circus? I could juggle enchanted apples, and you could be the 'Mystical Fire-Breather!'"

Alarion chuckled, imagining himself in a brightly colored costume, spitting fire like a dragon. "Somehow, I don't think that's quite my style. Besides, what if I set my eyebrows on fire? You'd have to fix that!"

Intro:
In the glow of the flame, we dream anew,
With laughter and love, there's nothing we can't do.
Through thick and thin, with friends by our side,
We'll chart a new course, and together we'll glide!
A Quirky Conversation

Lila plopped down on the grass, a wide grin on her face. "Okay, okay! How about we open a bakery? 'Alarion's Enchanted Treats'! I can picture it now: magical muffins that make you dance!"

"Or pastries that cause spontaneous singing," Alarion added, feigning seriousness. "Imagine the chaos in the kitchen! Flour everywhere, and everyone singing off-key!"

"Exactly!" Lila laughed, rolling onto her back and looking up at the sky. "But what if our singing is so enchanting that it brings the whole town together for a concert? We could have the 'Festival of Flavors!'"

"Festival of Flavors sounds amazing! But do we have to bake everything?" Alarion mused, picturing the sweet aroma of treats wafting through the air. "I mean, I'm more of a 'taste tester' than a baker."

The Song: "A New Beginning"
(A light-hearted reflection on their future together)
Verse 1:
With the flame restored, we've got dreams to chase,
Hand in hand, we'll explore every place.
From circus tents to bakeries, oh what a thrill,
With laughter and love, we'll climb every hill!

Just then, a sudden rustle in the bushes caught their attention. They exchanged curious glances, their playful mood interrupted. "Did you hear that?" Lila whispered; her playful tone replaced with intrigue.

"Could be a stray cat, or maybe a squirrel plotting world domination," Alarion said, winking.

Lila burst into laughter, imagining a squirrel wearing a tiny crown. "Or a tiny villain with a dastardly plan! I'll bet he's trying to steal the flame!"

An Unexpected Showdown

Before they could react further, a figure emerged from the bushes—a ragged-looking man with a wild beard and dirt-stained clothes. He brandished a makeshift sword, and his eyes glimmered with desperation. "You there! Hand over the Eternal Flame, or face my wrath!"

Alarion and Lila exchanged bemused looks. "Seriously?" Alarion said, raising an eyebrow. "That sword looks like it was made from a tree branch."

"It's an ancient weapon!" the man insisted, brandishing his sword dramatically, but not quite achieving the intended effect. "And I am the dreaded... um... what was I again?"

"Dreaded... Squirrel King?" Lila quipped, trying to keep a straight face.

The man's face fell as he blinked at her. "No, wait! I'm the Sworn Enemy of the Flame! Yes, that's it!"

Chorus:
With laughter and love, we'll stand side by side,
Facing every challenge, with hearts open wide.
Together we'll conquer, whatever may come,
In this new beginning, our hearts will beat as one!

A Battle of Wits

Alarion stepped forward, trying to hold back his laughter. "Listen, friend, we don't want any trouble. You can't just barge in here and demand the Eternal Flame!"

"But... but it's mine by destiny!" the man cried, waving his sword wildly.

Lila put her hands on her hips, her eyes sparkling with mischief. "If you want the flame, you'll have to defeat us in a duel! But first, how about we settle this with a little game? A riddle contest?"

"A riddle contest?" Alarion said, incredulous.

"Absolutely! If you can stump us, we'll consider your request," Lila replied, grinning.

The man, now visibly confused but intrigued, nodded eagerly. "Very well! I accept your challenge!"

The Riddle Contest

"Okay, here's my riddle," the man said, puffing out his chest. "What has keys but can't open locks?"

"An enchanted piano!" Lila shouted, laughing.

"Okay, fine! My turn!" Alarion said, clearly enjoying the absurdity. "What runs but never walks, has a mouth but never talks?"

"A river!" Lila replied, feeling the excitement.

After a few rounds of this light-hearted banter, the man slumped down on the grass, utterly defeated but smiling. "Alright, you win. I never stood a chance against you two."

The Resolution

"Why don't you join us instead?" Alarion suggested, extending a hand. "We're looking to start a bakery. Want to help? We could use some—um—creative flair!"

"Creative flair? I can do that!" the man said, his face lighting up. "I've always dreamed of being a pastry chef!"

"Welcome aboard, then!" Lila said, clapping her hands together. "But you'll have to promise not to steal the Eternal Flame. It's more useful in the kitchen than as a weapon, trust me."

A Heartfelt Moment

As they sat down together, sharing stories and laughter, Alarion looked at Lila, feeling a swell of affection. "I love how we turn everything into an adventure, even when it gets silly."

Lila smiled warmly. "Life's too short to take everything seriously. Besides, with you, every day is an adventure."

Outro:
So, here's to new beginnings, with laughter and cheer,
With friends by our side, there's nothing to fear.
With love in our hearts, we'll conquer each day,

In this beautiful journey, together we'll stay!

With the sun setting behind them, Alarion and Lila knew that whatever awaited them in the future, they would face it together—hand in hand, heart to heart, and with laughter guiding their way. The flame was not just a source of power; it was a symbol of their love, their unity, and the beautiful journey that lay ahead.

Chapter 43: The Journey Home

Alarion and Lila embark on their journey home, sharing laughter and stories. Their relationship blossoms as they navigate the ups and downs of life together.

As Alarion and Lila began their trek home, the sun dipped low in the sky, casting a warm golden hue over the land. The Eternal Flame flickered brightly in Alarion's pack, a constant reminder of their victory and the bond they had forged through laughter and trials. With each step, they shared stories, memories, and dreams, weaving their futures together like the intricate patterns of a tapestry.

"Do you remember the time we accidentally turned that village's fountain into chocolate?"

Lila giggled, her eyes sparkling with mischief.

Alarion chuckled, shaking his head. "How could I forget? The villagers were both thrilled and horrified! I think some of them were contemplating how to bottle it."

"Or how to swim in it!" Lila replied, laughing. "I can still see that old man trying to paddle in chocolate, splashing everywhere!"

Intro:
With every step we take, together we'll roam,
Through laughter and stories, we'll find our way home.
In the dance of the stars, we'll twirl and spin,
With love in our hearts, let the journey begin!
A Song for the Road

As the road stretched before them, Lila suddenly broke into song, her voice light and melodic, perfectly capturing the spirit of their adventure.

Verse 1:
On the road to home, where the wildflowers bloom,
With laughter and love, we'll chase away the gloom.
Side by side, we'll conquer the day,
With every heartbeat, come what may!

"Very poetic, my dear bard!" Alarion teased, a grin spreading across his face. "You might just have to add 'professional singer' to your résumé!"

Lila twirled, her dress swirling around her like petals in the wind. "I'll have you know, I'm a multi-talented artist! But this is more about us, not just me!"

Chorus:
Through valleys and mountains, hand in hand we'll go,
Facing every challenge, together we'll grow.
With joy in our hearts and adventure our song,
We'll dance through the night, where we both belong!

Unexpected Trouble

Suddenly, as if summoned by their joy, a group of shadowy figures emerged from the trees lining the path. Alarion's playful demeanor shifted to one of alertness. "Looks like our joyful serenade has attracted some unwanted attention."

"Who are they?" Lila asked, her expression turning serious. "They don't look like friendly folk."

"Probably those bandits we heard about in the last village," Alarion said, squaring his shoulders. "Time to show them that this bard and his muse won't be taken lightly."

The leader of the group stepped forward, sneering. "Hand over the Eternal Flame, and we might just let you keep your heads!"

ALARION AND THE ETERNAL FLAME

Alarion shared a quick glance with Lila, both ready for action. "Let's show them what we've got!"

A Battle with Humor

"Are we fighting or singing?" Lila quipped, preparing her spells. "Because I can do both!"

"I'd say a little of both would be perfect!" Alarion replied, brandishing his staff with a flair. "Let's give them a show!"

Verse 2:
With courage in our hearts and a spark in our eyes,
We'll dance through the battle, like stars in the skies.
With laughter as our shield and love as our sword,
We'll fight for each other, let's strike the right chord!

Lila waved her hand dramatically, conjuring shimmering notes that flew toward their foes like shooting stars. The bandits stumbled back, confused and momentarily dazzled by the magical display.

"Is that all you've got?" Alarion shouted, launching a stream of flame from his staff that sizzled in the air, creating a wall of warmth around them.

"Now for the grand finale!" Lila grinned, and with a flourish, she sent a flurry of musical notes that exploded into colorful fireworks, dazzling the bandits and illuminating the night sky.

Chorus:
Through the fire and the laughter, we'll stand side by side,
With love as our armor, we'll take them for a ride.
For every blow they strike, we'll dance and we'll sing,
With the power of our hearts, we'll conquer everything!

The Turning Point

As the battle raged on, Lila and Alarion fought as one, weaving between the attackers with grace. Alarion spotted the bandit leader, who was trying to rally his comrades with increasingly frantic shouts.

"Hey! You!" Alarion shouted, pointing dramatically. "Your swordsmanship is as good as your choice of friends!"

The leader turned, momentarily thrown off by Alarion's taunts. "What do you mean?"

"Didn't your mother tell you not to play with shadows?" Lila added, sending another wave of magical energy his way. The bandit stumbled backward, a look of shock and confusion on his face.

The Final Push

Realizing they were losing; the bandits began to retreat. Alarion and Lila seized the moment. "Let's finish this!" Alarion called.

With one final surge of power, Lila and Alarion combined their magic. They created a massive wave of light that swept toward the retreating bandits, causing them to scatter into the trees, vanishing into the shadows.

A Moment of Victory

With the threat gone, Alarion and Lila stood together, panting and laughing. "Did we just defeat a band of shadowy bandits with song and laughter?" Alarion asked disbelief etched on his face.

Lila grinned, wiping a tear of joy from her eye. "I think we did! And we did it together!"

Outro:
Now the path is clear, our spirits set free,
With laughter and love, it's just you and me.
Through the trials we face, we'll find our way home,
Together forever, no longer alone!

The Journey Continues

As they resumed their journey home, hand in hand, Alarion felt a warmth that transcended the glow of the Eternal Flame. "You know," he said, glancing sideways at Lila, "with you by my side, every adventure feels like a new beginning."

Lila squeezed his hand, her eyes shimmering with affection. "And with you, I know I'll never face a challenge alone."

Together, they walked under the starlit sky, their laughter echoing into the night, ready to embrace whatever awaited them on their journey home. Each step forward was a promise of love, laughter, and the endless adventures that lay ahead.

Chapter 44: The Celebration

A grand celebration awaits them in Emberwood. Amid the festivities, Alarion and Lila find moments of intimacy and humor, deepening their connection as they embrace their victory.

The sun dipped below the horizon as Alarion and Lila entered the vibrant village of Emberwood. Lanterns of every color hung from trees and rooftops, illuminating the streets with a warm, welcoming glow. The air was filled with the sounds of laughter, music, and the tantalizing aroma of roasted meats and sweet pastries. The villagers had gathered to celebrate not just the return of their beloved heroes but the restoration of hope after the battle against darkness.

"Wow, this place knows how to throw a party!" Lila exclaimed, her eyes sparkling with excitement. "I feel like I'm in a fairy tale!"

"Let's make the most of it, then!" Alarion replied, grinning as he twirled her around in a playful spin. "But first, let's grab some food before we dance our hearts out."

As they walked through the bustling streets, Lila spotted a stall piled high with colorful sweets. "Look at those! Can we please have some?" She pointed eagerly, her eyes wide with anticipation.

"Only if you promise to share!" Alarion said with a chuckle, knowing full well she wouldn't hold back.

A Sweet Treat

With their hands filled with sugary confections, they wandered toward the village square, where musicians were playing lively tunes. Lila took a bite of her candied apple and exclaimed, "This is delicious! We should have these for every victory celebration!"

Alarion laughed. "And what if we win a lot? We might end up with a candy empire!"

Lila giggled, the sound echoing through the square. "I can already see it: 'Lila's Luscious Candies'! We'd be millionaires, and I'd need a sparkly crown!"

Intro:
In the heart of Emberwood, where laughter fills the air,
We celebrate our victories, without a single care.
With sweets and music guiding our way,
Together we'll dance, come what may!

A Dance of Joy

As the sun fully set, the villagers invited Alarion and Lila to join in the festivities. The music swelled, and Lila pulled Alarion onto the dance floor, where couples spun and twirled under the stars.

Verse 1:
With every twirl and every spin,
We'll laugh together, let the fun begin.
With joy in our hearts and stars in our eyes,
In the dance of the night, let our spirits rise!

"Just follow my lead!" Lila shouted over the music; her eyes alight with mischief. Alarion nodded, trying to keep up with her exuberance. They danced like no one was watching, spinning wildly and laughing until their sides hurt.

"Don't step on my toes!" Alarion joked, narrowly avoiding a misstep.

Lila mockingly gasped, "I would never! Only if you stomp on my heart!"

Chorus:
Let's dance in the moonlight, hand in hand,
With laughter and love, together we'll stand.
In the joy of this moment, we'll find our way,
As we celebrate love on this glorious day!

A Shadow in the Celebration

As the night wore on, the atmosphere buzzed with excitement. But in the shadows of the festival, not all was well. A group of strangers lingered at the edge of the celebration; their eyes filled with malice. Alarion spotted them, his senses sharpening.

"Lila," he whispered, leaning close, "I think we have trouble. Those people don't look like they're here to celebrate."

"What do we do?" Lila asked, her voice dropping to a serious tone.

"Stay close to me," Alarion instructed, scanning the area. "We might need to handle this."

The Clash of Shadows

Just as the music reached a crescendo, the strangers made their move. They surged forward, knocking over tables and sending villagers scattering in fear. Alarion and Lila stood firm, ready to defend their newfound friends.

"Time for a little action!" Alarion declared, brandishing his staff as the crowd erupted into chaos.

Lila quickly conjured a barrier of light, shielding a group of frightened villagers. "I've got your back, Alarion! Just give me a signal!"

With a determined nod, Alarion charged at the nearest intruder, summoning flames that danced around him. "You picked the wrong celebration to crash!"

Verse 2:
In the heat of the moment, with laughter and fear,
We'll fight together, with love drawing near.
With every blow we strike, we'll find our way,
Through darkness and danger, come what may!

Lila joined the fray, weaving magic into her movements. She sent sparks flying, creating dazzling illusions that confused their attackers. "Ever seen a fire-breathing dragon?" she shouted, conjuring a giant, glowing dragon that roared with laughter.

"What? I thought we were doing a unicorn!" Alarion exclaimed, ducking a blow from a bandit.

"Unicorns are so last year!" she teased, giggling even as she fought.

The Turning Point

The battle intensified, but through the chaos, Alarion and Lila found a rhythm. They moved in tandem, their hearts beating as one. With every spell and strike, their bond deepened, each laugh breaking the tension around them.

Just then, the leader of the attackers stepped forward, his eyes filled with rage. "You think you can protect them? You're nothing but a pair of fools!"

Alarion stepped up, flames swirling around him. "Maybe so, but fools have a way of winning when they fight for what they love!"

Chorus:
In the heat of battle, with hearts full of light,
We'll dance with our magic; we'll stand up and fight.
For every ounce of courage, we'll make our stand,
Together forever, hand in hand!

The Final Showdown

With a final rallying cry, Alarion and Lila unleashed their combined power. They summoned a wave of light that enveloped the attackers, forcing them back. The leader sneered but faltered as he faced the united front of the couple.

"Enough!" he shouted, raising his weapon, but it was too late. With a flick of Alarion's wrist, the flame surged forward, surrounding the bandits in a brilliant light that left them scrambling for cover.

The villagers, emboldened by their bravery, rallied behind Alarion and Lila, joining the fight against the intruders. With one final push, the bandits retreated, disappearing into the night with a promise of vengeance.

A Celebration Renewed

As the dust settled, the villagers erupted into cheers. Lila and Alarion stood at the center of the square, panting but victorious. "That was quite the celebration," Alarion said, grinning at Lila.

"Nothing like a little drama to liven things up!" she replied, her laughter ringing in the night air. "But I think I preferred the dancing part better."

"And the sweets!" Alarion added, pulling her close.

Outro:
Now the night is ours, with laughter in the air,
We celebrate together, without a single care.
Through trials we've faced, our love will shine bright,
In the heart of Emberwood, we'll dance through the night!

As the music resumed, Alarion and Lila stepped back onto the dance floor, joining the villagers in celebration. Their laughter filled the air, the joy of victory igniting their spirits anew. Amid the festivities, they found moments of intimacy, sharing sweet kisses and playful banter that only deepened their connection.

With the stars shining above, they knew this was just the beginning of their journey together, filled with love, laughter, and endless adventures. The world was vast, but with each other by their side, they could conquer anything.

Chapter 45: Whispers of the Heart

In the aftermath of their adventure, Alarion and Lila explore their feelings for each other. Their light-hearted banter reveals the depth of their bond, teasing the potential for romance.

The night was calm as the stars twinkled above the quiet woods, their gentle light casting a silver glow on the path ahead. Alarion and Lila walked side by side, the soft crunch of leaves beneath their feet the only sound breaking the stillness. The air was cool, and a light breeze whispered through the trees, carrying with it the scent of pine and earth. It had been a long and eventful day, filled with celebrations, battles, and the overwhelming joy of victory. But now, in the aftermath, something else lingered between them—something unspoken but felt in every glance, every smile.

Lila broke the silence first, her voice light and teasing. "So, Alarion, do you always save the world with a charming grin and a flair for dramatics, or is that just for special occasions?"

Alarion chuckled, his eyes twinkling with amusement. "I like to think it's a natural gift. But you, Lila, you steal the show with your magical fireworks. I'm starting to think you just like showing off."

She nudged him playfully. "Maybe I do. But you can't deny it was effective! Besides, who else can say they've summoned a glowing dragon and won a dance contest in the same day?"

Their laughter echoed through the forest, but beneath the surface of their banter, something deeper stirred. Every time their eyes met; a quiet tension hummed between them—a spark waiting to ignite.

A Song in the Air

As they continued walking, Lila's eyes drifted to the stars. "You know," she mused, "I've always wondered if the stars sing. Sometimes, when it's this quiet, I swear I can hear them."

Alarion raised an eyebrow, intrigued. "The stars? Singing?"

Lila grinned, her voice softening. "Yeah. I imagine they hum little melodies, whispering secrets to those who care to listen."

Without warning, she began to hum a tune, soft and sweet, as if testing the air. Alarion, charmed, listened closely.

Intro:
In the stillness of the night, under the sky so bright,
A melody whispers low, where only the heart will go.
With every star, a secret lies, a song sung in the skies.
If you listen closely, you'll hear, the music drawing near.

Alarion couldn't help but smile as her hum grew into a soft melody. He glanced at her, seeing the playful joy on her face, and without hesitation, he joined in, adding lyrics as the song formed in the air around them.

Verse 1:
In the glow of the stars above, we find our way through love,
With laughter in our hearts, together we'll make our start.
Through every trial we've faced, side by side we've embraced,
And now the whispers of the night, guide us to the light.

Lila's laughter bubbled up, surprised at how quickly Alarion had joined her impromptu song. "Not bad, hero," she teased. "I didn't know you could sing."

"Only for you," he replied with a wink, causing her to blush slightly, though she quickly hid it behind a playful grin.

Chorus:
With whispers of the heart, we'll never be apart,
The stars will lead us home, no matter where we roam.
In the quiet of the night, our love will shine so brightly,

ALARION AND THE ETERNAL FLAME

With every whispered word, our song will be heard.

Hidden Feelings, Revealed

Their song faded into the quiet of the woods, but the warmth it left lingered. Alarion's hand brushed Lila's, and for a moment, they both froze. The accidental touch felt like a spark, sending a shiver down their spines.

"So," Lila began, her voice unusually soft, "about today... I mean, we've fought battles before, but this one felt... different."

Alarion nodded, his gaze steady on her. "It was different. Not because of the enemies or the magic, but because of us."

Lila's eyes widened, caught off guard by his straightforwardness. "Us?"

Alarion smiled gently, his tone light but sincere. "Lila, we've been through so much together. Every battle, every laugh, every ridiculous plan you've come up with—it's all led to this moment. And I think... I think there's more to this—more to us."

For once, Lila was at a loss for words. She stared at him, her heart pounding in her chest, and in that moment, all her teasing, all her bravado, melted away. "I... I think so too," she admitted, her voice barely a whisper.

Alarion took a step closer, his eyes searching hers. "I've never been good with words, not like you. But I know what I feel. And what I feel for you—it's more than just friendship, Lila. It's something I can't ignore anymore."

The Battle of Words and Hearts

Before Lila could respond, a rustling sound interrupted the moment. They both tensed, instinctively reaching for their weapons, but what emerged from the shadows wasn't a friend—it was a group of cloaked figures, their eyes glinting with malice.

"Great," Lila muttered under her breath, rolling her eyes. "Just when we were getting to the good part."

The strangers stepped forward; weapons drawn. "You thought the battle was over," their leader sneered. "But we've been waiting for this moment—when your guard is down, and your hearts are distracted."

Alarion's hand tightened around his staff. "Big mistake," he growled. "We're never distracted when it comes to defending what matters."

Lila, despite the looming threat, couldn't resist a smirk. "Guess you'll just have to wait a little longer for the romantic confession," she quipped. "I've got some bandits to fry."

Verse 2:
In the heat of the fight, we'll shine our light,
With love and magic strong, we'll right the wrong.
No matter what may come, we'll never run,
Together we stand tall, we'll fight them all.

The fight erupted with a burst of magic and steel. Alarion and Lila moved in sync, their bond evident in every motion. Lila sent waves of light crashing into the attackers, while Alarion's flames danced in the air, a blazing shield of protection around them.

The battle was fierce, but it was short-lived. The strangers, underestimating the power of a united front, soon found themselves retreating into the shadows from which they came.

Love's Quiet Victory

As the last of the attackers fled, the forest returned to its peaceful stillness. Alarion turned to Lila, his chest heaving from the exertion, but his eyes were soft. "Now, where were we?"

Lila laughed, wiping a stray lock of hair from her face. "I believe you were about to make a grand romantic declaration."

"Right." Alarion stepped closer, his hand brushing against hers once more, but this time, it lingered. "I'm in love with you, Lila. I think I have been for a long time."

Lila's heart raced, but her smile was soft and genuine. "Took you long enough," she teased, her voice barely a whisper as she closed the distance between them.

Outro:
With whispers of the heart, we'll never be apart,
The stars will lead us home, no matter where we roam.
In the quiet of the night, our love will shine so brightly,
With every whispered word, our song will be heard.

Their lips met in a soft, lingering kiss, and in that moment, the world faded away. It was just them—no enemies, no battles, no magic. Just two hearts finding their way to each other, guided by the whispers of the night.

As they pulled apart, Alarion smiled, his forehead resting against hers. "I guess we'll have to save the next battle for tomorrow."

Lila grinned, her eyes twinkling. "Good. Because right now, I'd rather just enjoy the quiet—and maybe one more song."

Hand in hand, they continued their walk through the woods, the whispers of their hearts guiding them toward whatever adventure lay ahead.

Chapter 46: A Gift of Flame

Alarion creates a special gift for Lila, a symbol of their journey and love. The humorous mishaps during the crafting process led to heartfelt moments and laughter.

The day was crisp, the sun casting golden light over the hills as Alarion worked tirelessly in the makeshift forge deep in the heart of Emberwood. Sweat beaded on his brow as he hammered the metal, sparks flying in every direction. The Eternal Flame flickered nearby, a reminder of the power they had harnessed and the journey they had endured. Yet today, the flame wasn't for battle or magic—it was for something far more personal.

Alarion smiled to himself, the memory of Lila's laugh ringing in his ears. This wasn't just any project. It was a gift—something to symbolize everything they had been through together, from their first bickering encounter to the moment their hearts intertwined. But crafting something like this wasn't easy, especially when magical flames and metal were involved.

"What could go wrong?" he muttered to himself, wiping his hands on his tunic, leaving a streak of soot across his cheek. "It's only a gift for the most unpredictable person I know..."

As if on cue, Lila's voice echoed from behind him. "Talking to yourself now, are we? That's the first sign of madness, you know."

Alarion whirled around, nearly knocking over the bucket of water beside him. Lila stood at the entrance of the forge, arms crossed and an amused grin tugging at her lips. She was clearly enjoying herself.

"Oh, you know me," Alarion replied with a sheepish grin. "Just thinking out loud. What brings you here?"

"I could ask you the same thing," she said, walking closer and peering over his shoulder to see what he was working on. "You've been avoiding me all morning. And here I thought we were past the whole 'keeping secrets' phase."

Alarion hastily tried to cover the object he was working on, but Lila was quicker. Her eyes lit up when she caught sight of the half-finished creation on the anvil.

"Is that... are you making something for me?" she asked a note of curiosity and delight creeping into her voice.

"Uh... maybe," Alarion stammered, scratching the back of his neck. "It's, um, a surprise."

Lila's grin widened. "A surprise? Now you've really piqued my interest."

The Crafting Mishaps Begin

Alarion turned back to the forge, trying to maintain his focus. The truth was, that crafting wasn't exactly his forte. Sure, he could wield a sword, cast a spell, and save the day—but making something by hand? That was an entirely different challenge.

"I'm guessing this isn't going as smoothly as you hoped?" Lila teased, leaning against a nearby workbench, her eyes twinkling.

Alarion sighed, shaking his head. "You could say that. The Eternal Flame is a bit... temperamental when it comes to forging."

As if to prove his point, a sudden burst of fire shot from the forge, singeing the edge of his tunic. Alarion yelped, quickly patting out the flames, while Lila dissolved into a fit of laughter.

"Maybe I should help," she offered between giggles. "You know, before you set yourself on fire again."

"No, no, I've got this," Alarion insisted, though his tone betrayed his own doubts. "This is something I need to do myself. It's important."

Lila raised an eyebrow, her expression softening. "Important, huh? Alright, I'll leave you to it. But just so you know, I'm very curious now."

She gave him one last playful smile before turning and leaving the forge, her laughter still echoing in the air. Alarion watched her go, feeling both relieved and even more determined. This had to be perfect.

A Song of Flame

As the day wore on, Alarion worked tirelessly, but with every swing of the hammer, another mishap seemed to occur. The metal warped in strange ways, the magic of the Eternal Flame making the crafting process unpredictable. At one point, the entire project caught fire, forcing Alarion to frantically douse it with water while muttering a string of curses under his breath.

Frustrated but undeterred, he wiped the sweat from his brow and took a deep breath. Maybe what this needed wasn't brute force or magic. Maybe... it needed heart.

Humming to himself, Alarion began to think of a song—a song that embodied everything he felt for Lila, their journey, and the gift he was trying to create. As he hummed, the flames in the forge seemed to calm, the metal responding more smoothly to his touch.

Intro:
From fire's light and love's embrace,
A gift is born from time and space.
With every swing, with every beat,
Our hearts, they find their rhythm sweet.

Alarion smiled as the words flowed into his mind. The rhythm of his hammer strikes matched the tune, and the crafting process seemed to take on a life of its own.

Verse 1:
Through battles fought and nights so long,
We've found our way, where we belong.

With laughter shared and moments bright,
Our love is forged in endless light.
Chorus:
With flames that burn, but never die,
Our hearts will soar beyond the sky.
In every spark, in every glow,
Our love will guide us where we go.

The metal gleamed brighter as the song continued, almost as if the Eternal Flame itself was listening. Alarion felt his frustrations melt away, replaced by a deep sense of purpose. This gift wasn't just a token—it was a piece of his heart.

Verse 2:
With every step, with every turn,
The fires of love, they brightly burn.
And though the road may twist and bend,
Our love will carry to the end.
Chorus:
With flames that burn, but never die,
Our hearts will soar beyond the sky.
In every spark, in every glow,
Our love will guide us where we go.

The Gift Revealed

Hours later, as the sun dipped below the horizon, Alarion finally stepped back from the anvil, a satisfied grin spreading across his face. In his hands, he held a pendant—small but intricate, with a delicate flame-shaped design that flickered faintly with the magic of the Eternal Flame. It shimmered in the fading light, capturing the essence of everything he had poured into it: love, laughter, and the unbreakable bond he shared with Lila.

Just as he finished, Lila reappeared at the entrance, her eyes immediately drawn to the glowing pendant in his hands. "Wow," she whispered, her usual playful tone replaced by awe. "Is that... for me?"

Alarion nodded, feeling his heart race a little faster. "It's a symbol," he explained. "Of us. Of everything we've been through together. The flame won't ever go out, just like... well, just like how I feel about you."

Lila's eyes softened, her teasing smile replaced by something warmer, deeper. "You really made this for me?"

"I did," Alarion said, stepping forward. "And, uh... it wasn't easy. I may have accidentally set myself on fire once or twice."

Lila laughed, the sound like music to his ears. "That sounds about right."

He carefully placed the pendant around her neck, his fingers lingering on her skin for just a moment. The flame glowed softly against her collarbone, its light reflecting in her eyes.

"It's beautiful," she whispered, her voice filled with emotion. "Thank you, Alarion."

He smiled, his heart swelling with affection. "You're welcome."

The Final Battle

Just as the moment turned sweet, the ground beneath them rumbled ominously. Alarion's instincts kicked in immediately. He drew his staff, scanning the area for any signs of danger. From the shadows emerged cloaked figures—hidden enemies who had been watching, waiting for the right time to strike.

"So much for a quiet moment," Lila muttered, drawing her own weapon. "Why do these guys always show up when things are getting romantic?"

Alarion grinned. "Maybe they're jealous."

The battle was fierce but short. The enemies had clearly underestimated the strength of the bond between Alarion and Lila. With the Eternal Flame's power coursing through them, they fought in perfect harmony—every move, every spell, every strike executed with the precision of two souls perfectly in sync.

In the end, the hidden enemies retreated into the shadows, defeated and vanquished.

The Gift of Love

As the dust settled, Alarion turned to Lila, his heart still racing from the battle. "Maybe now we can have a quiet moment."

Lila laughed, stepping closer to him. "I'd like that."

They stood together in the fading light, the warmth of the Eternal Flame flickering between them. Alarion reached for her hand, and Lila smiled, her fingers intertwining with his.

"Thank you for the gift," she whispered. "It's perfect."

Alarion smiled, leaning in to press a soft kiss to her forehead. "So are you."

Outro:
With flames that burn, but never die,
Our hearts will soar beyond the sky.
In every spark, in every glow,
Our love will guide us where we go.

And as the night fell around them, Alarion and Lila stood together, their love as bright and unyielding as the flame that had brought them together.

Chapter 47: The Flame of Love

As they prepare to share their lives together, Alarion and Lila navigate the joys and challenges of love. Their banter reveals the playful side of their relationship.

The sun was setting over the rolling hills of Emberwood, casting a golden glow over the village as Alarion and Lila sat side by side, gazing out at the horizon. It had been weeks since their last battle, and the village had returned to its peaceful rhythm. Yet, for Alarion and Lila, life had taken on a new kind of adventure—one that wasn't about magic or hidden enemies, but about love and the funny, often unpredictable path it took them on.

Lila leaned her head on Alarion's shoulder, sighing contentedly. "You know, I think the hardest battle we've ever fought is figuring out who's going to cook dinner tonight."

Alarion chuckled, wrapping his arm around her. "You're just saying that because I burn everything."

"Well, you did set the soup on fire last week. How is that even possible?" Lila teased, nudging him playfully. "It's soup! It's mostly water!"

Alarion grinned, shaking his head. "It's a special talent. Not everyone can summon flames while making broth."

Their banter was easy and natural. They had been through so much together—facing off against enemies, unlocking ancient powers, and navigating the complicated maze of emotions. Now, with the world at peace for once, they were discovering what it meant to truly be together.

A Dance in the Dark

The night was approaching, and as the sky darkened, the village square began to fill with the soft glow of lanterns. Music floated through the air from the nearby tavern, and a gentle breeze carried the scent of wildflowers. Alarion stood and extended his hand to Lila with a smile.

"Shall we dance?" he asked, his eyes twinkling with playful mischief.

Lila looked up at him with mock suspicion. "Are you planning to step on my feet like last time?"

Alarion laughed, taking her hand and pulling her to her feet. "Only if you step on mine first."

They moved to the rhythm of the music, their bodies swaying in time with the soft melody. The world around them seemed to fade, leaving only the two of them. As they danced, Alarion began to hum a familiar tune, the one they had shared during their last adventure.

Intro:
In the glow of a thousand stars,
We danced through battles near and far.
But here in your arms, I've found my light,
In the warmth of love's gentle fight.

Lila laughed softly, resting her head against his chest. "You're singing again. Is this going to be another one of your 'epic' songs?"

"You love my songs," Alarion said with a grin. "And this one's special. It's just for you."

Verse 1:
Through shadowed woods and starlit skies,
We've faced the dark, and silenced lies.
But nothing's sweeter than your smile,
It makes this journey all worthwhile.

Lila rolled her eyes but couldn't hide the smile spreading across her face. Alarion's voice, while not perfect, carried a warmth that made her heart flutter.

Chorus:
So, hold me close, we'll take it slow,
Through love's great flame, we'll let it grow.
In every laugh, in every sigh,
Together we'll reach beyond the sky.

As the music continued, the other villagers joined in the dancing, but Alarion and Lila were lost in their own world. Every twirl, every step, was filled with joy and love.

Verse 2:
From whispered words to daring fights,
We've found our way through endless nights.
And though the road ahead is long,
With you beside me, I'll stay strong.

Chorus:
So, hold me close, we'll take it slow,
Through love's great flame, we'll let it grow.
In every laugh, in every sigh,
Together we'll reach beyond the sky.

Lila couldn't help but laugh as Alarion tried to spin her, only to stumble over his own feet. She caught him before he fell, the both of them dissolving into laughter.

"You're hopeless," she teased.

"And yet, you still love me," Alarion shot back with a wink.

The Hidden Enemy Strikes

But just as the night seemed perfect, a sudden chill filled the air. Alarion felt it first—the unmistakable presence of dark magic lurking just beyond the edge of the village. His body tensed, and his grip on Lila's hand tightened.

Lila, sensing the shift, glanced at him. "What is it?"

"Something's coming," Alarion said, his voice low.

The village square grew silent as the wind shifted, carrying with it a sinister whisper. From the shadows at the edge of the forest, cloaked figures emerged—strangers with dark intentions. Hidden enemies, waiting for the perfect moment to strike.

"They never let us have a peaceful night, do they?" Lila muttered, reaching for her dagger.

"Nope," Alarion said, drawing his staff. "But they'll regret interrupting our dance."

The strangers moved quickly, their figures shifting like smoke. They charged toward the village, blades drawn, their magic crackling in the air. But Alarion and Lila were ready. This was their home now, and they would protect it together.

The Battle Unfolds

As the attackers rushed forward, Alarion called upon the power of the Eternal Flame. His staff glowed with fiery light, casting a warm glow over the village square. With a single motion, he sent a wave of fire sweeping toward the enemies, forcing them to scatter.

Lila, swift as ever, darted through the chaos, her dagger flashing as she took down one enemy after another. Her movements were graceful, almost like a continuation of their dance from earlier.

"Is this how we fight now?" Lila called out as she ducked under a sword swing. "Turn battles into dances?"

Alarion grinned as he blocked an incoming spell with a shield of flame. "I thought you liked a good dance."

"I do," she replied, kicking an enemy into the dirt. "But I like it better when I'm not being stabbed at."

The battle raged on, but Alarion and Lila fought in perfect sync, their banter keeping the mood light despite the danger. The villagers watched in awe as the couple took down the attackers, their love and teamwork shining through with every move.

But just when it seemed like the fight was over, the leader of the enemies appeared—a towering figure clad in dark armor, his eyes glowing with malevolent magic. He raised his hand, summoning a bolt of dark energy aimed straight at Alarion.

Lila saw it first. Without thinking, she threw herself in front of him, raising her dagger to deflect the blast. The force knocked her backward, sending her crashing into the ground.

"Lila!" Alarion shouted, rushing to her side.

She groaned, sitting up with a grimace. "I'm fine. Just... next time, maybe you can block the evil magic blasts, okay?"

Alarion helped her to her feet, his heart pounding. "I'll try to do better."

Together, they faced the enemy leader. With one final surge of magic, Alarion unleashed the full power of the Eternal Flame, engulfing the dark figure in a whirlwind of fire. The leader screamed, his form dissolving into ash.

The battle was over.

The Flame of Love

As the dust settled, the villagers erupted into cheers. But Alarion didn't care about the victory—his only concern was Lila. He turned to her, his eyes filled with worry.

"Are you sure you're alright?" he asked, his voice soft.

Lila smiled, brushing the dirt from her tunic. "I'm fine, Alarion. I've survived worse."

He reached out, gently tucking a strand of hair behind her ear. "You're incredible, you know that?"

Lila raised an eyebrow, her playful smile returning. "It took you this long to figure that out?"

Alarion laughed, pulling her into his arms. "No, I've known it all along."

They stood there, holding each other, the warmth of the Eternal Flame still flickering around them. The battle was over, but the love they shared had only grown stronger.

Outro:
With flames that burn, but never die,
Our hearts will soar beyond the sky.
In every laugh, in every sigh,
Together, we'll reach beyond the sky.

As the night continued, Alarion and Lila danced once more, their love shining brighter than ever. The flame of their bond would never fade, no matter what challenges or battles lay ahead.

Chapter 48: The Eternal Flame Ceremony

A ceremony to honor the Eternal Flame brings the community together. Alarion and Lila's vows are filled with humor and sincerity, showcasing the strength of their love.

The village of Emberwood had never seen such a grand gathering. The Eternal Flame, burning brightly atop the hill, was the heart of the ceremony, casting its warm, golden glow over the entire valley. Every villager had come out to witness the special occasion—the Eternal Flame Ceremony. But tonight, it wasn't just about the sacred fire that had protected their village for generations. Tonight, it was about Alarion and Lila, whose love had become as legendary as the flame itself.

As the sun began to set, the lanterns were lit, and a path of shimmering light led from the village square to the Eternal Flame. Alarion, standing nervously near the altar, tugged at his tunic for the hundredth time.

"Stop fidgeting, you look fine," grumbled his best friend, Rowan, a smirk on his face.

"I'm not fidgeting," Alarion replied, pulling at the collar of his ceremonial robes. "I just can't breathe in this thing. Whose idea was it to wear all these layers?"

Rowan raised an eyebrow. "Yours. You insisted on 'looking like a proper mage' for your own ceremony."

Alarion groaned, shaking his head. "Next time, I'll go with something more comfortable. Like—like dragonhide."

Rowan clapped him on the back, his grin widening. "Too late for that now. Just try not to set anything on fire."

Across the square, Lila stood with her closest friends, a vision in her flowing gown that shimmered like the stars. She glanced over at Alarion, catching him pulling at his collar again, and laughed softly.

"He's a mess," she said, shaking her head.

Her friend Tessa grinned. "He's only a mess because he loves you."

Lila smiled, her heart swelling with affection. "I know. And that's why he's perfect."

The Vows of Fire and Love

As the music began to play—a soft, lilting tune that filled the night air—Alarion took his place near the Eternal Flame, the fire crackling behind him. The villagers gathered around, their faces glowing with excitement and warmth.

Lila approached the altar, her steps graceful yet lighthearted, as if she were floating. When their eyes met, all the nerves that had been plaguing Alarion seemed to melt away. She was his anchor, his guiding star, and he couldn't believe he was lucky enough to have her by his side.

The village elder, a wise and gentle man named Eamon, stepped forward, his deep voice carrying across the square. "Tonight, we gather not only to honor the Eternal Flame that has protected us for centuries but to witness the vows of two souls bound together by love, laughter, and an unbreakable bond."

Alarion smiled nervously, and Lila, ever the mischievous one, whispered, "Don't trip over your words."

He smirked back. "Only if you promise not to set anything on fire."

They stood before the Eternal Flame, hands clasped together, and the ceremony began.

Alarion's Vow

Taking a deep breath, Alarion began his vow. His voice was steady but filled with emotion as if each word carried the weight of the universe.

Verse 1:
Through darkened woods and stormy nights,
We've faced the world; we've won our fights.
But nothing shines as bright as you,
My guiding flame, forever true.

He paused, grinning sheepishly. "Sorry, I know I said I wouldn't sing."

Lila chuckled, giving his hand a squeeze. "It's fine, as long as you don't make it a habit."

Alarion continued, his eyes never leaving hers.
Chorus:
In the fire's glow, I make this vow,
To love you then, to love you now.
Through laughter, tears, and all that's new,
I choose this life, with only you.

The villagers "aww'd" softly, and Lila rolled her eyes at the sweet sentiment, though her smile gave away how much she loved it.

Lila's Vow

Lila took a step closer, her voice soft but filled with humor and sincerity.

Verse 1:
You're terrible at cooking, can't sew for your life,
You've caused a few explosions, but still—no strife.
But through all the chaos, you've been my light,
Even if you sometimes set soup alight.

The crowd erupted into laughter, and even Alarion had to wipe a tear from his eye, trying not to lose it in the middle of the ceremony.

Lila grinned and continued:
Chorus:

In the fire's glow, I stand by you,
Through all the messes, through all we do.
Your heart is kind, your soul is bright,
I choose you now, for all our nights.

The villagers clapped softly, the warmth of the moment filling the air.

The Battle Unfolds

But just as the ceremony seemed perfect, an unsettling chill filled the air. From the shadows of the forest surrounding Emberwood, a group of cloaked strangers appeared, their faces hidden behind dark masks. Their leader, a tall figure cloaked in black, stepped forward, his voice low and threatening.

"We've come for the Eternal Flame," the leader growled. "And we'll take it by force if we must."

Alarion's heart sank. "Can't we have one night of peace?" he muttered under his breath.

Lila, however, had already drawn her dagger. "Looks like we're going to have to fight for our happily ever after."

Without hesitation, the villagers leaped into action. The attackers rushed toward the altar, their dark magic swirling around them. Alarion raised his staff, summoning a wall of fire to block their path.

"Rowan!" Alarion called. "Take the left flank!"

Rowan, ever the warrior, charged into the fray with his sword drawn, fending off the attackers.

The villagers rallied behind him, forming a defensive line. But the enemies were stronger than anticipated, their dark magic crackling in the air.

Lila, quick as ever, darted through the battlefield, her movements as graceful as when they danced. She took down enemy after enemy, her dagger flashing in the firelight.

But the leader of the attackers had his eyes set on the Eternal Flame. He raised his hands, summoning a dark spell that would extinguish the sacred fire. Alarion saw it just in time.

"No!" he shouted, raising his staff. With a wave of his hand, he unleashed a torrent of flame, colliding with the dark magic in a brilliant display of light and power.

The battle raged on, but with the combined strength of Alarion, Lila, and the villagers, the enemies were pushed back. The leader, seeing he was outmatched, snarled in defeat.

"This isn't over," he hissed before disappearing into the shadows.

As the dust settled and the enemies retreated, the villagers cheered, their voices echoing through the night. Alarion and Lila stood together, breathless but victorious.

The Flame of Love Burns Bright

With the danger passed, the ceremony resumed, though now it felt even more powerful.

Alarion and Lila, having fought side by side once again, stood before the Eternal Flame with renewed determination.

The village elder smiled warmly. "Through fire and battle, your love has proven unbreakable."

Alarion took Lila's hand once more. "So, how about we finish those vows?"

Lila grinned. "I thought you'd never ask."

Outro:
Through battles fought and fires burned,
Our hearts have met, our love's returned.
With every fight, with every flame,
I'll choose you, always the same.

With the vows completed, Alarion and Lila sealed their promises with a kiss, the Eternal Flame burning brighter than ever. The villagers cheered, and the night erupted in celebration.

The ceremony wasn't just about honoring the sacred flame anymore—it was about the flame of love that burned brightly between two souls, destined to face the world together.

As the festivities continued, Alarion looked down at Lila, his heart full. "You know, I think we're pretty good at this whole 'saving the day' thing."

Lila laughed, leaning into him. "Yeah, but next time, can we skip the enemies and go straight to the celebration?"

He kissed her forehead. "Deal."

Chapter 49: The Future Beckons

With their journey complete, Alarion and Lila look toward the future, filled with promise and excitement. Their laughter echoes as they dream of adventures yet to come.

The sun rose gently over Emberwood, casting golden rays over the village, and setting the horizon alight with soft hues of pink and orange. The morning was peaceful—a stark contrast to the battles they had faced, the enemies they had vanquished, and the magic that had tested them. Today, however, was different. It wasn't a day for battles. It was a day for new beginnings.

Alarion stood on the edge of the village, gazing into the distance where the mountains met the sky. His heart felt lighter, as if the weight of their recent trials had been lifted, leaving behind a sense of calm. It wasn't just peace that filled him—it was the quiet excitement of possibility.

Behind him, Lila approached, her footsteps light as always. She wrapped her arms around him from behind, resting her chin on his shoulder.

"You're lost in thought again," she teased softly.

Alarion smiled, turning his head to meet her eyes. "I'm just thinking about what comes next."

Lila raised an eyebrow, playfully nudging him. "Oh, you mean after saving the world from dark forces, fighting shadowy enemies, and nearly setting your robes on fire multiple times?"

He chuckled, his heart swelling with affection. "Yeah, after that. I was thinking about…us."

A Promise of Adventure

They stood there for a moment, wrapped in each other's warmth, watching the world wake up.

"I've been thinking," Alarion began, his voice soft but filled with a spark of excitement. "We've been through so much, Lila. Every battle, every challenge, every ridiculous mess we've gotten ourselves into—"

"Mostly your fault," she interrupted with a smirk.

He grinned, nodding. "Mostly my fault, but we've come out stronger every time. And now, we're here, together. But what if this isn't the end of our journey? What if it's just the beginning?"

Lila's eyes twinkled with mischief, the same playful gleam that had first drawn him to her. "What exactly are you proposing, Alarion? Another grand adventure? A quest to the unknown? A battle against even more terrifying enemies?"

Alarion turned to face her fully, his gaze steady and filled with affection. "Yes. All of that. But I'm also proposing...a future together. No matter what comes next, no matter how many more enemies we face or how many mountains we climb, I want to face it all with you."

For a moment, Lila was silent, her heart skipping a beat. Then, in true Lila fashion, she leaned closer, whispering in his ear, "You had me at 'mostly my fault.'"

They laughed, their voices mingling with the wind, a sound so pure it felt like magic.

The Song of Their Future

As they sat down on a grassy hill, watching the sun climb higher, Alarion picked up his lute—a gift from Rowan, who claimed it would help Alarion "charm more than just magical creatures." He had no intention of becoming a bard, but there was something about this moment that called for a song.

He strummed a few soft chords, and Lila gave him a teasing smile. "Oh, this should be good."

He cleared his throat dramatically. "I'll have you know, I've been working on this song for at least...five minutes."

Lila giggled, crossing her legs as she leaned in, eager to hear what he had come up with.

Intro:
We've danced with danger, and fought the night,
We've laughed through fear and held each other tight.
Now the world is wide, our hearts set free,
What lies ahead, just you and me.

Alarion grinned as he moved into the next part, his voice soft but steady.

Verse 1:
Through battles fought, and lands unknown,
You've been my guide, my heart, my home.
No storm too strong, no spell too wild,
With you, life's always worth the while.

Lila's smile softened as she listened, her heart swelling with affection.

Chorus:
So, let's chase the stars, let's sail the seas,
Face every foe with love and ease.
The future's bright, the road is long,
But together, we'll always belong.

As Alarion played, his fingers moving deftly over the strings, Lila found herself lost in the melody, in the promise of what lay ahead.

Verse 2:
From mountain peaks to the ocean's shore,
Every journey opens a door.
With you, my love, the world's a song,
And in your arms, is where I belong.
Chorus:
So, let's chase the stars, let's sail the seas,

Face every foe with love and ease.
The future's bright, the road is long,
But together, we'll always belong.

Alarion ended the song with a flourish, strumming the final chord and giving Lila a look that was equal parts proud and playful.

"Not bad for five minutes, right?" he said with a wink.

Lila leaned over and kissed his cheek. "Not bad at all. You might have a future in songwriting if the whole 'saving the world' thing doesn't work out."

The Battle Lurking in the Shadows

But as much as the future felt like it was filled with nothing but promise and joy, the shadow of past enemies still loomed. Just as Alarion set his lute down, a strange chill ran through the air. The wind shifted, and in the distance, dark figures began to emerge from the tree line. Cloaked in shadows, their presence was an unwelcome reminder that danger was never far behind.

Alarion was on his feet in an instant, his hand instinctively reaching for his staff. Lila followed, her dagger already drawn, her body tense but ready.

"Looks like the future beckons sooner than we thought," Alarion muttered.

From the shadows, a voice echoed—cold and sharp. "You thought your journey was over, but we are the ones who will see it end. The Eternal Flame belongs to us."

The leader of the shadowy figures stepped forward; his face hidden beneath a dark hood.

Alarion felt a surge of anger and determination rise within him.

"You won't take it," Alarion said firmly. "Not now, not ever."

The battle began in a flash. Alarion and Lila fought side by side, their movements perfectly in sync as they faced the enemies that had emerged from the darkness. Fire and magic lit up the clearing as Alarion summoned his power, while Lila danced through the battlefield with her dagger, striking down foes with precision.

But these enemies were unlike any they had faced before. Their dark magic twisted the air, and their shadows seemed to grow stronger with each passing moment.

"We need to stop their leader!" Lila shouted over the din of battle.

Alarion nodded, his eyes locking on the hooded figure who commanded the shadows. With a surge of energy, he raised his staff and sent a powerful blast of flame toward the leader. But the figure simply waved his hand, dispersing the fire with ease.

"You'll have to do better than that, mage," the leader taunted.

Alarion gritted his teeth. "Lila, distract him."

Lila nodded, slipping into the shadows herself, moving swiftly and silently toward the leader.

As she approached, she threw her dagger with precision, aiming for his hand.

The leader deflected it with a sneer, but the distraction was enough. Alarion summoned every ounce of his magic, calling upon the power of the Eternal Flame. The fire roared to life, engulfing the leader in a blaze of light and heat.

With a scream of fury, the leader and his shadows dissipated into the air, leaving nothing behind but the faint scent of smoke.

The Future Beckons

As the last of the enemies vanished, Alarion and Lila stood together, breathless but victorious once again.

"Well," Lila said, wiping her brow, "that was fun."

Alarion laughed, pulling her into a tight embrace. "You know, we really need to stop meeting new enemies at the end of every chapter."

She smiled up at him, her eyes twinkling. "Maybe. But it makes life interesting."

Alarion looked into the distance, the horizon stretching before them. "The future's out there, waiting for us."

"And whatever it brings," Lila said, taking his hand, "we'll face it together."

With their laughter echoing through the hills, Alarion and Lila turned toward the future, ready for whatever adventure came next, their hearts full of love, laughter, and the promise of a lifetime shared.

The world was wide, and their path was uncertain, but together, they knew they could face anything. And in that moment, the future beckoned with endless possibilities.

Chapter 50: A New Quest

As they embark on a new quest together, Alarion and Lila reflect on their experiences. The final chapter closes with laughter, love, and the promise of many more adventures ahead, as they embrace the warmth of the Eternal Flame together.

The morning air was crisp, tinged with the scent of pine and the distant sound of rushing water. Alarion and Lila stood on the edge of Emberwood, looking out over the endless horizon. Their journey had been long—filled with battles, mysteries, and a love that had grown stronger with every challenge. Now, after facing their darkest foes and embracing the warmth of the Eternal Flame, they found themselves at the start of something new.

"Another quest?" Lila asked, half-teasing as she glanced at Alarion. "I thought we were done with all the life-threatening adventures for at least a week."

Alarion grinned, his eyes sparkling with mischief. "Come on, what's life without a little danger? Plus, I think we've learned that trouble tends to find us no matter where we go."

She shook her head, laughing. "You're hopeless."

As they stood there, basking in the warmth of the rising sun, Alarion pulled out a scroll from his satchel, one that had been handed to him by a mysterious messenger the night before. It was sealed with a strange symbol—a flame intertwined with a serpent. He hadn't opened it yet, but something told him this wasn't the end of their adventures.

"We should read it together," Alarion said, handing the scroll to Lila.

She raised an eyebrow but accepted it. Slowly, she broke the seal and unfurled the parchment, her eyes scanning the neat, cryptic handwriting.

"It's a map," she said, her voice quiet with intrigue. "A new quest?"

Alarion leaned in closer, examining the intricate lines and symbols. "Looks like it. It leads to the mountains of Eldathar...and something called the Heart of Ember."

Lila sighed, though there was a smile tugging at her lips. "Of course it does. So much for that peaceful week."

They stood there in comfortable silence for a moment, the anticipation of a new journey bubbling up between them. And though the road ahead was once again uncertain, they both felt the thrill of it—the pull of adventure, the joy of discovery, and most of all, the knowledge that they would face it together.

The Song of Adventure

Before they could get lost in planning their next steps, Alarion took a step back, his hand drifting toward the small lute strapped to his side.

Lila raised an eyebrow, amusement dancing in her eyes. "Oh no. Not again."

"Oh yes," Alarion replied with a wide grin. "I've been working on a new song. It's called 'The Quest for Love and Laughter.' Perfect for our next adventure, don't you think?"

Lila rolled her eyes, but the affection in her gaze was undeniable. "Alright, let's hear it, troubadour."

Alarion cleared his throat dramatically, then strummed a bright, playful chord. The melody that followed was light, and joyful—like the feeling of setting off on a new journey with someone you love by your side.

Intro:
We've sailed the seas, we've climbed the peaks,
Through every battle, we find what we seek.
With love and laughter, by my side,
We're ready now for one more ride.

Lila couldn't help but smile, shaking her head as Alarion continued. His voice was clear, filled with warmth and humor, perfectly capturing the essence of their adventures.

Verse 1:
The road ahead is full of surprises,
With hidden foes and cloudy skies.
But with you here, I'll face it all,
From shadowy caves to castle walls.

She chuckled at the memory of their past quests—the countless times they had stumbled into trouble, only to emerge victorious through sheer stubbornness and a little magic.

Chorus:
So, let's chase the dawn, let's find the flame,
Through every storm, through every game.
With you, my love, I'll never fall,
We're stronger when we stand tall.

Alarion leaned in, eyes twinkling with mischief, as he moved into the next verse.

Verse 2:
We've danced with danger, laughed through fear,
Every moment, you've been near.
And now, my love, a quest anew,
With every step, I'll follow you.

Chorus:
So, let's chase the dawn, let's find the flame,
Through every storm, through every game.
With you, my love, I'll never fall,

We're stronger when we stand tall.

Lila clapped softly when he finished, her heart swelling with affection. "You know, for someone who claims to be a mage, you're quite the bard."

Alarion bowed dramatically, his lute still in hand. "I'll take that as a compliment."

The Hidden Enemies Return

Just as their laughter began to echo across the meadow, a sharp rustle from the woods interrupted the moment. Alarion's hand instinctively went to his staff, and Lila, ever alert, was already drawing her dagger.

The trees shifted unnaturally, and from the shadows emerged a group of cloaked figures.

Their movements were silent, but the air around them hummed with dark magic. These were no ordinary travelers.

"Really?" Lila muttered under her breath. "Can't we just have one peaceful morning?"

Alarion sighed but readied himself for the inevitable. "Looks like the new quest starts sooner than we thought."

The leader of the cloaked group stepped forward, his voice low and menacing. "The Heart of Ember does not belong to you. It never will."

Alarion narrowed his eyes, gripping his staff. "We'll see about that."

The battle that followed was swift and intense. Alarion and Lila fought in perfect harmony, their movements synchronized from years of practice. Alarion summoned bursts of flame, lighting up the clearing with flashes of fire, while Lila darted through the shadows, her dagger striking with precision.

But these enemies were different. They moved with unnatural speed, their dark magic weaving through the air like poison.

One of the attackers lunged at Lila, but with a graceful spin, she dodged and struck back, her dagger slicing through the air. Alarion, meanwhile, was locked in a fierce duel with the leader, their magic colliding in a brilliant display of light and shadow.

"Your power is nothing compared to the Heart of Ember," the leader hissed, his voice dripping with malice.

Alarion's eyes blazed with determination. "Maybe. But you've never faced the power of love."

With a final surge of energy, he unleashed a wave of flame, driving the leader and his followers back into the shadows. The clearing was once again silent, save for the crackling of the remaining embers.

Lila sheathed her dagger, glancing at Alarion with a smirk. "Did you really just say 'the power of love' in the middle of a battle?"

Alarion shrugged, grinning. "It felt appropriate."

The Promise of More Adventures

As the last of the enemies disappeared into the woods, Alarion and Lila stood side by side, their hearts still racing from the fight.

"Well," Lila said, brushing a stray lock of hair from her face, "that was...unexpected."

Alarion laughed, shaking his head. "Seems like trouble really does follow us."

But even as the adrenaline from the battle faded, there was a sense of excitement that lingered in the air. They had faced enemies before, and they would face them again. But together, they were unstoppable.

As they gathered their belongings and prepared to follow the mysterious map to the Heart of Ember, Alarion turned to Lila, his eyes soft with affection. "No matter what happens next, we'll face it together. Right?"

Lila smiled, taking his hand. "Always."

The sun was high in the sky now, casting long shadows as they began their journey toward the mountains of Eldathar. And though the road ahead was uncertain, there was one thing Alarion knew for sure: with Lila by his side, every quest, every battle, and every adventure would be filled with laughter, love, and a promise of something more.

As they walked hand in hand, their footsteps in sync with each other's, Alarion began to hum the tune of their song once more.

Outro:
So here we go, on paths unknown,
With love and laughter, we've always grown.
The future's bright, the world is wide,
But with you, my love, I'll always stride.

With that, they set off toward the horizon, ready for the next chapter of their lives, filled with new quests, untold stories, and the warmth of the Eternal Flame lighting their way.

The future beckoned, and they were ready to embrace it—together.

————-THE END OF THE SERIES————-

A Thank You Note to the Readers

Dear Readers,

As we reach the end of Alarion and the Eternal Flame, I want to take a moment to express my heartfelt gratitude for joining Alarion on this incredible journey through all seven books in the series. Your unwavering support and enthusiasm have fueled my passion for storytelling, making each chapter an adventure I was excited to share.

This final book marks the culmination of Alarion's quest, where he sought not just the legendary Eternal Flame but also his true self. Together, we explored a world brimming with magic, laughter, and love. Each character you've encountered—every challenge faced and every bond forged—has contributed to the rich tapestry of Alarion's story, and I hope you found joy, excitement, and perhaps a touch of inspiration along the way.

While this is the last installment of the Alarion series, it is by no means the end of our adventures together. I am thrilled to announce that a new series is on the horizon, filled with fresh characters, exciting plots, and even more magical journeys. I can't wait to share those stories with you and continue exploring the realms of imagination together.

Thank you once again for your incredible support, and encouragement, and for being a part of this journey. Your enthusiasm for Alarion's tale has meant the world to me, and I hope you carry the lessons of courage, friendship, and love from this series into your own lives.

Until we meet again in the next series, may your paths be bright, your adventures bold, and your hearts forever filled with the warmth of magic.

With heartfelt gratitude,
[ANANT RAM BOSS]

Acknowledgments

As I pen this acknowledgment for Alarion and the Eternal Flame, I find myself reflecting on the incredible journey that has unfolded throughout this series. This final book is not just a culmination of Alarion's adventures; it is also a testament to the support and encouragement I have received from so many wonderful individuals along the way.

First and foremost, I want to express my deepest gratitude to my readers. Your enthusiasm for Alarion's story has been a constant source of inspiration. Every message, review, and word of encouragement has fueled my passion for writing and kept me motivated through the challenges of crafting this series. Thank you for believing in Alarion and for embarking on this magical journey with me. It has been an honor to share these adventures with you, and I hope that the characters and tales resonate in your hearts long after you close the final page.

I would also like to extend my heartfelt thanks to my family and friends, who have stood by me throughout this creative process. Your patience, understanding, and unwavering belief in my ability to weave tales of magic and wonder have been invaluable. You have been my sounding board for ideas, my first readers, and my greatest cheerleaders. Thank you for your support during late-night writing sessions, your feedback during brainstorming, and for always reminding me of the joy in storytelling.

A special acknowledgment goes to my editor and literary team, who have played an essential role in shaping this series. Your keen insights, constructive criticism, and unwavering dedication to the craft have elevated my writing and helped me stay true to Alarion's voice and journey. I am incredibly grateful for your expertise and your commitment to ensuring that this story is the best it can be.

To the amazing artists and illustrators who brought the world of Alarion to life with your vibrant and imaginative work, thank you. Your talent has enriched the pages of this series and has made the characters and settings leap off the page. It is a joy to see my words transformed into such beautiful visuals, and I appreciate the passion you poured into your art.

Lastly, I want to acknowledge the countless storytellers, authors, and creatives who have inspired me over the years. Your works ignited the spark that led me to write my own stories. From childhood tales that whisked me away to fantastical realms to modern narratives that challenged my imagination, your influence is woven into every word I write.

As we bid farewell to Alarion and his quest, I am filled with excitement for what lies ahead. Although this is the conclusion of one chapter, it is merely the beginning of new adventures waiting to be told. I look forward to sharing more stories with you in the future, stories that will spark joy, ignite the imagination, and remind us all of the magic that exists in our lives.

Thank you once again for joining me on this incredible journey. Your support means the world, and I can't wait for us to meet again in the realms of imagination.

With warmest regards,

[ANANT RAM BOSS]

Disclaimer

The following pages of Alarion and the Eternal Flame are intended as a work of fiction. Any resemblance to actual persons, living or dead, events, or locales is purely coincidental. The characters and situations presented within this story are products of the author's imagination and are crafted for entertainment purposes. While inspired by various myths, legends, and cultural narratives, this tale is not meant to reflect any specific belief system or historical event.

As you delve into Alarion's world—a realm filled with magic, adventure, and romance—please remember that the events and characters are fictional constructs. Any magical elements, creatures, or settings described in this book are purely imaginative, drawn from the rich tapestry of fantasy literature. The landscapes, spells, and enchanted beings are creations meant to evoke wonder and spark the imagination, and they should not be interpreted as representative of any real-world phenomena.

This book also explores themes of love, friendship, and the complexity of human emotions. While the relationships depicted within the story may resonate with readers on a personal level, they are ultimately fictional and dramatized for narrative effect. Readers are encouraged to interpret the themes and character dynamics in ways that are meaningful to them while recognizing that the specific scenarios and experiences of Alarion and his companions are unique to this narrative.

In crafting Alarion's journey, the author has drawn from a wealth of storytelling traditions and artistic expressions, resulting in a tale that pays homage to the universal struggles and triumphs we all face. The lessons learned and the adventures undertaken by Alarion are meant to inspire and entertain, but they should not be construed as prescriptive or normative in any way.

While this book seeks to provide an engaging and immersive reading experience, it is important to approach it as a work of fiction. Any opinions, ideas, or viewpoints expressed by the characters are not necessarily reflective of the author's own beliefs or values. Instead, they serve to create a rich narrative landscape where readers can explore diverse perspectives and discover new insights.

Lastly, this story is part of a broader series, and as you journey through Alarion's final quest, be mindful that the characters and their relationships have evolved throughout the previous books. To fully appreciate the depth of their journeys, readers are encouraged to explore the earlier installments of the series. This context enriches the narrative, providing a more comprehensive understanding of the stakes involved and the transformations each character has undergone.

Thank you for joining Alarion on this magical journey toward the Eternal Flame. As you turn these pages, let your imagination soar and remember: the magic of storytelling lies not just in the adventures of its characters, but in the connections, we forge with them and the reflections they inspire within ourselves. Enjoy the adventure!

With endless gratitude,

[ANANT RAM BOSS]

Author of the **Series "The Chronicles of Alarion" Book 7: "Alarion and the Eternal Flame"**

Please contact us for any quarry/suggestions if any at: anantramboss@gmail.com

About the Author: Anant Ram Boss

Anant Ram Boss is a dynamic author whose creative works blend the realms of fiction and non-fiction, captivating audiences with both imaginative storytelling and practical insights. A passionate storyteller, Anant crafts narratives that not only entertain but also inspire and empower his readers to explore new possibilities in their own lives.

In his fictional works, Anant weaves stories that transport readers to extraordinary worlds. Whether it's an epic adventure or a touching tale of friendship, his characters come to life with depth and emotion. His stories are marked by wonder, humor, and a profound sense of humanity, making them relatable and impactful for readers of all ages. Through his fiction, Anant encourages readers to dream big, embrace their creativity, and believe in the endless possibilities of their imagination.

On the other hand, Anant's non-fiction works are grounded in actionable knowledge and real-world strategies. He empowers his audience with the tools they need to thrive in a fast-paced and ever-changing world. From personal development and wealth-building to entrepreneurial guidance and mastering social media, his writing offers clear, practical advice designed to help readers take meaningful steps toward success. Anant's approachable style ensures his books are not only informative but also engaging, making complex topics accessible and motivating.

One of the central themes in Anant's writing is the importance of relationships, particularly between parents and children. In his reflections on family dynamics, Anant explores the disconnect that often exists between generations, where children idolize external role models while undervaluing the wisdom and sacrifices of their parents. He poses a thought-provoking question: Why do children often see others as role models rather than their parents? Through his writing, he advocates for a deeper understanding and connection between parents and children, encouraging both sides to nurture mutual respect, strengthen their bond, and work together for positive change.

Anant believes that the relationship between parents and children can evolve into a friendship, built on open communication, understanding, and a shared commitment to personal growth. In his vision, this approach can bridge the gap between generations and foster a family environment that is both supportive and empowering.

Beyond his writing, Anant is a dedicated artist, an enthusiastic learner, and a seeker of inspiration. He values the connections he builds with his readers, constantly learning from their stories and encouraging them to realize their potential. With a growing body of work that spans both fiction and non-fiction, Anant Ram Boss is committed to leaving a lasting impact, inspiring others to embark on their own journeys of discovery and self-improvement.

"Stories that ignite the imagination, insights that spark transformation—that is the legacy Anant Ram Boss aspires to leave behind."

Don't miss out!

Visit the website below and you can sign up to receive emails whenever ANANT RAM BOSS publishes a new book. There's no charge and no obligation.

https://books2read.com/r/B-A-GGLBB-FFPJF

BOOKS2READ

Connecting independent readers to independent writers.

Did you love *Alarion and the Eternal Flame*? Then you should read *Alarion and the Rift of Arcane Fates*[1] by ANANT RAM BOSS!

In *Alarion and the Rift of Arcane Fates*, the sixth book in *The Chronicles of Alarion*, a new and darker chapter unfolds in the young sorcerer's journey. Alarion's fate has always been intertwined with magic, but as he ventures into the mysterious Rift of Arcane Fates, he finds himself standing at the very crossroads of destiny and chaos. The Rift is no ordinary realm— it is a swirling convergence of ancient magics, long forgotten and wildly unpredictable, holding the power to either elevate him to unimaginable heights or plunge him into realms of destruction.

Alarion's arrival in this enigmatic world opens a door to both wonders and dangers, unlike anything he has ever faced. With

---

1. https://books2read.com/u/m21yLO

2. https://books2read.com/u/m21yLO

landscapes that defy the laws of nature, every step he takes seems to lead him deeper into a web of impossible choices. The Rift speaks to him, urging him to harness the untamed powers of the Arcane, promising him the ability to reshape his fate and control the very forces of magic itself. But at what cost? As the weight of his decisions grows, Alarion realizes that the power he seeks may come at the expense of everything he holds dear—his friendships, his love for Lila, and perhaps even his own humanity.

But the Rift does not reveal its secrets easily. It tests Alarion at every turn, throwing him into epic battles with strange and formidable enemies, from shape-shifting beasts to dark, sentient forces that seem to have known him all his life. Each confrontation forces him to reconsider his beliefs about power, choice, and the cost of altering the future. Alongside these battles, Alarion finds unlikely allies in the most peculiar forms—a witty, riddle-speaking fox, an ancient, sarcastic artifact, and even a mysterious bard whose haunting songs seem to hold answers to questions Alarion has yet to ask.

Amid the turmoil of magic, battles, and betrayal, Alarion's relationship with Lila is pushed to its limits. Their bond has always been a source of strength, but the Rift presents them with challenges that even their love cannot shield them from. As their hearts grow closer, they are also torn apart by the dangerous forces at play. The choices Alarion must make could either preserve the world they've fought to protect or tear them—and their love—apart.

Alarion and the Rift of Arcane Fates is more than a tale of magic; it is a story about what it means to be human in the face of overwhelming power. It explores the tension between destiny and free will, the bravery required to choose between what we desire and what we must protect, and the sacrifices that define the path we walk. Alarion's journey is filled with moments of humor, heartache, and unexpected twists, making it an adventure that will keep you on the edge of your seat, questioning the very nature of fate itself.

As Alarion's decisions reverberate through realms, you too will be swept up in this thrilling narrative, where destiny and danger collide. The Rift is calling—will you dare to answer?

Also by ANANT RAM BOSS

1
The Chronicles of Alarion -Part-6 "Alarion and the Nexus of Netheron"
"The Chronicles of Alarion -Part-7-"Alarion and the Legacy of Luminarya"

2
Mystic Alliances

Alarion Chronicles Series
The Dawn of Magic
Shadows Embrace
Book#3: "Phoenix's Flight"
Book 4: "Warriors of Light"
Echoes of Wisdom
Captivated Woodland
Kingdom of Crystals
Book 8: "Lost Legacies"
Book 9: "Siege of Hope"
Book 10: "Veil of Light"

The Astral Chronicles
Awakening Shadows
Awakening Shadows
Celestial Convergence
Whispers of the Himalayas
Riddles of Rishikesh
Portals of the Past
Echoes from Vijayanagara
Veil of Varanasi
The Astral Nexus
Eclipse of Eternity
Beyond the Veil

The Chronicles of Alarion
Book # 1: Alarion and the Cryptic Key
Book # 2 Alarion and the Secrets of Tiderune
"Book # 3 "Alarion and the Oracle's Enigma
Book 4 Alarion and the Shattered Sigils
"The Chronicles of Alarion" A Magical Adventure Awaits
Book#4Alarion and the Shattered Sigils
Alarion and the Rift of Arcane Fates
Alarion and the Eternal Flame

Standalone
Love's Delectable Harmony
Adventures in Candy land
Adventures in Candy land
Canvas to Catalyst: Parenting Mastery

Guardians of Greatness: Our Children Are Our Property in Cultivating Tomorrow's Leaders
Guardians of Greatness: Cultivating Tomorrow's Leaders
Space Explorers Club
The Enchanted Forest Chronicles
Mystery at Monster Mansion
Robot Friends Forever
Underwater Kingdom
Underwater Kingdom
Time Travel Twins
Time Travel Twins
The Giggle Factory
Dreamland Chronicles
The Case of the Vanishing Cookies
Dragon Knight Chronicles
The Wishing Well
Trade Tactics Unveiled: Mastering Profit Secrets
Whispers in the Graveyard
Love after Dawn: A Second Chance Romance
Exodus: A Hopeful Dystopia
Death at Blackwood Manor
Orient Express: Murder Redefined
Poirot & the Raven: Digital Legacy
The Brave Little Elephant
The Little Robot That Could
The Adventures of Little Star
Dream World
Unique Friendship
The Courage of the Lion
The Art of Building Wealth: A Strategic Guide
Epic Savings Day

❖❖❖❖ ❖❖ ❖❖❖❖❖❖❖ ❖❖❖❖❖

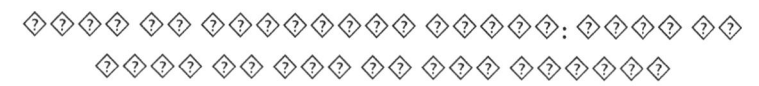

The Circle of Life
Alarion and the Veil of Duskspire
The Circle of Life: Embracing Childhood Again
The Circle of Life: Embracing Childhood Again
High-Ticket Marketing Mastery
Legacy of Sacrifice
Monetising Pinterest
Mastering Life: Small Habits, Big Wisdom

About the Author

Anant Ram Boss is an accomplished author with a passion for creating immersive worlds and captivating stories. His journey into the realm of writing began at an early age when he discovered the magic of words and the power of storytelling. Anant's dedication to his craft and his relentless pursuit of literary excellence have made him a notable figure in the world of fantasy literature.

With an imaginative mind that knows no bounds, Anant has the ability to transport readers to enchanting and mysterious realms. His writing is known for its vivid descriptions, well-drawn characters, and intricate plots that keep readers eagerly turning pages. He has an innate talent for weaving intricate tales filled with magic, adventure, and profound themes.

Throughout his career, Anant has received acclaim for his ability to craft epic sagas and captivating series that resonate with readers of all ages. The Sries, in particular, has garnered a devoted following, and it showcases Anant's mastery of the fantasy genre.

When he's not lost in the worlds he creates, Anant enjoys exploring the great outdoors, indulging in his love for photography, and seeking inspiration from the beauty of the natural world. His appreciation for nature often finds its way into his storytelling, enriching his narratives with a deep connection to the environment and the magic that exists within it.

Anant Ram Boss is not only a storyteller but also a world-builder, a dreamer, and an explorer of the human experience through the lens of fantasy literature. With each new book he writes, he invites readers to embark on journeys of the imagination, fostering a love for the magical and the wondrous that resides within us all.